"Two of my favourite authors have joined forces to create an engaging, sly mystery that is perfect for fans of Richard Osman and Louise Penny. With a heroine to root for, a quirky supporting cast, a charming but shadowy small-town setting, and a whodunit that had me turning pages as fast as I could, this novel is an absolute delight!"
—Marissa Stapley, *New York Times* bestselling author of *Lucky*

"A smart, devious whodunit filled with theatrical shadows and veils, *Bury the Lead* is both twisty and hilarious."
—Robyn Harding, bestselling author of *The Drowning Woman*

"A classic, but also topical, whodunit staged with humour and wit."
—Linwood Barclay, author of *The Lie Maker*

"Right from the hilariously brilliant opening line, I was hooked, helpless to resist reading just one more chapter. This very witty, sharp, fun, and suspenseful cozy mystery is the best escape and also a thought-provoking novel. With pitch-perfect dialogue, beautiful flow, and the most relatable heroine, *Bury the Lead* showcases the immense talents of Kate Hilton and Elizabeth Renzetti. As a team, they're unstoppable."
—Samantha M. Bailey, *USA Today* and #1 national bestselling author of *Woman on the Edge* and *Watch Out for Her*

"Reading *Bury the Lead* is like having cocktails with your most fabulous friends. Liz and Kate tell you fantastic stories, and you laugh, gasp, say 'Wow!' and 'What?!' a lot, and learn a few tricks you're glad to know. They get the worlds of theatre and journalism exactly right, the stubborn talents and eggshell egos. The minute it's over, you can't wait to get together again."
—Johanna Schneller, Bigger Picture columnist, *Globe and Mail*

"*Bury the Lead* is a word-perfect romp through the world of small-town theatre, both hilarious and poignant, insightful and full of twists. I give it a standing ovation!"
—Roz Nay, bestselling author of *The Hunted*

"Giant egos, secret grievances, the locals vs. the artsy-farts: theatre towns were made for murder, and *Bury the Lead* was made for mystery lovers. Kate Hilton and Elizabeth Renzetti had a lot of fun with this, and so will you."
—Andrew Pyper, author of *The Demonologist* and *Oracle*

"*Bury the Lead* is the perfect cozy mystery novel ... fun, dark, and impossible to put down. Kate Hilton and Elizabeth Renzetti have built a wonderful world in Port Ellis and an excellent main character in Cat Conway. As readers we find ourselves rooting for her while also wondering if we can fully trust her, which is the perfect setup. The cast of characters feels both fresh and familiar, straight out of a hard-boiled detective novel. It's got to be hard to write a book that's both

touching and a little bit sinister, but *Bury the Lead* pulls it off. I truly loved this novel!"
—Amy Stuart, bestselling author of *A Death at the Party*

"A propulsive, juicy little ride—the perfect combination of Agatha Christie and Janet Evanovich—a gorgeously written, twisty, turny, small-town whodunit, that also seamlessly weaves together themes of a dying era of journalism, the ruthless nature of the 'theatah,' and the strength of a woman trying to reinvent herself, heal her heart, and hopefully catch a killer before it's too late. Kate Hilton and Elizabeth Renzetti have created a vivid, warm, hilarious character in Cat Conway, whose story surely doesn't end here ... I loved every page."
—Lisa Gabriele, author of *The Winters*

BURY THE LEAD

QUILL & PACKET MYSTERIES

Bury the Lead

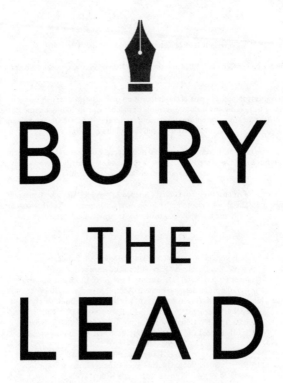

BURY THE LEAD

KATE HILTON AND ELIZABETH RENZETTI

SPIDERLINE

Published in Canada in 2024 and the USA in 2024 by House of Anansi Press Inc.
houseofanansi.com

House of Anansi Press is committed to protecting our natural environment.
This book is made of material from well-managed FSC®-certified forests, recycled
materials, and other controlled sources.

House of Anansi Press is a Global Certified Accessible™ (GCA by Benetech)
publisher. The ebook version of this book meets stringent accessibility standards
and is available to readers with print disabilities.

28 27 26 25 24   1 2 3 4 5

Library and Archives Canada Cataloguing in Publication
Title: Bury the lead / Kate Hilton and Elizabeth Renzetti.
Names: Hilton, Kate, 1972- author. | Renzetti, Elizabeth, author.
Description: Series statement: A Quill & Packet mystery
Identifiers: Canadiana (print) 20230524834 | Canadiana (ebook) 20230524842 |
ISBN 9781487012625 (softcover) | ISBN 9781487012632 (EPUB)
Subjects: LCGFT: Detective and mystery fiction. | LCGFT: Novels.
Classification: LCC PS8615.I48 B87 2024 | DDC C813/.6—dc23

Cover design: Greg Tabor
Cover image: Marta Lebek/Stocksy Images
Typesetting: Lucia Kim

*House of Anansi Press is grateful for the privilege to work on and create from the
Traditional Territory of many Nations, including the Anishinabeg, the Wendat, and the
Haudenosaunee, as well as the Treaty Lands of the Mississaugas of the Credit.*

Canada Council   Conseil des Arts
for the Arts   du Canada

ONTARIO ARTS COUNCIL
CONSEIL DES ARTS DE L'ONTARIO
an Ontario government agency
un organisme du gouvernement de l'Ontario

With the participation of the Government of Canada
Avec la participation du gouvernement du Canada

*We acknowledge for their financial support of our publishing program the Canada Council
for the Arts, the Ontario Arts Council, and the Government of Canada.*

Printed and bound in Canada

MIX
Paper from
responsible sources
FSC
www.fsc.org   FSC® C103567

To all the small-town journalists and
big-city scribes who hunt the truth every day,
and live to tell the tale.

SUMMER 2022

CHAPTER 1

ELIOT FRASER WANTED to show me the treasure he kept in his pants.

He beckoned for me to follow him into the depths of his dressing room. Torn between reluctance and curiosity—he was, after all, one of the most famous actors of his generation—I let him lead me to a closet. My feet squelched with every step. I'd cycled to the theatre in the rain, and even though I hadn't checked in Eliot's giant mirror, I was pretty sure I looked like the last drowning rat off the ship.

"Here," he said, removing a heap of dark cloth from a shelf. He fished around inside and pulled out a small glass object. A drinking glass. "Jason Robards himself gave it to me, not long after we set a monkey loose at

Sardi's. I believe the glass may be purloined but"—he put a flirtatious finger to his lips—"that will be our little secret, eh?"

He passed me the glass as gently as if it still contained a cocktail and Jason Robards was returning any minute for it. Eliot folded the pants over his arm. "Jason also bequeathed these to me after the run ended, though of course I was substantially the slimmer."

"*Long Day's Journey into Night*," I said. "I've read about that production. It was legendary. You were nominated for a Tony."

His face brightened, as I knew it would. It was a cheap move, and I felt slightly gross using it. Flattery was the grease that made the interview run smoothly, and you only had to use a dab. What amazed me was that even Eliot Fraser—Tony winner, Oscar nominee, star of one of the most beloved films of all time—was as thirsty for praise as a model hawking skincare on Instagram.

"The city lay at my feet like a drunken hoyden," he said, reaching to take the drinking glass from me. His fingers lingered against mine, and I snatched my hand back. I bent to take my digital recorder from my backpack, and when I looked up I found his eyes—famously blue, still so vivid—locked on the gaping neckline of my shirt.

So the stories were true. Old dog, old tricks.

"New York, such a world of wonders," he continued as he lowered himself into a chair. "Unlike this ... this"—one hand indicated the cluttered dressing room—"mausoleum of morality."

Did he mean the Port Ellis Playhouse, or the town of Port Ellis itself? Either way, I couldn't disagree with him. This smug little burg with its pretensions of grandeur had sucked us both back in. It had tempted Eliot with the promise of a leading role in *Inherit the Wind* (and a fat paycheque). And me? I'd scurried back to Port Ellis six months earlier with the smell of burning bridges in my hair.

Not that I would ever write anything quite so purple for my new employer, the Port Ellis *Quill & Packet*. I placed my notepad and recorder on the table between us and glanced up at Eliot. He was gazing at himself in the mirror, not in the furtive way that I might, but with the full-blown appreciation of a primatologist studying a fine silverback.

And he was quite a specimen, even at the age of seventy. A full head of white hair framed his face, which was long and bony, but in an appealing way. A way that gets described as leonine, if you're a man. And those eyes—they were still as bright as they were when he'd starred in the movie that made his career, *A Dream or Two*. He'd played a dying priest who coached a baseball team composed entirely of adorable urchins, and even though it was schmaltzy as hell I still stopped to watch it every time it came on. Everyone did.

Now those luminous eyes were fixed on me, and I sensed that the stories about his wandering hands were not just Broadway rumours. Time enough to ask about that at the end of our talk. You always save the tough questions for the end. If you get kicked out the door, at least you've still got your interview.

I switched on the recorder. "So, you haven't been back to the Port Ellis Playhouse since you appeared here thirty-five years ago—"

"And what role was I playing?" There was a challenge in his voice.

"Prince Hal in *Henry IV, Part 1* and *Part 2*. One of the critics said they could have turned down the lights and your energy would have lit the stage." I cringed as I said it, but again the flattery worked. Eliot Fraser beamed his approval. I remembered what the arts editor at my old newspaper had said: never underestimate the vanity of politicians or actors.

My old newspaper. Suddenly the rain that had soaked my shirt felt like ice, and I shivered. Fraser noticed, and something in his eyes shifted. "My dear, you must be frozen. They have the air conditioning set to Siberian climes. Perhaps a drink to warm you up?"

His long hand gestured toward his dressing table, where a collection of bottles stood: whisky, rum, brandy, something green that looked as lethal as one of those tiny toxic frogs. On my notepad I wrote: *old skool*. Not that any of this shocked me. I'd been in this business for two decades, and Eliot was not the first man I'd interviewed who thought he held the key to my happiness in his lap.

"I'm all right, thanks." I shivered again. "Maybe a coffee, if there's one available."

He looked disappointed. It occurred to me, with a rush of embarrassment, that I'd asked a national treasure to fetch me a coffee. I muttered, "I mean, I can go get it—" but he raised that elegant hand once more and bellowed, "Hadiya!"

The force of his pipes nearly knocked me off my seat. "Hadiya!" he shouted again, and he was muttering some choice backstage curses when the door to his dressing room opened. A woman stood in the doorway, young and very pretty. She wore a pair of lime cropped pants and a sleeveless shirt the colour of marigolds—a combination that worked only on preschoolers or supremely confident adults. It worked on her. Her dark hair was pulled into a bun, and she'd stuck a pen in it.

"Yes, Eliot?"

"There you are. Finally. Do you think you could perhaps procure a coffee for"—he stared at me for a minute, and we both knew he'd forgotten my name—"for our journalist friend here?"

The woman in the doorway made a face that I knew

all too well, which suggested that coffee-fetching was not in her job description but the fight was not worth having. She said, tightly, "Cream and sugar?"

I told her I'd like some milk, and she disappeared back into the theatre. Eliot Fraser let out a thunderous sigh. "Hadiya. My amanuensis." The blue eyes flashed at me. "You know what that is?"

I did, and it did not mean "she who runs errands." But I sensed he'd like to explain, so I shook my head.

"She is my literary assistant, helping to prepare my memoirs. My publisher is quite impatiently waiting for the manuscript, as you can imagine. But there's such a wealth of material—Broadway, the West End. That folly with Liz Taylor. It's taking longer than I ever imagined."

With another sigh, he reached for the row of bottles, as if the weight of his past had driven him to drink. He unscrewed the lid of the whisky bottle and poured a healthy measure into Jason Robards's purloined glass. "Are you sure you won't have one? No?" He raised the glass in a salute. "Confusion to our enemies."

No journalist likes to waste a good opening. "Now that you mention it," I said. "What's it like to be back working with your ex-wife?" Martha Mercer, the first of Fraser's wives, sat atop Port Ellis like a queen. The Mercers were the royal family of this little lakeside kingdom. They had substantial real estate holdings, and Martha was chair of the Port Ellis Playhouse board of directors. "The rumour is that she's the one who lured you back to Port Ellis," I said. "What's your working relationship like?"

Eliot scowled into his drink. "She did not lure me back. I am not a fly, though Martha could accurately be described as a spider. No, my dear, I returned for this magnificent role. Henry Drummond, the great rationalist and defender of free thought." His voice suddenly boomed from his diaphragm: "And soon you may ban books and newspapers!"

I stared at him for a second, and then realized he was quoting from the play. Fraser leaned forward and tapped my knee. "Is that not a crucial sentiment these days, eh? When the forces of puritanism are once again sweeping the land? When men are afraid to speak their minds?"

But not afraid to touch strangers, I thought. I crossed my legs and his hand slid off. In the mirror, I caught a glimpse of myself: my wavy dark hair was both flat and frizzy, thanks to my bike helmet, and there was a conspicuous ink stain on the hem of my shirt. I was literally an ink-stained wretch. But the dishevelment that would have sent my mother into cardiac arrest only seemed to have whetted Eliot Fraser's appetite. He was weighing his next move when the door opened again and Hadiya came in with my coffee.

"Wouldn't you say, Hadiya," Fraser continued, "that political correctness blankets the world like a shadow?"

I met her eyes in the mirror. There was a brief flash of something in her expression, and then it was gone. I had a sense of something simmering, a pot about to boil. I knew that look too. I'd boiled over once myself, and the ensuing eruption had unfortunately hurled me back to Port Ellis. But as soon as Hadiya opened her mouth, I realized that she kept a better grip on her lid than I ever had. Her voice was pleasant and modulated. "That's something we'll definitely explore in your book, Eliot."

She placed the coffee cup on the dressing table with something close to a bang. A bit of coffee slopped over the side, a tiny rivulet sliding toward Eliot's script. His mask slipped, the smooth operator replaced by the cranky old despot. "For God's sake, Hadiya!" he roared.

I wondered if they'd heard him out on the lake.

Hadiya muttered apologies and tried to mop up the spill with a ratty tissue she pulled from her pocket. But Eliot swatted her hand away and I said, instinctively, "Hey. Don't do that."

They both turned to look at me, Hadiya struggling to keep her emotions under control, Eliot's face flushed red. In fact, he looked alarmingly red, and his hands were shaking. Just what I needed: my jackpot interview going to hell right in front of me.

"Here, use this," I said, taking a microfibre cloth from my backpack.

She quickly wiped up the spill and returned the

wadded-up cloth. "I'll go top up your coffee." She departed without looking at me, but I noticed that she left the door open. An insignificant act, or something she did every time there was a woman alone in the room with Sir Grabby Hands?

Eliot watched her go, and then turned to me expectantly. I consulted my list of questions and lobbed him a soft one about his Tony, which he'd won for a revival of *Equus*. We spoke at length about his career, Eliot answering in a booming Hampstead accent that gave no hint of his birth above a Saskatoon hat shop. He gesticulated; he did imitations of famous colleagues; he refilled his glass more than once. Hadiya came back with my coffee, and once again she left the door open behind her when she left.

When he seemed properly softened, I consulted my final page of questions, where the tough ones lay.

"You were quoted last year saying that theatre is being ruined by 'weepy girls and grievance poets.' That statement offended many people. What exactly were you trying to say?"

Eliot blew out a mighty breath. "Offended. Exactly! These people find offence everywhere. In my day, you did the work and moved on. And if some old goat patted your bottom backstage you smiled and went on anyway. There was an esprit de corps that—hello there! Jonah!"

He appeared to be gesturing to someone out in

the corridor, and I turned to look. After a moment, a figure filled the doorway, and I felt my face freeze in a dumb smile. *Don't be a fawning idiot*, I told myself sternly. But here was Jonah Tiller—less famous than Eliot, but in my opinion a much greater actor. When I was in university, I'd scraped together the money to see him in a touring production of *Coriolanus*. His portrayal of the raging Roman general had made me see Shakespeare in a new light.

Now he stood in the doorway and nodded his head at Eliot, and then at me. A Black man about the same age as Eliot, he was equally compelling (and notably more sober). I knew that he was playing Matthew Harrison Brady, the other lead in *Inherit the Wind*. Casting Eliot and Jonah together was a coup that had padded the pockets of the Port Ellis Playhouse and brought an avaricious sheen to Martha Mercer's eyes. The play's gala opening on the first weekend of summer had been sold out for months.

Eliot batted the air with his hand. "Jonah!" he boomed. "Come in, man. Meet this lovely representative from the local fourth estate."

Tiller nodded politely at me but made no move from the door. "I'm just on my way to a fitting, Eliot."

"Nonsense!" Now Eliot was trying to rise from his chair, with limited success. "I was just saying how different it was in the old days. The camaraderie. The esprit de corps!"

Jonah opened his mouth as if to say something, and then closed it again. In his face there was an intensity I recognized from that production of *Coriolanus*, something cold and restrained. I looked back at Eliot—surely he could see it too? But Eliot was smoothing his eyebrows in the mirror.

"I really must be going," Tiller said. His voice was beautiful, the low rumble of an expensive car's engine. But the look he gave Eliot was far from friendly. Suddenly, I remembered something I'd read long ago, about a feud between the two of them. Was it over a stolen role? The half-memory sat in the back of my mind, irritating me. I made a note to ask Hadiya. If she was ghostwriting Eliot's memoir, she would know.

Eliot thumped back in his seat. As Tiller turned to leave, I said, "I've been trying to reach you. I'd love to set up an interview with you and get your perspective on the play."

He looked at me for a second, then gave a small nod. It was not a gesture that reeked of encouragement. What kind of actor didn't want publicity? When he was gone, I turned back to Eliot. "What's it been like working with Jonah Tiller?"

"Ah, Jonah." His gaze fell to the bottom of his glass, as if he expected to find the ghost of Jason Robards there. "I feel like I've known him since the dawn of time. An actor of rare force. He suits the Brady role,

KATE HILTON & ELIZABETH RENZETTI

all that fire and bombast barely contained. Alec is very good at modulating that force, focusing it."

"Alec Mercer?"

"Yes, our director." His eyes were suddenly sharp on my face, and I remembered that actors were observers too. "Why, do you know him? Everyone in this Podunk town seems to know everyone else."

I resisted the urge to snarl, "I'm not from this Podunk town. I just washed up here, like you." But that wasn't exactly true, was it? I'd been formed here, on the shores of Lake Marjorie. All those summers I'd spent with my grandparents at their cottage, when this was a town of screen doors and hot dogs rather than pizza ovens and basil gelato. At least the town could support a newspaper, even if that newspaper had only one section, and that section contained ads for tractors. It wasn't where I'd hoped to end up, but I was here, and I had a job to do. That job sat in front of me, scratching his belly. I wondered, for a second, if Eliot Fraser wore Spanx. Now there was a question that would get me thrown out.

Instead, I said: "I remember Alec Mercer when he was terrorizing Port Ellis from the top of his skateboard. I was a judgmental college student when he was a brat with no brakes." Eliot raised his eyebrows at me, and I explained: "I used to spend summers here with my grandparents. They were huge fans of the Playhouse. In fact, they saw every production that first season. There was a lot of buzz that summer you played Prince Hal."

His magnificent old head snapped up. When he spoke, his voice was deadly calm and suddenly not tipsy at all. "Why? What have you heard?"

"Um, nothing, nothing in particular," I stuttered, looking down at my notepad. No rescue there. I kicked myself for not writing down some of the juicier quotes I'd found in the newspaper's archive describing the Playhouse's first season. Something about a cast party where a sailboat caught fire, and a drunken punch-up between the two leads in *Guys and Dolls*. But there had been hints of something darker too, which at the time would have been filed under the general category "boys will be boys." I tried to remember the specifics, but with Eliot Fraser's blue lasers aimed at me, the memory fled my head.

This town was quite literally making me lose my mind.

I said, "My grandparents talked about your farewell scene with Falstaff for years after."

Eliot expanded in his chair and cast a disdainful glance my way, and suddenly he was salty young Prince Hal again. "'I know thee not, old man.'" His eyes half closed in a dreamy reverie. "It was a magical summer. Far from the hurly-burly. No cameras or devices trained on you, not like now. A company of like-minded souls. One found one's pleasures where one could."

This seemed like an entry, possibly. "What kind of pleasures?" I probed. "Anything you'd regret now?"

One spectacular eyebrow rose halfway up his forehead. "Have you seen the Scottish play, my dear? There's much wisdom in it. Especially for this sensitive generation. 'Things without all remedy should be without regard. What's done, is done.'"

CHAPTER 2

AS I CYCLED back to the newsroom—the rain had cleared, and a gentle mist hovered over the lake— I couldn't get the words out of my head. Of course I'd seen *Macbeth*, a play about the crushing power of guilt. And the folly of pissing off witches. It seemed unlikely that an old perv like Eliot Fraser possessed the secret to a happy life, but it was clear from the state of my own that I certainly didn't. I wasn't averse to letting go of the past, cutting the lines and watching all my stupid mistakes drift off into the distance, but it wasn't so easy. What was the expression: "little kids, little problems; big kids, big problems"? Well, I had midlife-adult problems, and they weren't floating anywhere. They were scattered around my life like the Precambrian boulders that dotted the landscape around Port Ellis.

I coasted to a stop at the corner of Erie and Lakeshore, the main intersection in the historic district. I still experienced a kind of cognitive dissonance whenever I passed this spot, as if another town, spectral, existed beneath the surface of this one: the Port Ellis I'd known and loved in my childhood, where I'd spent summers with my grandparents. Back then, it had been a sleepy place without a lot of ostentatious wealth. In the intervening years, a few Hollywood stars and hockey players had decided that the pristine lakes, windblown pines, and rocky shorelines of the tri-lake area made for an ideal escape. Waves of tech titans and hedge fund managers had followed hot on their heels.

Economically, it was good for Port Ellis, and for several other towns around the three major lakes: Hilda, Jane, and Marjorie—the daughters of Joseph Ellis, the area's original settler—known collectively as the Three Sisters. The old-timers complained about how you couldn't afford much on Main Street anymore. McCracken's Hardware was now a fancy kitchenware shop called the Harvest Table, with a window display featuring Le Creuset pots in rainbow shades and hardcover copies of *The Complete Aga Cookbook*. Twinkle Toes Shoes had become a purveyor of crystal bracelets, dream catchers, and cashmere wraps.

And the Second Act, the gastropub that had replaced Treasure Garden Chinese Restaurant, promised that all its ingredients were sourced from within a fifty-kilometre radius. The Second Act was also where I'd found a second home: I rented the apartment above, and sometimes I picked up a shift at the bar. No one ever got rich working at a small-town paper.

Here and there, the old town peeked through. The Bijou, where I'd fallen in love with John Cusack in *Say Anything*, was still showing movies. Next door, the curio shop Mugs 'n Things continued its inexplicable existence. I'd always thought of it as "crap you don't need until you do." Dog bowls shaped like bones. Barbecue aprons telling dads that it was beer o'clock. In other words, birthday presents for when you'd forgotten the birthday.

I kept pedalling, cruising past Glenda's Country Bakehouse, the unofficial bridge between the old town and the new one. Everyone, tourists and locals alike, loved the bakery, and if the *Quill & Packet* had a second newsroom, it was sandwiched somewhere between the almond croissants and the sourdough loaves. The menu and signage had been updated since Glenda had taken the business over from her grandmother, but the bakery's mouth-watering scents were as irresistible as ever.

My eye was caught by a sign in the window, and I slowed down to read it. It was a publicity photo of

Eliot Fraser with a red line running through it diagonally and a bold-type tagline: WE DON'T SERVE A-HOLES.

I burst out laughing. While the message appeared to be specific to Eliot Fraser—and I'd be asking Kaydence for the backstory—it struck me that it wasn't a bad philosophy for life.

TWENTY MINUTES LATER I was attending the *Quill & Packet*'s weekly editorial conference, which was a pretty grand way of describing a handful of sandal-wearing journalists sitting around a table with a wonky leg. Except for Amir, my old friend and now boss. He would never stoop to sandals.

"And so this week's Soapbox will be"—Dorothy Talbott squinted down at the paper in front of her— "Joyce Chesney on the shameful scam of septic-tank cleaning companies."

From the opposite end of the table, Bruce Collinghurst piped up. "I think we all know that Joyce Chesney is full of—"

"*Bruce,*" Dorothy Talbott's voice contained a note of warning, but also affection. Dorothy was the *Quill & Packet*'s owner and publisher, and Bruce a mere reporter-photographer, but they had the easy camaraderie that came with working together for decades. If not centuries. I pictured them delivering the paper together in the early days, Bruce unloading the wagon and Dorothy driving the team of horses.

Dorothy put down her glasses, which had lenses so thick they looked like they'd been designed by NASA. Everything about her was built for comfort, not speed, from her short-cropped grey hair to the wardrobe she'd bought at an Eddie Bauer outlet in 1982 and never saw the need to update. "Joyce Chesney is a cherished member of this community, three times elected head of the Port Ellis Business Improvement Area."

Bruce, who was as lean as a piece of licorice and had the wild grey hair of a folk singer, shrugged. He was quirky and non-conformist in a Grateful Dead–inspired way, and evidently unimpressed by Joyce's history in elected office. Next to him at the table, Kaydence Johnson was examining her fingernails, each painted a different colour in honour of Pride Month. She sold ads for the *Quill & Packet*, but the job took less and less time as the ads dried up, so she was also in charge of the paper's social media and marketing. This mainly involved answering people's questions on Facebook about what time the weekly fireworks at Centennial Park began. Every week they began at the same time; every week people asked. Kaydence responded to every dumb question with blithe good humour. Possibly she was cheery because she spent her spare time on her true passion, collecting vintage clothing and selling the bits that did not suit her red hair and pale complexion.

Generationally, I fell in between Bruce and Kaydence, and I liked them both. If I stayed in Port Ellis, they had the potential to become friends.

And then there was Amir Mahar, our editor-in-chief. We had history that should have bound us together: we'd been the best of friends during those summers when we'd both worked at Camp Ravenhead, had even started flirting with something more. We'd kept in touch over the years, especially once we'd landed in the same profession, and he'd lobbied hard to get me to return to Port Ellis.

But now that he was my boss he was ... *frosty* wasn't the right word. Cool? Proper? Managerial? And while he looked crisp as a fresh lettuce leaf in his business attire, he was the only person in Port Ellis who routinely wore a tie and wasn't on his way to a funeral or wedding. He didn't look as if he'd put on an ounce in three decades, and when I'd asked him his secret he'd said it was illegal to buy carbs in San Francisco. His mouth didn't laugh when he said this, but his eyes did—the dark eyes I'd once found so alluring, gold-flecked and Maybelline-lashed. There were shadows under them now, and twin grooves between his brows, but his eyes were still captivating. Not that I'd noticed.

I wasn't sure how to relate to him now, which was slightly weird considering all we had in common, notably our status as big-city backwash. He'd been running a tech-news site in the Bay Area when he'd been reeled back to Port Ellis to help out his parents, who'd lost their jobs when Camp Ravenhead closed. My walk of shame had been much shorter; I'd only had to slink back from Toronto. I had to assume that he was feeling as conflicted about the change in his circumstances as I was, but he didn't seem open to that line of conversation.

"Bruce does have a point," Amir said. "I've been thinking about ways to make Soapbox more relevant." Dorothy shot him a look. As publisher and owner of the paper, she was his boss, even if he held the exalted title of editor-in-chief. (*More like editor-in-brief*, I'd joked to him on my first day, referring to the tiny paper and the tinier staff; I'd received a tight smile in return.) He tolerated her interference—mostly harmless—in the editorial decisions of the paper. He'd told me that he preferred it to the alternative he might have to face sooner rather than later: a new owner. We all knew that Dorothy's macular degeneration was getting worse, and that her children, who arrived from the city every weekend in a fleet of expensive cars, wanted her to sell the money-losing paper. *Your expensive hobby*, they called it. Even though it was a hobby that had been in the Talbott family for generations.

Amir smiled at Dorothy. "We need to encourage different people in town to express their views," he said. "For example, I had a submission from the people who run the solar panel outlet—"

"Damn hippies," Dorothy muttered.

"They sent in an opinion piece about how the new retirement facility is going to tax the town's power grid. With all the new demand we could be looking at brownouts in a few years."

Dorothy's watery eyes suddenly snapped into focus. "Martha Mercer's new retirement village?"

Amir's expression turned wary. "Yes, it's the Mercers' development. Out at the old summer camp. Why?"

"No reason," said Dorothy innocently. "Sounds like an op-ed you might want to run."

"Right," said Amir. "I'll look into it. Moving on to you, Cat, what's the status on your Eliot Fraser profile?"

"It's not going to be a problem. He gave me lots to work with." I flipped through my notes. "There was one weird thing that came up in our conversation. I mean, weird beyond the fact that he was pounding back Scotch at eleven in the morning. I asked him about the early days of the Playhouse and he got defensive. Super defensive, actually."

"What do you think that was about?" asked Amir.

"I have no idea. But I thought I'd ask around, dig a bit more in the archives."

"The archives" was a grand way of describing a poky corner in the basement that the mice considered their playroom.

"Do you really think people are going to be

interested in ancient gossip?" Dorothy asked. "Seems like the opening-night gala is a much bigger story."

I was about to tell her that readers loved gossip, both ancient and new, when Amir broke in, trying to hustle us along. "You're going to file on time, right?"

As if I'd forget my deadline, after twenty years in the news business. I'd spent fifteen years on the print side, much of it on the investigative team of a major Toronto newspaper, deciphering documents and coaxing sources to speak on the record. I'd left that job I loved—unwisely, it turned out—to become a TV reporter on a major network. My stories had run on the front page and aired at the top of the newscast. And now? I was being asked if I could handle a simple entertainment profile. It was like being asked if I could tie my own shoelaces. And as a forty-five-year-old divorced woman in journalism, it was hard to see any end to the relentless questioning of my competence.

The meeting broke up shortly afterwards, and I tried to shake off the dark mood that had wrapped around me. I picked up a copy of last Saturday's paper and stared at the byline above my story about kids drag-racing on Rural Route 4. I still wasn't used to seeing Conway, my maiden name, there. For years I'd been Schultz, thanks to an ex-husband who wanted his line to carry on. I'd given in, taken his name, produced a son. Now I was taking my name back. Our son, unfortunately, was still in his clutches.

"Hey." I spun around to see Bruce, holding a baggie of raw carrots. The baggie, as far as I could tell, was almost as old as Bruce; he diligently washed it out in the office sink at the end of each day and returned with fresh roughage in the morning.

He walked over to my desk and held out the baggie. I took a carrot, and we crunched in solidarity. Bruce was totally comfortable in his own skin, a quality I both envied and admired. He knew what he was about and didn't feel the need to prove it to anyone. He was a jack of all newspaper trades: he could take pictures and lay out pages, interview queens of the fall fair and grieving parents of car crash victims, all in the same week. It was a rare skill set, disappearing along with the small-town papers that depended on people like him.

When his mouth was empty, he said: "If you want to know more about the first few years of the Playhouse, you should ask Martha Mercer."

"Dorothy's BFF?"

Bruce grinned. "Those ladies have a history. Remind me to tell you about it sometime. Dorothy loves nothing more than publishing stories that piss Martha off. But that's not the reason I'm telling you to talk to her. Martha was every bit as involved in the Playhouse back then as she is now, like a tick stuck to a deer's back. If there's dirt to know, she knows it."

"She was married to Eliot Fraser back then, right?" I took another carrot.

"Married." Bruce snorted. "I guess you could call it that. Eliot was peeing on every pole he could find, if you know what I mean."

I slid my notepad closer. "So he was a groper even then?"

"You'd hear stories," Bruce said. He stretched, exposing his skinny midriff above his cargo shorts. "I was never a theatre person, myself. More a live music guy. And I was fairly new to town then too. But even I felt ... an atmosphere, I guess you'd say, without really knowing any details. Anyway"—he tapped my notepad—"keep asking around. You've got the nose for it. Martha Mercer is a serious piece of work, but the way I see it, it's a win-win. If she talks to you, you get a story. If she doesn't?" His smile was impish. "You'll have scored points with Team Talbott."

CHAPTER 3

FROM MY APARTMENT above the gastropub, I could see its sign, glowing red: The Second Act. A promise of the future or the coffin lid closing? I didn't really like to think about it.

My landlord was Adeline Chen, owner of the Second Act and a homegrown success story. I hadn't known her growing up—she was ten years older than I was—but she'd taken me under her wing since my arrival in Port Ellis, giving me a few bartending shifts a month to supplement my tiny newspaper income. During my first stunned weeks in town, she'd seemed to intuit my need for undemanding company, and given me an open invitation to grab a free coffee and sit at the bar anytime I wanted. Adeline was a good listener. She let me moan about my divorce, my sulky kid, and the mistake that had changed my life in one dumb minute.

And then she did the kindest thing possible. She told me it was time to stop feeling sorry for myself and get on with the business of living.

I liked my apartment, with its two small bedrooms and galley kitchen. In the pocket-sized living room was a couch from Goodwill, a vinyl recliner that let out a gassy sigh when you sat in it, and almost enough shelves for my books. When I'd married Mark he'd insisted that I shelve my books according to the colour of their spines. I should have known then that he was a sociopath.

I hung my bike helmet in the pocket closet and opened the door to what I was already calling Jake's room in my mind. Jake had balked at visiting so far, and I'd decided not to engage directly with his excuses. Instead, I'd been driving back to Toronto once a month to visit him at my parents' home, which was both palatial and convenient to Mark's house. I was counting on a shift in Jake's attitude now that the warmer weather was here. I stood in his doorway feeling a rare moment of maternal accomplishment: I'd bought him a snorkel set in case he wanted to swim, and a bike helmet if he wanted to join me for a ride on the lakeside trail. There was also a gaming console that I could not really afford, in the much more likely event that he wanted to stay in all weekend pretending he didn't have a mother.

I carried my backpack over to the old sofa and flopped down. In my notebook I'd written the names of all the people I'd need to talk to for the Eliot Fraser profile: Hadiya Hussein, Alec Mercer, Martha Mercer, Declan Chen-Martin, Jonah Tiller. I tapped my pen next to Hadiya's name. She had the potential to be a gold mine of information, and she might just be angry enough at Eliot to offer up a nugget or two. I made a note to call her in the morning and feel her out.

I put my notebook aside and headed for the shower. I had half an hour to get myself looking respectable, and I had work to do. It wasn't every night I had dinner with a celebrity.

ADELINE GAVE ME and her son a prime table in the centre of the restaurant. "Dinner's on the house," she said, quelling our protests. "I don't get that many opportunities to feed my son a home-cooked meal these days. And it's not like you have an expense account, Cat."

She brought us a bottle of sparkling water, took our orders, and then bustled off to look after her other guests. Even on a weekday night, the red velvet curtain that draped the front door swished repeatedly as women in sundresses and men in deck shoes arrived for dinner.

"I couldn't believe the change in this place when I came back," I said. "It doesn't seem fair that your mom's a genius with the menu and the decor at the same time."

Declan nodded, looking around the gastropub. "When my grandfather died, Mom did a full gut job. I sent emotional support from LA." He grinned. "Best I could do. It's not like I know which end of a hammer is up."

He was too modest to say that he'd been busy acting in *Special Forces*, the prime-time series in which he'd played a clairvoyant coroner, part of a medical team that all had superpowers. His face had stared at me from a billboard across from our newsroom in Toronto, above the words "The doctor will see you now." When the show was cancelled, its small but rabid fanbase had mutinied on social media. And now Declan was in Port Ellis, co-starring with Eliot Fraser and Jonah Tiller in *Inherit the Wind*.

I'd thought maybe there had been some dark magic afoot to make him look like a god on that billboard, but nope. Even in the dimness of the Second Act, Declan's face was beautiful in every facet, like a well-cut diamond. Glowing and healthy, with no sign whatsoever of the bout of problematic drinking that had sent his character to hospital in a coma for several months of the third season while real-life Declan did a stint in rehab.

The food arrived, artful and elegant. "Bon appétit," said Declan, tucking into his lake-caught pickerel, displayed on a cedar slab with a side order of fries nestled in a miniature shopping cart alongside.

I would have loved a glass of crisp white wine, but I wasn't going to be so rude as to make Declan watch me drink. I took a bite of my tart. Locally foraged mushrooms were layered with goat cheese that came from a farm overlooking Lake Marjorie, and crowned with a puff of briny foam that tasted like summer and the sea. *I would happily bathe in that sauce*, I thought, banishing any regrets about the wine; the meal was perfect without accompaniment.

Declan saw my expression and laughed. "My mom's a wizard with the foam." He nodded to the back of the restaurant, where Adeline stood behind the bar giving directions to a bartender who was doing his best not to look irritated. Declan watched her with genuine affection. "She's also a backseat bartender."

"It's certainly an improvement over the number-twelve special," I said, and then kicked myself. "I mean, no offence to your grandfather. The number twelve rocked. Who doesn't want a grilled cheese with a spring roll on the side?"

Declan smiled and started to answer a question I'd asked earlier about the relevance of *Inherit the Wind* to a modern audience. But my mind was lost in the past. When I was a kid, my grandparents used to take me to Treasure Garden, a local institution, after we'd seen a matinee at the Playhouse. We'd come in and find teenaged Adeline and her father yelling at each other, until Adeline stomped over to take our order. Where there'd once been a mural of the Yellow River, there was now a wall of antique bottles gleaming in the dim light. The renovation must have cost a mint.

"—and the role seemed pertinent to today, you know? The idea that we need to have the bravery to question and not just blindly obey." Declan tilted his head at me as if to say, *You still listening?* I gave him my best serious listening face, and glanced down at my recorder. We'd been talking for thirty-seven minutes, and I thought I'd been paying attention for three of them.

I roused myself in my seat. "And what's it been like working with Eliot Fraser?"

Declan bent his head back to laugh, and there was something familiar in the gesture. A worm of curiosity wriggled through my brain. Where had I seen that? Maybe I'd just watched too many episodes of *Special Forces*. Or maybe actors only had so many gestures, which they shared between them.

"Eliot's a legend," Declan said. "On the stage. In movies. I'd be lucky to have a career like that."

"Very diplomatic," I said.

He tilted his head and again I felt the flash of familiarity. "What do you mean?" he said.

"Look, Declan, you know his reputation. People say he's 'old-school.'" I crooked my fingers around the words. "But that's code for all kinds of gross behaviour."

Declan touched a french fry, as if weighing pleasure against calories. "I try to keep my head down and just do my work. He hasn't said anything off-colour to me, which is nice. Believe me, I've heard some crazy shit on set. I had one makeup lady tell me she couldn't do anything with 'Asian hair.'"

Suddenly, his attention was drawn to the restaurant's door, and I followed his gaze. Jonah Tiller, Declan's co-star, was entering the Second Act with Hadiya Hussein. They looked like a game of hide-and-seek brought to life: Jonah aiming for anonymity with a trilby hat pulled low over his eyes, Hadiya glowing like a flame in a burnt-orange jumpsuit.

Declan leaned across the table toward me. "Now Jonah, he might have a different opinion about Eliot. But you didn't hear it from me. Excuse me for a minute, would you?"

I watched him snake-hip his way between the tables to greet his co-star, and I could appreciate why Kaydence had nearly fainted when I'd said I was meeting Declan. "Just try to find out who he's seeing, would you?" she'd whispered to me in the office, and I'd had to remind her that I had not yet embarked on my career Plan B—professional matchmaker.

I watched Declan snag a lovely window table for Jonah and Hadiya. I felt sure Jonah had seen me, but he avoided my gaze in the same way he'd been avoiding my phone calls. I was starting to feel like a bill collector. Clearly, whatever feelings he had about Eliot Fraser were not for publication.

"Did you enjoy the conifer fizz on the tart?"

I spun around to find Adeline at my shoulder. Like her son, she had the silent, economical movements of a panther—and the black wardrobe to match, today a sleeveless turtleneck and slim-fitting pants. Under the faint worry lines I could still see Adeline as a girl, bussing tables at Treasure Garden. I wondered if she could see my younger self, if both of us looked in the mirror and were surprised at the careworn stranger who appeared there sometimes.

"I'm sorry," she laughed. She refilled our water glasses from a vintage crystal bottle. "I know you were extremely suspicious of the idea when I suggested we put it on the menu. What did you call it? Tree spume?"

I shrugged in surrender. "You were right, as always." I picked up the pen that was sitting on top of my notepad. "Adeline, I'm doing a story on the first season at the Playhouse, for this profile I'm writing on Eliot Fraser. I wondered if you might have any juicy stories from serving the theatre crowd back then."

"Oh," she said, "I—" A glass exploded on the other side of the room, and Adeline and I both jumped at the sudden, shocking sound. The bartender who'd been so irritated earlier now looked like a toddler bracing himself for a spanking. "Excuse me, Cat. Bradley doesn't have your skills behind the bar." Adeline's narrow shoulders squared into fighting posture and she marched over to deal with the mess.

It was only later, staring down at the blank page in my notebook, that I realized she had never answered my question.

Declan arrived back at the table, bringing with him the delicious scent of a store that sold cashmere scarves. "Sorry," he said. "I had to check in with Jonah. We start rehearsals of *Much Ado About Nothing* tomorrow. I saw you talking with my mom—did she tell you to write only nice things about me?"

"We didn't get to talk, unfortunately. Butterfingers the Bartender dropped a glass. I was hoping to ask her about the early days of the Playhouse."

"Yeah, good luck with that. She's a vault when it comes to her customers. She says restaurant owners are like therapists—confidentiality is the key to success. Not that she's chatty about her own stuff either. Did you know that my parents separated a year ago?"

"She told me," I said. "I'm so sorry. It must be difficult for you."

He nodded. "The hardest part is that neither of them will discuss it. They say it was a long time coming, but I never saw it. And now Dad's in Maine, where his family is from." Declan ran his hands through his perfect hair. "I guess you never really see your parents as adults with their own problems, no matter how old you are."

We ate for a few moments in silence. I turned to look at the table where Jonah and Hadiya were framed against the early-evening sky. Jonah was hunched forward, his wide shoulders bunched and tense. He was shaking his head like he was trying to dislodge a pesky fly. Hadiya's hand shot out and she bolted half her glass of wine.

I glanced at my list of questions. "You're playing Claudio in *Much Ado*, right? That's amazing. Two juicy roles in one season."

Declan's head jerked up. His eyes were suddenly narrow and wary. I knew this body language: it was the classic pose of an interview subject who'd been touched in a sore spot.

"Do you think it's weird?" he said. "I mean, I know that I'm known mostly for my TV work—"

"No, not at all," I said, putting my hands up in a position of surrender. If there was a prize for offending theatrical egos, I was going home a winner tonight. "You're a big star, Declan, and a local—"

"It's just that Alec thought I had the right qualities for both roles. 'A certain physicality' is how I think he put it."

His insecurity was unexpected and touching.

"I don't think audiences make much of a distinction between screen and stage actors these days," I said. "If you love an actor on television, it's exciting to be in the same room with them. I'd bet that your name on the marquee has sold as many tickets as Eliot Fraser's."

His smile blazed like a fire on a winter night. "You're a kind person, Cat. Thank you."

Sensitivity was hardly a rare affliction in Declan's business, but I didn't want to derail the interview again. I was thinking about my next question when the door to the restaurant opened once more.

This time, the atmosphere changed. I'd felt this frisson before, at the Toronto International Film Festival, when Brad Pitt walked through a hotel lobby looking like the sun captured in a bottle. I knew without turning that it was Eliot at the door. A wave of whispers rippled through the room, and people reached for their phones.

Jonah hadn't been greeted with that kind of excitement. Neither had Declan. I wondered if it chewed at them.

I heard Declan sigh. Adeline, standing by our table, was starstruck into stillness. In a moment, I smelled a hint of cologne with a top note of Scotch. Eliot placed a hand on my shoulder and began to knead.

"If it isn't our fair scribe," he boomed, and I knew he'd forgotten my name again—if he'd ever bothered to learn it in the first place. "And Bertram, freed from the classroom!"

"Eliot, it's nice to see you." Declan's face betrayed nothing. "You know Cat, and this is my mother, Adeline. The Second Act is her place."

"My dear." Eliot bent at the waist and reached for Adeline's hand. "How marvellous to meet the progenitor of this splendid young man." Adeline was staring at him wordlessly, a blank look on her face. Fame stunned people, as I well knew. I'd run smack into Mr. Pitt on the way to the hotel bathroom and he'd said "Sorry, pal" and I couldn't speak for the next hour.

Eliot took this dumbfounded silence as his due, and filled it. "We're supremely fortunate to have your son in our production. And I think we've managed to erase nearly every bad habit he learned in front of the television camera!"

Even Declan wasn't talented enough to disguise that gut punch. He took a deep breath and said, "I'm learning so much from you, Eliot. What to do. What not to do."

But Eliot's attention had already left us. With a nod in our direction, he turned and headed for the table where Hadiya sat with Jonah. He sailed through the restaurant like a majestic old barge, and phones were lifted, discreetly, in his wake.

Adeline still hadn't moved, but Declan shoved his chair back. "What a dick," he muttered. He caught my eye. "Don't write that down."

CHAPTER 4

I FASTENED A strand of pearls around my neck, a gift
from my mother. "Take these," she'd said. "Your father
gave them to me on our fifteenth anniversary. I know
you don't have many nice things." It was one of her
talents, the ability to make devastating insults seem
like generosity. It had been my own fifteenth anniversary at the time, and I'd been sitting at my parents'
kitchen table reviewing a draft separation agreement.
I fingered the clasp, hesitating. I was headed out to
the opening gala at the Playhouse and I didn't want
bad memories cramping my style. But my mother had
been right, as she often was: I didn't own many nice
things. The pearls would stay.

I stood in front of the full-length mirror fastened to

the inside of my closet door, and gave myself a frank appraisal, top to bottom.

My hair, liberated from its four-hundred-dollar city treatments, was usually a frizzy disaster, but I'd managed to tame it into a reasonably chic updo for the occasion. My skin looked healthy and tan without foundation or bronzer. The sickly pallor of the post-divorce period was finally gone, along with the grooves of sadness around my mouth. The squint lines had deepened at the corners of my eyes, but I could live with that.

In my fitted yellow dress, I could see that I'd filled out a bit after months of eating at Adeline's, but that too was welcome. When I'd arrived in Port Ellis, I hadn't had an appetite in months; it had vanished along with my marriage and career. It was a relief to feel strong again, and to see a version of my old self reflected back, wearing a stunning pair of high-heeled sandals in a bright floral pattern—a huge online shopping victory. I looked hopeful, and happy, and the realization made tears catch in my throat. It had been such an awful year. Maybe the gala marked more than the opening of theatre season in Port Ellis. Maybe it was the beginning of a new season for me as well.

Everyone from the *Quill & Packet* was attending tonight's gala, and we were all working the event. Bruce was taking red carpet photos as guests arrived. Kaydence was set to circulate in the crowd, shooting video and candid snaps for social media, tagging everyone she shot. Human vanity being what it was, it seemed like an opportunity to grow our online audience. Amir was playing squire to Dorothy, ensuring that she found and chatted with our key advertisers. An excerpt from my interview with Eliot Fraser had just been published online, generating more buzz than we'd had at the paper in a good long while. I was still working on a longer profile of Eliot, and Amir was keen to give Jonah and Declan the same treatment in upcoming editions. My job tonight was to keep my ears open and my notebook handy.

I took my sandals off and threw them into my oversized purse along with my notebook and a bottle of water, slipping my feet into Birkenstocks for the drive over. I ran downstairs, waving to the waiters taking a smoke break behind the building, and climbed into my aging Honda CR-V. It hadn't been washed in months, and it was as filthy as a teenager's imagination. I didn't need a car this size anymore, but it was sturdy on the winter highways up here, and it reminded me of all the years I'd driven Jake and his friends to hockey practice. I tried to make up for putting sentimentality ahead of environmental responsibility by riding my bike for short trips around town and carpooling with others whenever I could.

Today, I'd offered to drive Adeline to the gala but she'd declined, hoping for a few private minutes with

Declan before the crowds descended. "I still get nervous for him," she'd said. "You'll see: you're always their mother, no matter how old they get." I could see the wisdom of her plan to arrive early as I slowed to a crawl a kilometre away from the theatre; the whole town was out for opening night, and they'd all brought their cars. Harried attendants ran through the traffic in neon vests, directing angry people to auxiliary parking lots. I did a U-turn, found a side street as yet untouched by the chaos, ditched the CR-V, and strolled back in my sandals.

Perching on the ledge of a planter at the theatre entrance to swap my shoes, I nodded to a bony woman in a strapless gown as she sailed past on the arm of a tuxedoed man. We'd never been introduced, but I recognized Martha Mercer from the pages of the *Quill & Packet*. Up close, her face was as smooth as a cyborg's, while her husband, Rod—shorter and chubbier than his wife, with tufts of hair framing a dome of speckled pink scalp—looked like a mad scientist displaying his robot bride. Not entirely devoid of expression, she absorbed my ankle-down striptease and pursed her lips in a small moue of distaste.

I followed at a safe distance, skirting past them as they posed for a red carpet photo in front of a backdrop emblazoned with the logo of the Playhouse's major sponsor, Mercer Developments. Signs pointed me toward the north lawn, where the opening cocktail party was in full swing. The north lawn doubled as a local park, with stately oaks and maples that offered shade to picnickers, and extensive flower beds maintained by the Port Ellis Garden Club. In the centre of the lawn was a large reflecting pool, the bane of every child custodian; the designer had made it stupidly deep, more than a metre, and the low marble lip offered little protection for curious kids who wanted to peer down at the koi swimming in its depths. Most summer afternoons, the peace of the park was shattered by the sounds of annoyed adults fishing their wailing charges out of the water.

At the centre of the pool was a fountain, sculpted in the form of two male figures standing back to back, one holding a larger fish than I'd ever seen emerge from the lakes hereabouts, and the other resting a booted foot on a dead stag. The men depicted were, the plaque announced, Buck Mercer and Grey Talbott, founders of the Port Ellis Chamber of Commerce. Water jetted from the mouths of the fish and the stag, to ghoulish effect.

From the fountain, there was a much-photographed view of the Playhouse, a Frankenstructure that had resulted from grafting a 1980s concert hall onto a neoclassical veteran's hospital. Seen from this vantage point, the building was formal and somewhat institutional; the original hospital was three storeys of sensible brick with no ornamentation other than the portico, a hulking structure held up by two enormous white pillars framing a set of tall doors, typically locked to the public. Viewed from the south, however, the whimsy of the eighties was on full display with a massive circular construction inspired by a circus tent, its roof a cone clad in bronze that exploded at the tip into a profusion of metal ribbons, like a sparkler on a showstopper cake. I liked to think of the Playhouse as a metaphor for theatre life: sobriety at the front-of-house and frivolity backstage.

I caught sight of Adeline and Declan and made my way over to them. "How are the nerves?" I asked.

"Are you asking me or my mother?" said Declan. "Her opening-night jitters are way worse than mine."

I pulled my notebook out of my purse. "Do you have time for a few questions?"

He kissed Adeline on the cheek. "Sorry, Cat. I've got to head in. Curtain's in an hour. And I want to check on Eliot. He was looking a bit unsteady this morning."

"He isn't schmoozing out here?" I hadn't pegged Eliot as someone who would pass up a free drink, but then again, he had plenty in his dressing room.

He grinned. "He took a pass. Maybe he still gets anxious before an opening, even after nine hundred years onstage. You can ask him about that next time you talk to him."

"Break a leg," I told him, and he strode off toward the Playhouse.

I turned back to Adeline, who seemed distracted by a point over my left shoulder. I was about to ask her if she was okay when she said, "Is that your friend? The one waving over there?"

I turned to see Kaydence gesticulating wildly and heading toward me. I sighed and tucked my notebook away. "It is. And she looks upset. I'd better go and see what's wrong." I gave her a quick hug goodbye. "Declan knows what he's doing. Try to enjoy yourself."

As Kaydence looped her arm through mine and pulled me away, I asked, "What's going on?"

"It's Glenda," she said. "She's totally losing it." She was walking quickly toward the Playhouse. "You know she was on *Baking with the Stars*, right?"

"I heard something about that," I said. In truth, I wasn't much of a cook, and even less of a reality TV enthusiast. A competitive baking show sounded about as much fun as a full-body wax.

"She got eliminated in Pies and Tarts Week. Eliot Fraser was the celebrity judge. He didn't like her butter tarts."

"But her butter tarts are legendary."

"It wasn't about the tarts, Cat. Glenda wouldn't fuck him when he suggested it was the road to first place. She said no, and he said fine, there's the door. Not in so many words, of course. He's too smart for that."

The shoe dropped. "Oh, I get it now. The sign in the bakery window."

Kaydence grabbed a fistful of cocktail napkins from a passing server as we rounded the side of the building. "It gets worse," she said.

Glenda was sitting on a bench, her face damp and puffy. I sat down next to her. "What's going on?" I asked.

"It's an outrage," said Kaydence, sitting on the other side and putting a protective arm around Glenda. "Eliot Fraser can go suck a bag of dicks." Glenda dissolved into a fresh round of tears, dabbing at her face with the napkins. Kaydence turned to me. "He got her concession contract cancelled."

"The Playhouse told me they were only doing chips and candy this year to save on costs," said Glenda. She was crying so hard I could barely understand her. "But I was in there just now and they have all the same baked goods I used to make for them. I made Kelly tell me what was going on. She said that Eliot Fraser told the board they had to cancel my contract. He said that he insists on the highest quality in every aspect of his productions, and I didn't meet his standards."

"Are you sure? How can that be right?"

"Kelly went to high school with us," said Kaydence. "She works in the HR office at the theatre. She oversees all the employment contracts. If she says that's what happened, that's what happened."

"How could he do this to me?" wailed Glenda. "Do you know how bad it makes me look? That they're bringing in butter tarts from three towns away when my shop is down the street? All because I wouldn't sleep with a disgusting old man? I should sue him."

I felt my own anger rising at the endlessness of it all. I imagined a voice in my ear, taunting, and suddenly I was thrown back into the past. To my disgrace, which I'd thought I'd left behind. But then I checked myself. Kaydence had called me over to help manage the situation. I wasn't going to let her down by losing my cool. "Glenda, you have to calm down," I said. "People are looking. Let's not draw attention to the problem. It's opening weekend, right? Maybe we can put some pressure on and get the issue resolved before anyone really notices. Okay? Can you try to breathe?" I patted her on the shoulder.

"Maybe you could do a story about it," said Kaydence. "An exposé on Eliot Fraser's campaign of sexual harassment right here in Port Ellis."

"We can absolutely talk about it," I said. "If the evidence is there, I promise, I will."

Glenda's head whipped from side to side. "No," she said. "He's already taken up too much of my headspace. I want people to know me as a baker, not a victim."

"I'm here if you ever want to talk." I knew that too much coaxing could backfire and push a source away. Speaking out came with consequences, and the desire had to come from within them.

Glenda said, standing up, "This is my town, not his." She gave me a wobbly smile. "Thank you both. I have the best friends." Glenda gave us a damp group hug and headed for the rear entrance to the building. "I have my ticket. I'll see you in there."

"Is she going to be okay?" I asked Kaydence.

"Are you going to help get her some justice?" she countered. "Eliot Fraser is on a mission to destroy her. We can't let that happen."

"I agree," I said. "I'll talk to Amir first thing tomorrow." Across the lawn, I heard the chime ring out, summoning the audience to their seats. We joined the crowd gathered at the entrance, and I found myself crushed up against Hadiya as I passed through the main doors.

"I read that excerpt from your profile of Eliot," she said. "He absolutely loved it, no surprise there."

"And you didn't?"

"The writing was generous, let's just say," she said. "I didn't think you were the type for puff-piece celebrity journalism." I was surprised at how much her comment stung. We barely knew each other, but we were both writers trying to make a buck doing the work we loved. And honestly, what gave her the high ground? I wasn't ghostwriting anyone's memoirs, at least not yet.

"I haven't filed it," I said. "I'm still doing my research. I'd love to sit down with you. You know from your own work that secondary interviews add the most depth."

She glanced away, as if she were trying to collect her thoughts. I wondered if she was particularly nervous on Eliot's behalf or if she was always this twitchy. "Maybe," she said. She slid me a look from the corner of her eye. "Or maybe there's a way this works for both of us. An exchange of information. Shit has gone down this past week, let me tell you."

"Such as?"

She swung her head to peer over one shoulder and then the other. Possibly she was trying to be unobtrusive, but she was wearing the same orange jumpsuit she'd worn to dinner, with a few more buttons undone, and a sea of theatregoers surrounded us. Secrecy was not in the cards.

She beckoned me closer, and I leaned in. "I can tell you it's no lovefest around here. Just for starters, Jonah and Eliot have been at each other's throats for weeks."

"Really? What's the—"

"Tickets, please." A beaming usher held his hand out, and I showed him my ticket. Hadiya opened her clutch to search for hers. The current of bodies carried me up the steps.

"I'll drop you a line to follow up," I called over my shoulder. "Enjoy the show."

"I've seen it fifty times," Hadiya said. "But you'll like it. It's a crowd-pleaser." This felt like a veiled insult, not least because it was true. I loved *Inherit the Wind*. It was bombastic and opinionated and ripe for scenery-chewing and I couldn't wait. If that made me a cultural peasant, so be it.

I took my seat on the aisle beside Amir and Dorothy. In short order, the lights dimmed and the curtain rose on a minimalist set with a square cell in the middle, flanked by two large screens suspended from above. Declan sat inside the cell on a metal bench, dressed in a prison tracksuit and facing away from the audience.

As the action began, the screens flickered to life, Eliot on one and Jonah on the other. They were in their dressing rooms, each with a small tray table in front of them as if they were airline passengers: Eliot with a laptop, a plastic glass, and a travel-sized bottle of vodka; Jonah with a Styrofoam cup and a Bible. Evidently, Alec had decided to try a modern staging, and I was curious to see whether he would be able to carry it off.

The audience's attention was focused on Declan in his cell, but my eyes were drawn to the screen showing Eliot. His skin was an odd shade, dusky, and he grimaced as if in pain. Maybe these were the nerves Declan had been worried about. Or was this part of his method? Was he trying to convey Henry Drummond's inner torment? He shifted awkwardly in his chair.

No one else seemed to notice, so I dropped my gaze back to the stage. Declan's love interest, Rachel, entered the scene, and the prison guard unlocked the cell. Declan emerged, slowly, his body radiating fear and exhaustion, and when he turned to face the audience, I felt a physical jolt. I'd seen him on television but never onstage, and his presence was astonishing. I could feel the whole room leaning forward in their seats, caught in his spell.

As Declan embraced his lover there was a sudden movement from Eliot's screen; someone in the audience screamed. The lovers broke apart in confusion. I watched the screen and gasped. Eliot's face was contorted, his eyes bugging. One hand clutched his throat and the other clawed the air, a gesture so hammy that I thought for a moment he might still be acting.

And then he toppled from the chair.

Another scream from the audience. Someone in my aisle yelled "What the hell?" Onstage Declan was frozen, unsure what to do in the sudden chaos. Jonah's face, on the second screen, was blank with confusion.

Bucking the collective paralysis, I kicked off my sandals. "Call 911," I told Amir as I took off down the aisle, pushing an usher aside as I went. If Eliot was having some kind of attack, I could try CPR at least; it was more than anyone else was doing.

A door at the bottom of the aisle led backstage and I shoved it open. Behind me, I could hear the uproar in the audience. No time to think about that. Ahead of me, the corridor branched, and I raced along the one I thought led to Eliot's dressing room.

There was already a group of people blocking his door, men and women in black wearing headsets. I forced my way through them. Eliot was lying on the floor, making horrible rasping noises. His famous blue eyes were open but unseeing, and his skin ... In the bright light of the dressing room, his skin looked faintly blue too.

As I fell to my knees next to him, I heard someone else arrive and looked up to see Alec Mercer, his face disbelieving.

"No," he said. "No, no, no."

I started chest compressions, counting out the beats: *one and two and three and four ...*

"Alec," I said. He didn't register me at all, and so I shouted his name. He turned to look at me, but there was only shock there. No recognition.

"Alec." I tried to keep my voice calm. My hands pumped, an automatic motion. "911 has been called. You need to go out to the front of the house and ask for a doctor."

I heard a voice from the doorway say, "I'll do it."

Suddenly, I heard Alec swear, and he moved quickly around Eliot's splayed body. I looked up at him; anything so that I didn't have to stare at that poor twisted face.

"Jesus Christ," Alec said. "The video feed is on." He stepped over Eliot's outstretched hand to a tripod that I hadn't even noticed was there, supporting a camera with a blinking red light. There was a table next to it with a monitor showing the stage, now empty. There was a woman projected on the screen, feet bare, face pale, eyes wide and blank. It took me a full second to recognize myself.

Alec's hands shook as he removed the camera from the stand and turned it away from me and the scene on the floor. I watched myself disappear, and then the screen went dark.

CHAPTER 5

IF IT WAS possible to have a thunderstorm in your brain, I had one. Foggy, menacing, so loud it drowned out thoughts. I sat with Kaydence at Glenda's café and tried to fight the disbelief that arose every time I thought about the past few days. Eliot Fraser was dead.

My brain fog wasn't helped by the fact that I'd taken a Xanax so that I could sleep the previous night. And maybe also one of the nighttime antihistamines I'd found in the medicine cabinet, courtesy of Adeline's previous tenant. Perhaps I'd washed it all back with the tiniest mouthful of brandy from the bar at the Second Act.

Could you blame me? A national treasure had died under my useless hands. Eliot had lasted twelve hours in the intensive care unit of the local hospital. According to the town rumour mill—also known as Kaydence's friend Carly, the ER nurse—Eliot had slipped away just as doctors were preparing to transfer him via air ambulance to the nearest trauma centre. It gutted me to think that my panicky eyes had been the last thing he saw.

Kaydence, sitting across from me, put a comforting hand on my arm. She looked like she'd been beaten with a broom. I knew that if I were brave enough to risk a mirror I'd look just as bad.

We'd spent the day before tearing up the paper. Bruce and I worked the phones and wrote stories. Amir handled our copy and laid out the pages. Dorothy reached out to her web of contacts for any bits of information we could use. Even Kaydence was writing headlines by the end of the day. There was only one story that anyone cared about: the death of Eliot Fraser.

The *murder* of Eliot Fraser, I should say. Two senior officers from the Ontario Provincial Police had been spotted checking into the Lakeside B & B the day before, and all our calls to the local detachment, which had doubled in size overnight, were being forwarded to the media office at OPP headquarters, who assured us that community safety was the OPP's top priority. For more information we would have to wait for the press conference, which would be held at some point between now and the end of time.

"Cat, are you okay?" Kaydence's voice was full of concern. She was dressed for shuffleboard on a cruise ship—baggy T-shirt and cargo shorts—further evidence that everything was wrong side up. Before I could respond, there was a clatter of cups as Glenda dragged over a chair, jostling the table as she did. Her face was as white as the bleached flour she disdained.

Her voice came out as a yelp. "They think that I—" Several customers turned to stare, and Glenda fought to lower her voice. "They think—the police think that I did it."

"What?" Kaydence squawked.

"Wait a second," I said. "Hold on. Glenda, what makes you think that?"

Her hands shook in the pockets of her apron. "I had a call from them this morning. They want to talk to me, they said. As if I could have had anything to do with it. I don't even like flushing spiders down the john!" She lifted a napkin to her eyes, her mascara leaving a Rorschach-like blob behind.

"Look, Glenda, there's nothing to worry about," I said. Behind Glenda's hunched shoulders, I could see everyone in the café staring at us. The place was packed, the customers hungrier for gossip than chocolate croissants. It would get more crowded still as media descended on the town like locusts. I knew this because I had been, in happier days, one of the locusts.

I lowered my voice. "They'll want to talk to everyone who was at the gala. That's how they investigate."

"But I was—I was so angry. And people heard! I'm going to spend my life in prison because of freaking butter tarts!"

As Kaydence comforted her, my tired brain began to creak to life. Who would have wanted Eliot dead? Hadiya had looked like she was ready to slit his throat, that first day I met her. Had he tried to get up her skirt too?

Jonah had also looked like he could barely stand Eliot. I'd done a quick search on their history and hadn't found anything about a feud, but I'd keep looking. My gut told me there was no love lost. And perhaps Eliot's first wife, Martha Mercer, had been holding a grudge for decades? There was a reason that people called the Mercers "the Cosa Nostra of cottage country." They valued loyalty, and silence, and money—although not in that order.

"Cat." Glenda turned her tear-blotched face to me. "What do I do? Should I call a lawyer?" I recognized her tone. For some reason, locals asked me for advice on major questions, as if my time living in a big city gave me access to wisdom that they didn't possess. The voice in my head knew the truth: *Honey, I'm just as clueless as you are.* I took a tiny pillow and smothered the voice.

"It can't be a bad idea to call a lawyer and ask a few questions," I said. "I mean, it's not every day the cops want to ask you about whether you had anything to do with the death of a famous actor."

Glenda's face crumpled and I immediately regretted my flippant words. "There's nothing to worry about, Glenda. It's just routine. There's no way the cops will think a butter tart feud is enough motive to kill someone. This isn't *Midsomer Murders*."

After a giant honk into her napkin, Glenda squared her shoulders. "I'll call my cousin's wife," she said. "She's a lawyer. I mean, she mostly solves property-line disputes but ..." She bounced from the chair, erect, looking around her crowded café. "I have strudel to attend to."

I watched her stride back into the kitchen, marvelling at her ability to dump her troubles into some canister in her mind and snap a lid on top. I took a sip of my coffee, but my hand wouldn't obey my brain and half of it ended up on the table.

"You're a mess," Kaydence said, simply and without judgment. This directness was one of the things I liked about her, even when it was aimed at me. She pushed the remains of her maple-walnut scone toward me. "I don't know what happened before you came here. I only know what I see now. And I think you're pretty awesome. I mean, the way you ran from your seat like your ass was on fire. And then when you saw him lying there you didn't freak out. You did the whole CPR thing."

"I learned first aid when I was a counsellor at Ravenhead," I said. "And I got recertified when Jake was a baby." Kaydence cocked her head at me, and I realized how little I'd told her about my life before landing in Port Ellis this time around. "He's fifteen now, but when he was a toddler, I was haunted by the thought that he'd get locked in a hot car or choke on a grape. I used to cut each grape into a dozen tiny pieces. The only thing I could do to keep myself off the path to crazy-land was learning first aid. I take a refresher course every year. You know, CPR. Burns. Arterial bleeding."

I pressed my finger into the scone like I was stopping a fountain of blood, and Kaydence grimaced. Eliot Fraser's face swam in front of me—the bulging eyes, the contorted mouth. I'd seen dead bodies before, of course. Me and my camera guy on the safe side of the police tape. But I'd never been part of the story. Not like this.

I shuddered. I cast my mind back to opening night, and I pictured the crowd standing around the reflecting pool in front of the theatre. No one had been acting particularly weird, but what did I know about the behaviour of small-town killers, or any killers for that matter?

Many of the faces outside the Playhouse had

been new to me: rich cottage owners up from the city by helicopter, a local TV crew with its cameras interviewing patrons holding glasses of champagne. Everyone cheerfully expecting an evening of middle-brow theatre, not actual tragedy.

I suddenly sat up straight in my chair.

"What is it?" Kaydence asked.

"The cameras," I said. "Everyone had their cameras out before the show. Hoping to catch a glimpse of somebody vaguely famous, like Declan. People would have been filming. What if we could put out a call for the footage so we could comb through it, see if there's anything suspicious?"

Kaydence looked dubious. "Wouldn't the police want to see that?"

I grinned at her. "No reason we can't do it first."

A bell chimed, and I looked up to see Declan Chen-Martin entering the café. Normally he'd fill the room with his magnificence, but this morning he looked awful. His eyes were still chocolate pools, but the effect was marred by dark circles. And was that a bit of stress acne on his forehead? At least I wasn't the only one not at my best.

Kaydence, meanwhile, looked like my parents' cocker spaniel in the presence of chicken: eyes wide and fixed on Declan, mouth hanging open, attention unwavering. I kicked her gently under the table, and she snapped out of it.

His eyes scanned the bustling café, looking for a seat. "Declan," I called. "Come join us."

He lifted his chin and came over to our table, flopping heavily into the empty chair. He sat hunched over, and I noticed his hands trembling. He saw my gaze and tucked his fingers under his thighs.

"Can I get you a coffee?" Kaydence asked. He thanked her and she blushed and scurried to the counter.

"You've been through the wringer," I said.

He let out a hollow, barking laugh. "You could say that. I had no desire ever to see a real dead body. I'm not a coroner. I just played one on TV."

"So what now?"

"We're locked out of the theatre for now, while the police investigate. We've cancelled a week of performances for *Inherit the Wind*, but *Much Ado* is supposed to go ahead in two weeks. The police have promised Alec that we'll be able to use the theatre by then. We pick up rehearsals soon."

"That seems fast," I said. "Will you be ready to go back to ..." I almost said "the scene of the crime," but I managed to catch the melodrama before it left my lips. Declan, in his own world, didn't seem to notice.

"Alec insists that both shows must go on, and the sooner the better. We're booked solid all summer and the Playhouse will go under if we cancel, so I get where he's coming from, but we've got a cast and crew literally sobbing all day at the community centre, where we're supposed to be rehearsing. Not that we can get any rehearsing done, since the police are in and out constantly with more questions. Alec says we need to get ourselves together, but I think he needs to cut people some slack. They're traumatized. I don't know why he doesn't get that. He's usually so attuned to emotion. I think his mother is putting pressure on him to save the season."

I didn't pretend to know the Mercer family well, but emotional attunement didn't strike me as a big part of their genetic inheritance. "What kinds of questions are the police asking?"

"Did Eliot have any symptoms that anyone noticed? Was there anything unusual happening that day? Were there any strangers around? Which there were, obviously, and everything was unusual, because it was the gala. It was the one day when no one would have noticed Eliot's symptoms, assuming he had them. He was a prima donna, and normally he got a lot of attention paid to him. But we were all going flat out perfecting the performance that day, then schmoozing a park full of strangers, and then running inside to get onstage."

Kaydence came back with his coffee and he offered a quick nod, which I think might have given the poor girl third-degree burns. "Oh, and the police want to know about all the costume elements Eliot would have touched—who handled them, how they were stored, that sort of thing. The props and wardrobe staff are losing their minds."

So was Glenda, I thought, but Declan didn't need to know that.

"It must have been poison," said Kaydence, startling us both. "What else could it have been? The police wouldn't be interested in the props otherwise."

"Have they told any of the rest of you that you might have been exposed?" I asked. I agreed with Kaydence, even if I wasn't ready to say so on the record. If Eliot's death wasn't due to a natural heart attack or stroke, the likeliest culprit was a toxin. I'd spent some time researching poisons when I was covering the trial of a Russian assassin living under an assumed name in Canada. His weapon of choice had been the nerve agent Novichok, but the case had generated a lot of curiosity about poisons in general. I'd done a report on the most notorious poisonings of the last ten years, and unfortunately still had a catalogue of gruesome symptoms lodged in my brain.

"No," said Declan. "They said that they wanted to make sure the theatre was safe before we went back in. But nothing about a risk to anyone else who was there that day." He looked worried. "Should we get some kind of testing done to make sure the rest of us are okay?"

"Not at all," I told him. "The police would have

a duty to tell you if you were in any danger. I'm just thinking out loud. It's an occupational hazard." I caught Kaydence's eye. Alec might not be sensitive, but Declan was, and I didn't want to start a panic among the Playhouse staff. A change of subject was in order. "Who was Eliot's understudy?"

"I was. Am." He took another sip of his coffee, his expression glum. "Talk about a promotion no one would ever want."

"Declan, listen. I want to ask you something."

He lifted his gaze, glassy and numb, to meet mine.

"Was there bad blood between Eliot and Jonah?"

Those lovely broad shoulders slumped. I could see Kaydence was on the verge of offering him the comfort of her bosom.

He dragged a hand through his hair, which already looked like a badger had crawled through it. "Look, the thing is, Jonah and I talk. But it's between us, because … well, it just is." He sighed. "The cops are going to ask me about it anyway, aren't they? It's going to come out."

"What is?"

"Jonah told me that Eliot stole a role from him early in his career. A live television broadcast of *Hamlet*. He would have been one of the first African American actors to play Hamlet on a stage like that. On TV. It would have been—" His fingers popped open, miming an explosion.

"Jonah must have been hugely pissed off."

Declan sat back. "It's worse than that. The way Jonah tells it, Eliot stabbed him twice. He told the producer that Jonah was a drunk, that he wouldn't turn up. So not only did Jonah lose the gig, but nobody wanted to cast him for years after."

That tracked. I'd done some research on Jonah's career in preparation for my profile on him, and he'd had a decade or so in the wilderness. There had been some notable episodes of public drunkenness that had produced cruel headlines. That hadn't been written off as hijinks with Jason Robards.

It seemed odd that Eliot was so threatened by Jonah. I'd met lots of Eliot Frasers in my time—hard-drinking, skirt-chasing, self-loving—but they didn't usually have their elbows out. Why should they? Opportunities washed up on their shores with every tide.

"I don't get it," I said. "I mean, why steal *Hamlet*? He could have had any other role he wanted."

"Are you serious? Those old bastards thought they were entitled to everything. Eliot's ass was kissed more often than the pope's ring." Declan leaned forward, lowering his voice. "He complained to Alec about me, if you can believe it. He thought I was upstaging him. It was ridiculous. He was an annoying goddamn baby." Suddenly Declan caught himself. "I mean, not so annoying you'd want him dead or anything."

Just at that moment, his phone rang and he snatched it up. "Gotta go," he said, and headed for the door. A young woman tried to grab him for a selfie on the way out, but Declan declined, bowing his head in humility. From where I sat, it almost looked real.

CHAPTER 6

"I THINK SOME idiot from CNN just stole my parking space," said Bruce. "I would have called him out but I was blinded by the sun reflecting off his teeth."

Kaydence helped herself to a dried cherry from Bruce's stash. "Some British dude offered me fifty pounds if I could produce a photo of Eliot at a bar. I asked him how much that was in real money."

At the morning news meeting, everyone was sharing their run-ins with the international press who had descended on the town. I said nothing; it wasn't so long since I had been one of the people with gleaming teeth and straightened hair, shoving a microphone in the face of Jane Citizen.

Amir let the chatter go on for a moment, and then

he held up one hand, like the world's most Zen first-grade teacher. The hubbub died down.

"Okay," Amir said. "Let's see where we're at."

We published our newspaper in print twice a week. The weekday edition tended to cover issues under the broad heading of business and politics, including reports from city hall and the chamber of commerce. The weekend edition had the puzzles, recipes, and lifestyle stories. Our online readership was reasonably healthy, and it had seen a huge spike after Eliot's death. The print edition was another matter. In a rare moment of defeatism, Dorothy had told me that the average age of subscribers was "one year away from death."

The real action lived online, where we published new stories every day. For the foreseeable future, the *Quill & Packet* would be concentrating its efforts, print and digital, on the untimely demise of Eliot Fraser. The weekday edition was headed for the printer by midafternoon today, so we had a few hours to pull together a smart package with everything we knew. Which, at this point, was not much.

"I have a call in to the investigating officer in the Fraser case," said Amir. He looked down at his phone. "Detective Inspector Cheryl Bell. Not that I have any hope that she'll actually tell us anything. But I have Dorothy working her connections in the local cop shop."

I nodded, hoping I was keeping a straight face. The local cop shop consisted of two uniformed officers: Sergeant Dick Friesen, an old-timer who spent his days giving tickets to people illegally fishing, and Constable Ele James, who was studying part-time for her forestry degree.

"Other thoughts?" Amir asked.

"We saw Declan Chen-Martin today," I said. "Apparently the police are asking a lot of questions of the cast, and the props and wardrobe people. Whoever interviews Cheryl Bell should ask about that. Also the cast and crew are struggling to process the news. Maybe a human interest story on the impact of Eliot's death on his co-workers?"

"Good," said Amir. "Bruce, do you want to take that one?"

"Sure," said Bruce. "If CNN didn't get there first."

"Thanks. Other leads?"

Kaydence's expression was pleading. We couldn't keep silent about Glenda forever—Kaydence knew that—and if she continued to be a suspect we'd have no choice but to report on it. There was another avenue I wanted to explore first, however. "There was apparently some tension between Jonah and Eliot in rehearsal," I said. "We were planning to run a profile on Jonah at some point soon anyway. Maybe I could start prepping for that piece and plan a few questions about his relationship with Eliot?"

"Sounds like a good start," said Amir. "Okay, every-one, I think that's it for this morning. Keep in touch with developments, please."

As my colleagues returned to their desks, my phone vibrated. I turned it over and stared at the screen. "What is it?" Kaydence asked, seeing my face. She must have been tired of asking that question.

Cat, the text said. No salutation. The number wasn't in my contact list but I knew immediately who had sent it. *I know it's been a long time. One day we'll talk over a glass of something strong and brown. But right now I need a stringer in Port Ellis. Call me.*

Claire Silverberg was the national editor at the newspaper where I'd worked for a dozen years before I'd been seduced away to the land of television. She hadn't taken my departure well, let's just say. On my farewell card she'd written: *Good luck. You're going to need it.* And then she'd never spoken to me again. At least not until this moment, when she needed my help.

Kaydence stalked away, miffed at my silence. But I was still staring at my phone, which had become something much more: a path to the outside world, a highway back to the high life. If I wanted it. Did I want it?

"Cat?" Amir was standing on the other side of the table. I recognized his quizzical look from years ago, when we were camp counsellors and he was trying to solve a problem: how to get marshmallow out of hair, how to unlock two adolescents accidentally joined at the braces.

But he wasn't that young man anymore. He was my boss, and a mystery.

"Cat, can I talk to you for a minute? Maybe in my office?" I felt my anxiety spike. I'd had some bad closed-door meetings in the too-recent past. Had he seen the message from Claire on my phone?

I followed him into his tiny office, which was as calm and tidy as its occupant. "What's up?" I asked, trying for nonchalance and failing.

"You seem pretty stressed," he said. I started to protest and he held up a hand. "Come on, Cat. I know you. So does Kaydence, and she sees it too." I'd need to have a word with Kaydence about the friend code, I thought. "You had a tough experience the other night. No one would blame you if you were thrown by it. But I need to know if you can handle the reporting on this story."

"If I can't, I'm in the wrong business," I said. Amir didn't respond with the smile I'd expected. "I'm perfectly capable of doing my job, Amir. I've covered serious crime before, in bigger places than Port Ellis. I've got this."

"If you start to feel differently, you need to tell me right away," he said. "Port Ellis may be an outpost, but it just handed you an international story, and you're the reporter with the local advantage. Don't squander it. I need you at the top of your game."

"Has anyone ever told you that you worry too much?"

"Once or twice." He smiled, a rare event these days, and I caught a glimpse of the boy who'd been my favourite companion all those years ago. "Most often my mother."

I HAD AN hour before the police press conference was to begin at five, so I stopped by the Hasty Mart to load up on snacks that a fifteen-year-old would love: beef jerky, chips, chocolate bars. I stopped at the fridge, staring at the psychedelically coloured cans of energy drink inside. Impulsively, I reached in and grabbed a few. Jake's energy seemed to be drained merely by being in my presence.

With my arms full, I batted the door to the Second Act open with my hip and headed up the stairs to my apartment. I'd have to tell Adeline that I couldn't work my usual evening shift when Jake was visiting. That was another reason to answer Claire's message: if I took on some freelance work, I wouldn't have to supplement my income slinging drinks for rich jerks from the city like the one I'd divorced.

As I came back downstairs, I saw Adeline framed in the doorway to the street, her arms folded across her chest. She was staring at a camera crew who'd set up on the sidewalk. I went to stand beside her, feeling my heart constrict a little.

"They asked if they could shoot inside my place, but I said no. Then they asked if I'd talk to them about Eliot Fraser, and I told them I had nothing to say." There was an uncharacteristic stoniness in Adeline's tone. "They remind me of the weevils I find in the flour sometimes." She turned to me with an apologetic smile. "Sorry, Cat. I know you're one of them. Kind of."

But I didn't say anything. I couldn't stop staring at the TV reporter across the street, who radiated the brittle energy of someone trying to fly a plane with one wing. She'd have a producer on the line, asking for more. Always asking for more. She'd be thinking about getting her shots, getting her interviews, whether her lipstick had smeared. Worrying about that one asshole who could walk by and ruin her day's work. Her life's work.

I felt a sympathetic vibration, a tremor that shook me from the feet up.

I took a deep breath and closed my eyes. I was not one of them. Not anymore.

CHAPTER 7

WHEN INSPECTOR BELL came to stand at the lectern, she had to adjust the microphone slightly downwards. The junior constable who'd introduced her was almost a foot taller. I looked for him now, standing with his police colleagues, and I wondered if he felt embarrassed for failing to make the necessary correction for his boss. But he was whispering to the officer next to him, oblivious.

Men. They walked through the world as if it was designed for them, because it was.

Inspector Bell took it in stride and began by introducing herself to the assembled journalists. I imagined that she took a lot in stride: she was a small middle-aged Black woman in a profession that respected none of those things. The stories she must have. What an incredible profile she'd make for the *Quill & Packet*.

Not that she'd ever agree. Cops made monks look like blabbermouths. Officially, anyway. If you got them away from microphones, if you earned their trust, then you had a chance of learning interesting things. Always on background, and usually after a lot of diligent courting. I hadn't had time to woo any of the police in the tri-lake area. I was a wallflower at this particular dance.

"… given the high degree of interest in this case, we're setting up a command post here at the community centre," Inspector Bell was saying. She spoke quietly and with authority, not looking at the notes before her. She indicated the young officer behind her, who was still ignoring her. "Constable Symanski will be stationed here to act as community safety officer." Hearing his name, the gangly constable snapped to attention.

She was right about the interest in Eliot Fraser's murder. The lectern in front of Inspector Bell bristled with microphones from news networks around the world. A towering German reporter wedged himself in front of me until I kicked him in the Achilles tendon, at which point he swung on me with a filthy look. "Sorry," I said, in my best fake-cheery voice. "Entschuldigung!" He glared at me but sidled over so that I could see again.

Eliot Fraser's noble mug stared at me from a poster that had been propped on an easel. Instead of sitting beneath a movie title, his piercing blue eyes had top billing under a Crime Stoppers hotline. It was ridiculous, but I felt like his gaze was following me, as if to say: *Nice job on the CPR, Conway.*

"I'd just like to repeat my request to the public," Inspector Bell was saying. "If anyone has photos or video taken at the gala, that material could be pertinent to our investigation. Please get in touch if you have anything you think might be relevant to—"

A voice from the crowd interrupted her. "We don't let anyone take pictures inside the theatre."

The journalists shifted, buzzing, craning to see who'd been rude enough to interrupt the senior investigator. Inspector Bell showed no irritation. I couldn't imagine the scar tissue that would build up after a lifetime of biting your tongue.

A little space had opened up around the man who'd interrupted: Alec Mercer, cottage country's nepo baby. Inspector Bell gave the young director a glare set at half power. "Thank you, Mr. Mercer," she said. "I'm aware of the theatre's official policy. But human nature being what it is, one of the audience members might have taken the opportunity to grab a quick picture. If so, we'd like to see it."

Alec leaned against a table as if he owned the place. In truth, the community centre was one of the few things in Port Ellis safe from the Mercers' grasp. *They put the "merce" in "mercenary,"* Dorothy had snapped at me once, and I'd nearly laughed. There was nothing funny about that family, though.

Inspector Bell was still talking, but my attention was frozen for the moment on Alec. He cultivated a 1970s Robert Redford vibe, all shaggy blond hair, bright blue eyes, and stubble that invited a stroking hand. Like Declan, he was vibrant and magnetic, but I felt repulsed by him.

Money and beauty: together they bought everything. Such as two prime directing gigs at one of the country's premier summer festivals. Money and beauty also hid a multitude of sins.

"Even though this is now a homicide investigation," Inspector Bell was saying, "we're confident there is no risk to the public at this time." She consulted briefly with a fridge-shaped detective who'd been standing by her side. Where had they sent him from? You could bet that every level of policing wanted a piece of this action. She turned back to the journalists, who stood as tense and eager as cheetahs when the zookeeper arrived with a bucket of goat parts. "I'll take questions now."

I glanced at Alec, who was typing something into his phone. Alerting his mother, maybe. They'd be desperate to save the good name of the theatre that was the source of their cultural cachet. I stood up straighter, watching him. An electric thrill ran through me, so long-forgotten that it took me a minute to identify it. The voices around me faded as I grasped for that unfamiliar, comforting feeling: the joy and excitement of the chase. Everyone knew that Eliot Fraser had abandoned Martha for Broadway at the end of the Playhouse's first summer, dashing her dreams and leaving her to pick up the crumbs in a two-bit cottage town—which, in Martha's case, had involved marrying a local developer within months and producing the first in a brood of sons in short order. She was a survivor, that was for sure. My racing mind circled the other people in Eliot's orbit. Declan, his understudy. Jonah, his rival. Hadiya, his browbeaten assistant.

"Any more questions?" Inspector Bell was gathering her papers at the lectern. My hand shot up, and she nodded at me. "Cat Conway, from the Port Ellis *Quill & Packet*." Did I hear the German snort with laughter at the name of the paper? I sunk my elbow into his side, and he grunted. "I'm wondering what you can tell us about the toxicology results you've received."

"The office of the coroner continues to do its work and will provide us with the relevant information we require for our investigation as it becomes available," said Inspector Bell, and I wondered if she practised her non-answers at home.

As she turned to leave, I shouted, "I have a follow-up! Has your department identified a suspect yet?"

Inspector Bell had a file folder clasped to her chest. "We are at a preliminary stage of our investigation and continue to explore all avenues open to us. Which is why it's so important for anyone in the community to contact us with information. Even if they think it's inconsequential, it might provide a crucial piece of the puzzle."

With that, she strode toward the door. Her colleagues fell into line behind her like ducklings learning to swim. The camera crews began to pack up their gear. The reporters drifted into small clusters, gossiping, criticizing, trading tiny bits of information like currency. It was the way of my people. We all played the game, seeing how much we could get without giving much away. Everyone in that room wanted the story. Everyone wanted to know who had shut Eliot Fraser's eyes for good.

I picked up my bike helmet from the hook where I'd hung it, one thumb on my Twitter feed. Journalists used Twitter the way that European explorers had used the St. Lawrence River: for navigating new territory and trading valuable goods. Also dumb jokes and insults. It had become a bit polluted lately, but there was still room in the current for everything.

The hashtag #RIPEliotFraser was trending again. Someone had posted a picture of Inspector Bell alongside the words *fuck around and find out*. Someone else had tweeted *old pervs get what's coming sooner or later* alongside the hashtag #MeToo. I didn't recognize the account, but I bookmarked the tweet for later reference. I'd reach out to the account holder and see what they knew.

As I walked out the double glass doors, the sun hit me like a slap and I blinked. I was standing there, half-blind, when I heard a voice, low and pleasant and entirely unwelcome. "Hey, look who's here! If it isn't the runaway."

That voice. It was the aural equivalent of seeing the cops in your rear-view mirror, flashing their lights. For a moment, I thought about putting the pedal to the metal and making a break for it—running away, just like he'd said.

Slowly I turned. He had a few more wrinkles and a bit less hair than when I'd last seen him, staring at me over a luridly coloured cocktail at the end of my going-away party. Nick Dhalla had been my colleague when I'd worked at the newspaper, the nicotine-stained soul of the investigative team. I'd abandoned the team for a job in television, and he'd made me understand with a glance that I'd stomped on his heart.

"No hello for an old friend?" He held out his hand, and I walked over to shake it. I hoped he wouldn't notice how wet my palm was. He gestured to the man standing beside him, a tall pale guy with hair the colour of an Irish setter's. "Do you know Detective Mike Hayward?"

I did not. I shook the detective's hand and told him my name, and he looked at me quizzically. "You're the one who administered CPR. Have you been interviewed yet?"

"I'll talk if you will," I said.

Nick laughed and said, "Cat's with the local paper." He leaned closer to the detective, man to man: "You'll want to watch out for her. She'll find a way in when you're least expecting it."

A HALF-HOUR LATER Nick and I were sitting in Centennial Park overlooking the lake. To the left was the private marina, cruisers and sailboats waiting for their owners to be free from the tyranny of the phone and the laptop. On the right was the public dock, where you could catch a ferry to one of the sister lakes. The *Maiden of the Lakes* (a.k.a. the *Old Maid*), a paddle steamer refitted as a party boat, sat at the dock with the sun glistening on her giant wheel.

"So," he said. "Nice new byline, Ms. Conway. You're on the run and you've got an alias."

"Not an alias," I said. "Just going back to my roots. I was Conway until Mark convinced me that I needed to take his surname or the Schultzes would be lost to history. It was like *Titanic*. My name had to die to save his."

He snorted, stretching out his legs so that his

motorcycle boots reached for the lake. If his boots hadn't already marked him as an alien in the land of deck shoes and flip-flops, then the hand-rolled cigarette between his fingers finished the job.

It was a mistake to write him off because of the way he dressed, I knew. He had the laser focus of a forensic accountant and the tenacity of a cat with a half-dead bird in its jaws. He could find a scandal in a footnote.

Nick stubbed his cigarette out on the sole of his boot. "You sure picked the right place to hole up," he said.

"Because it's pretty or because there's a famous corpse here?"

"Does it have to be one or the other?"

"You're here to write about Eliot Fraser," I said. Not a question but a statement.

"Well, you didn't reply to Claire's message this morning."

This was true. I'd start to write a text to the national editor, and then I'd delete it. I'd done this twenty times over the course of the day.

"So they sent me," Nick said. "The Opticon numbers on the Fraser story are off the scale, apparently. Not that I give a shit." Opticon was my old newspaper's audience-engagement software. It told editors what stories readers wanted, and when they wanted them. It knew who was on the verge of buying a subscription, and precisely which story about the royal family—or a dead celebrity—would make them reach for their wallets. Nick used to say that Opticon knew when readers were taking a crap and had ten minutes to read a long feature.

"I saw the footage of you giving the old guy CPR." He turned to me, hazel eyes searching mine. He was such a good listener. He listened with his whole face, even his eyebrows. "You've never missed a detail in your life. What did you notice when you were down there?"

"You did not drive two hundred kilometres to blow smoke up my ass."

He grinned at me, the grin that had bagged him three wives. And me.

I turned my head back to the lake, playing for time. Trying to forget what had happened between us such a long time ago.

I'd been split from Mark for six months on a trial separation—the first of three over the course of our failing marriage. Jake was five, made up of equal parts Lego and ear infection. Mark and I were trying to see if there was a way ahead, but not speaking to each other much.

Jake was staying with Mark that week. I was working with Nick on a series about a parking-lot magnate and his connections to city hall. It was even less exciting than it sounds, but somehow spreadsheets acted like porn on my dormant libido. We had dinner and then worked late at his apartment, which smelled like cigarettes and Old Spice. I'd been living in a house that smelled only of hand sanitizer and resentment, and I found Nick's shabby apartment oddly erotic.

It was no surprise, then, that we fell into bed. My doing as much as his. What was surprising, though, was that he avoided me at the office afterwards. I thought I'd have to beat him off with a stick, but he ducked into offices when he saw me coming. And then I was pissed.

I cornered him one day in the line at the cafeteria, and he told me, sheepishly, that he was on the short walkway between wives two and three. He wanted to be a better man this time around.

We'd had one night, and it never happened again. Which didn't mean that I never thought about it.

The sun sent shards of brilliance off the waves. I felt Nick's eyes on my face, and I felt them when they moved away. "Did it work?" he said. "Running away?"

I had no idea how to answer that. I felt like I was in the middle of running and it was too early to tell. "It was a pretty big explosion I had to escape," I said.

Nick was rolling another cigarette. He shrugged, brought the paper up to his lips to lick it shut. "We all make mistakes," he said. "Did I tell you I'm getting married again? Fourth time lucky."

AS I RODE back to my apartment, my mind raced. It was as if twenty crazed hamsters had been set loose in my brain, and they all had different ideas about where the food dish was. I tried to keep everything straight—Eliot Fraser's murder and Jake's visit and Nick's unexpected arrival—but it was hopeless.

The traffic crawled along Lakeshore, and I whizzed past a Prius whose owner was leaning on the horn. Good luck with that, buddy. Every ghoul and rubber-necker in the tri-lake area had landed in Port Ellis to see if Eliot Fraser would make an appearance, like the ghost of Hamlet's father.

Had Eliot really stolen Hamlet from Jonah? That'd be enough to make me reach for a dagger. But then, I had a bit of a short fuse. As I pulled up outside the Second Act, I noticed that the same camera crew was across the street. They'd moved a few metres down to get a different backdrop.

I saw the young reporter glance at her phone, then quickly nod to the cameraman, then do a quick scan of the street. A dim echo of panic filled my ears. I'd never felt comfortable when I was in her position, trying to look presentable and sound intelligent, juggling my own thoughts and the producer's voice in my ear. And always keeping an eye open for the assholes on the street.

A pair of young men approached the reporter, who had turned her bright smile to the camera. They slowed. My breath caught.

Suddenly I was back there, the day everything changed. It wasn't summer anymore; it was January, with my feet frozen and my cameraman trying to hide his frustration. It should have been a simple story, city hall debating whether or not to cut the police budget. But every time we tried to shoot, something happened: the siren of a passing ambulance, a pigeon flying in front of the camera, a group of school kids stopping to ask, *Hey Miss, are you fake news?*

I was already on edge when it happened. The thing every woman on camera dreads. The thing she knows could happen any given day. The thing she's supposed to ignore, if she's a good girl.

I was not a good girl that day.

A shadow passed by my shoulder as I was explaining the police department's new wage demands. Too close. Then the shout, an explosion in my ear. Someone screamed, "Fuck her right in the pussy!" Out of the corner of my eye, I could see this jackass high-fiving his friend and squawking with laughter.

My cameraman, Tony, threw up his free hand in exasperation and gestured at me to start again. But something had invaded my body, a streak of rage as real as my own breath. I felt possessed. Every indignity of that day, and the years before it, crashed together in one atomic moment.

Without thinking, I grabbed a fistful of hoodie. Suddenly there was a face in front of mine. His eyes flew open in shock, as if his chicken dinner had sprung to life and kicked him in the balls.

"Hey—" he said and tried to back away. "Get off me!"

But I hauled him closer, my hand moving to circle his throat. I could feel his Adam's apple jerking under my fingers. Tony was beside me now, trying to keep us apart. My rage had an inevitability, though. It felt oddly like childbirth, like something that had to be finished. I screamed into his face, spittle flying: "I think you're the pussy, and you should go fuck yourself."

It wasn't particularly witty, really. I wish I'd had a better retort to end on. Especially when a video taken by a bystander went viral, making me a hero to a bunch of women who had also had enough. A hero for a day, until the next one came along.

My bosses at the station didn't quite share that view. I was out on my ass by lunch.

CHAPTER 8

WHAT DID YOU notice when you were down there? Nick had asked. He'd always had a magpie's eye for the elements of a case that glittered with investigative potential. It was a gift, but it could be an annoying one, especially when he flew off with a gem you'd had ample opportunity to seize for yourself.

I'd seen the body up close. What had I noticed? I'd been so focused at the time on saving Eliot, and so distressed afterwards at my failure, that I hadn't really processed what I'd seen. Now, days later, the images refused to fade.

I was sitting in the basement at the *Quill & Packet*, a grim, windowless space that housed a microfiche station, a few rows of metal storage units piled high with dusty cardboard boxes and discarded technology, and a couple of 1980s-era tweed-upholstered office chairs with squeaky caster wheels. Not an ideal setting for meditation, but I could improvise. I closed my eyes, took a few deep breaths, and let my mind drift back to the night of the gala, and the floor of Eliot's dressing room.

Eliot's skin had been oddly tinged—unnatural, horrible. Even with all of my first-aid training, I'd hesitated to touch him for a fraction of a second. His famous eyes were bloodshot. His tongue was protruded, swollen and twisted. As hard as I'd tried to bring him back from the brink, I'd been sure he was dead when the paramedics rushed in, put him on a gurney, and rolled him out of his dressing room.

I opened my eyes with a shiver. The police didn't think he'd been taken out by natural causes, like a heart attack or aneurysm. Which left the unnatural possibilities: drugs that interfered with oxygen uptake, ingested accidentally or by design. Poison, in other words. If the police were right, Eliot had been a goner before I even touched him. He'd been as tough as old boots to have survived even briefly on life support.

I exhaled, feeling a scaly layer of guilt moulting off like snakeskin. Trust Nick to get me back on the right track. It was time to stop blaming myself and start acting like the investigative journalist I'd once been—one who knew a thing or two about poison.

It was a weapon of premeditation, requiring a

certain amount of knowledge—admittedly available to anyone with internet service—and access to the victim's food, drink, or medication. Historically, it had been viewed as a woman's strategy: secretive, cunning, intimate. Like witchcraft. These days it wasn't witches we needed to worry about; it was government agents poisoning the underpants of freedom-loving dissidents. Either way, poison was a nasty way to go, designed for maximum suffering. Eliot had been a randy old narcissist—but who in Port Ellis could have hated him enough to inflict that kind of torture?

I stood, stretching, and walked to the wall where the old issues of the *Quill* were archived. The earliest, more than a century old, were bound in blue leather and sat on specially built shelves. The microfiche spools holding more recent issues had been shoved into several deep drawers. An apt metaphor for daily newspapers.

If Glenda and anonymous Twitter users were to be believed, Eliot Fraser had been a sexual predator of the highest order. Surely there'd be some record of it in the *Quill* during that first summer he'd appeared at the Playhouse. But as I unspooled and squinted, my eyes assuming the quality of grated horseradish, I could find nothing, apart from the vague gossip items about hijinks and fistfights backstage. No news story, no editorial, no opinion column that mentioned his terrible behaviour. It was a different time—there were a lot of ads for double-breasted suits—and if Eliot had misbehaved, the *Quill* had decided to look the other way.

My phone buzzed and I glanced down to see Jake's name. He'd be getting on the bus in Toronto right around now, arriving in Port Ellis in three hours. I opened his message and felt my stomach drop.

Change of plans. Staying in the city.

I grabbed my phone in a stranglehold, scrolled through my contacts for "Disorder, Personality," and stabbed at the call button with my index finger. "Mark Schultz," said a voice I knew as well as my own.

"What the hell, Mark," I hissed. "We agreed that Jake would come to Port Ellis this summer. I can't keep driving down to Toronto every time I want to see my son. He hasn't made the trip up here once since I moved." I needed my anger. Anger was the only thing keeping me upright.

"Whose choice was it to move to the middle of nowhere?" my ex-husband said dismissively. "Not mine, and certainly not Jake's. You can't be surprised that a teenage boy has better things to do than spend his whole summer with his mother. He wants to see his friends too."

"Let me get this straight," I said. "Instead of encouraging him to visit me, you're letting him hang out with his friends at your house?"

"I'm supporting his choices," said Mark. "He's a young man and he deserves to have his agency respected."

I bit back the snarky observation that Mark had never once advocated for Jake's individual preferences unless they aligned with his own wishes. I'd learned the hard way that he was a man who disliked the inconvenience of accommodating others. "He's fifteen, Mark."

"That's old enough to make decisions about where he wants to be. If you're upset, you can take it up with Jake."

I kicked out savagely at the wall behind the desk, feeling the moist drywall give way. "Our son is supposed to spend a weekend every month and all of his school vacations with me. You agreed to that arrangement."

"I did. And Jake is aware of the agreement. But any lawyer will tell you that teenagers vote with their feet. I'm not going to stuff him onto a bus against his will. If you want to see him more often, you can move back to the city. Or you can take me to court. But they'll ask Jake where he wants to live and we both know what he'll say. So I don't see that working out for you." He murmured something to someone in the background. "I have to go."

"Mark," I said, but the call disconnected.

I stood up violently, a howl lodged in my throat. My chair skittered away on its casters, clanging into the shelving unit behind me.

Who could have hated Eliot enough to poison him? An ex-wife, that's who.

"You could throw the other chair," said a voice from the door. "It's already broken. No one would miss it." Bruce was leaning against the door frame. His eyes were kind. "Or we could go outside for some air if you don't want to get your Hulk Hogan on?"

I nodded, and Bruce ushered me out of the storage room, up the stairs, and out into the sunshine. We walked across the street to the park, Bruce putting up a hand to stop cars as we crossed. "Here," he said, stopping in front of a bench near the bandshell. "Sit."

I did. I couldn't speak. I didn't know what would come out of my mouth if I opened it.

Bruce turned his face up toward the sun, his eyes hidden behind mirrored shades. "I never had kids of my own," he said. "But I came to Port Ellis to help my sister raise her boy, almost forty years ago now. My sister's husband walked out on her, the useless son of a bitch. She was in a bad way, so I came for the summer. Ryan was a toddler." He paused, as if deciding whether or not to continue. I'd never heard him mention his famous nephew, and I knew from Kaydence that he was incredibly private about their relationship. I could understand why. Ryan Marlow was the frontman for Things That Go Bump, a band that had been generating hits and tabloid stories in equal measure for a couple of decades. "Summer turned into a year, and then another one. Meghan, my sister, was a drinker. Still is. And Ryan grew up wild. He was smart as a whip, even then. But he'd have these outbursts, and Meghan couldn't manage him."

I found that I could speak. "They were lucky to have you."

"I don't know. I got a lot wrong. I'd never had that kind of responsibility for anything, and I had no idea what I was doing. But I mostly figured it out. When Ryan was seventeen, he begged me to take him down to Toronto to audition for *Show Us Your Hits*. It was a tiny cable show but he was amazing on it. He swept the competition." I'd read enough profiles on Ryan to know what had happened next. His new manager—one of the judges from the show—had assembled a band around him and turned them into a music-industry fairy tale. "As soon as Ryan earned his first buck as a performer, his father crawled out from under a rock and wanted a relationship with him. No surprise there. He told Ryan that we'd blocked him from visiting or calling. It wasn't true, but Ryan was furious with us. He cut off all contact for a couple of years. Worst time in my life."

"I'm so sorry," I sniffled. Somewhere in the middle of Bruce's story, the tears had started, first a dribble and then a swell that swamped my defences. I had no more ability to stop the water than a twig caught in the rapids. Was I crying for Bruce? For Ryan? For my shitty divorce? My lost career? My once-sweet son, now transformed into a seething, resentful teenager? I didn't know, and it didn't matter, really.

Bruce rummaged in the pocket of his khaki shorts and pulled out a package of tissues for me. He patted my hand. "It was a long time ago now," he said. "Eventually, Ryan matured enough to get some perspective on his parents and on me. And now we're tight and his father is pretty much out of the picture."

I blew my nose, drew a few hiccupping breaths. "So you're saying it'll be fine?"

He laughed. "That depends what you mean by fine, Cat. Sooner or later, your teenager will grow a frontal lobe, and he'll become slightly less self-involved and angry about the divorce, and he'll figure out that his father is at least as annoying as you are. And if you use that time to work out your own shit, you'll end up more or less where you want to be."

We sat in the sunshine, and I could feel sadness oozing out of my pores and dissipating in the warm air. "I don't know if that's Port Ellis," I said. "Where I want to be, I mean."

"I would have said the same. It sneaks up on you, though. Don't say I didn't warn you." He glanced at his watch. "Oh, crap. We need to go. We're going to be late."

"Late for what?" As far as I knew, the workday was basically over.

"We need to be at the Pinerock by four. There's a presentation on the retirement village, the one proposed for the Ravenhead site. I'm taking photos, and you're doing a story—Amir said you can decide what it is. That's what I came downstairs to tell you in the first place. Are you up for it?"

"Yeah," I said. "Thanks to you. Can I buy you a drink after? I hear they have a swanky bar at the Pinerock."

"They have a swanky everything," he said. "And if you want to pay fifteen bucks for a beer, I'll be happy to drink it."

WE DROVE IN Bruce's aging Subaru, since he'd already loaded up his camera equipment. "Not exactly rustic," I said, as we pulled into the parking lot.

"It's eight hundred bucks a night, minimum," said Bruce.

I had to admit, the Pinerock Resort was impressive. The original building was a modified Tudor style, with four storeys of faux plaster and timber, bright white and warm brown. It was constructed in an elongated crescent shape that mimicked the shoreline. The roofline was dotted with turrets, shingled in red. It was the fanciest hotel in the region by far, with a five-star restaurant, a Scandinavian spa, and a competition-level golf course. At the front door, a young man with an iPad greeted us. "Are you here for the press conference?" he asked.

"Bruce Collinghurst and Cat Conway from the *Quill & Packet*," Bruce said.

The staffer tapped on his screen. "Welcome to the

Pinerock. You'll find your press packets on the table next to the elevator. You're going to the second-floor conference centre. Turn right out of the elevator and follow the signs to the end of the hallway. You'll want to hurry, though—they're about to start."

It was quiet on the second floor; we were late, and the doors were closed. We were hurrying along the curved corridor when I spotted Martha and Alec Mercer in a heated tête-à-tête up ahead. I stopped so suddenly that Bruce bumped into me, and pointed over my shoulder to an alcove a few steps behind us. We shuffled out of sight of my quarries, and I tapped my ear: *listen*. Bruce nodded. The conversation down the hall continued, and I gave Bruce the thumbs-up. They didn't know we were there.

Alec Mercer's voice carried clearly from his position outside the conference room. "What I'm saying is that we should have put this presentation on hold. Of course the turnout is low! Eliot Fraser's death is the only story anyone cares about. And we look like assholes, carrying on as if it's business as usual."

His mother's voice was cold. "Business doesn't stop for a second, Alec, not even for death. Which you would know if you took even the slightest interest in our holdings. I shouldn't need to remind you that the family business funds your salary and your mortgage and your car payments and god knows what else. We need this development. The theatre is hanging on by a thread. And you think I should take my foot off the gas because Eliot died? You think I should let him ruin me a second time? I don't think so."

"It's tacky, Mom. You're drawing attention to yourself. Attention you can't afford. Don't you get that? In a murder investigation. You've been questioned by the police. I'm trying to protect you. You need to keep a low profile. At least cancel the boat cruise."

"Out of the question," she snapped. "The Playhouse will go under without that fundraiser."

Alec was quiet for a moment, and when he spoke, his voice was urgent. "If you had anything to do with it, you need to tell me. Right now."

"Always so dramatic, Alec. Anything to do with what? Say it."

"With Eliot's death."

Martha laughed then, a short, harsh bark. "If I did, it was only what he deserved," she said. "And I'd scarcely tell you if I had. It's hard to know whose side you're on these days. Now, are you coming? I need to get back to work." I heard a door open and close, and then nothing more.

I peeled myself away from the wall and turned to Bruce. "Did you hear that?"

"Sure did. Your talents are wasted at the *Quill & Packet*, by the way."

"I took Skulking 101 in J-school," I said. "So what do you think? Could she have done it?"

Bruce raised an eyebrow. "Martha Mercer is a crappy human, but a murderer?"

"Someone around here is," I said.

We slipped into the conference room. The lights were low, but not enough to hide the sparseness of the audience. On a screen, renderings of the proposed development were interspersed with photographs of merry seniors swimming, doing yoga, dancing cheek-to-cheek, and toasting each other with champagne. "Luxury living, designed for the best years of your life," the narrator intoned, and the lights came up.

Martha stepped to the podium and invited questions. Bruce dutifully snapped photos while several residents grilled Martha about the electrical grid and the sewage treatment plans for the property. She deflected and took some other questions, obviously planted, about the world-class amenities at the facility and the health benefits of community living for seniors. Then she wound down the presser and headed for the exit.

I intercepted her. "Cat Conway from the *Quill & Packet*," I said. "Would you like to respond on the record to residents' concerns about stress on the power grid?"

"I wouldn't, actually," she said. "If you wanted a comment, you should have had the courtesy to show up on time."

"You have no response to accusations that you're putting your business's interests ahead of the town's?"

I'd intended to provoke her, and I succeeded. "The two are the same. They've always been the same. My businesses employ most of Port Ellis, one way or the other. You can mess with me if you want, young lady, but you'll only be hurting yourself. I'll make sure of it. And you can tell Dorothy Talbott I said so." She stalked out of the room, several terrified staffers hot on her heels.

I turned to face Alec, who had been watching our exchange with a concerned expression. "I apologize for my mother," he said. "Eliot Fraser was her ex-husband, as you probably know. His death has been quite upsetting for her. She was very fond of him. She always said he made a much better friend than a husband."

He'd opened the door a fraction, and I took the opportunity to wedge my foot in it. "If you have time to spare, I'd love to ask you a few questions."

"My brothers are much more involved in Mercer Developments than I am," he said. "I'm only here today as moral support for my mother. If you're looking for more information about the retirement village, I'd suggest calling the office and arranging an interview with Justin or Keiran."

"We'll do that," said Bruce. "Thanks for your time."

I shot a glance in his direction. I'd been hoping for an opportunity to speak to Alec, and here it was. Bruce, it seemed, was ready to call it a day. "Actually, I have some questions about the impact of Eliot's death on the cast and crew at the Playhouse. We were on our way downstairs for a drink, if you'd like to join us?"

Alec weighed his options and came down on the side of humouring the press. It was a skill he had certainly not learned from his mother.

"Sure," he said. "I can give you twenty minutes."

THE GREYBUCK BAR was outfitted in dark brown leather and brass, with a huge granite fireplace at one end and a wall of windows with a panoramic view of Lake Jane. Black-and-white photographs of men with rifles and fishing poles served as decoration, along with a few mounted stag's heads. We were seated at the best table within seconds of arriving.

"The service here is amazing," said Bruce with a hint of irony in his voice.

"That's our priority," said Alec, and I saw Bruce look up at the ceiling as if seeking strength from a higher power. I wondered if Alec genuinely didn't understand that people tended to spring to attention when they worked for you.

"Are those photos from the original Greybuck Lodge?" asked Bruce.

Alec nodded. "Our designer went to the town archives. She wanted to play up the history of the hotel. What do you think?"

"I love it," I said. "How old is the hotel?"

"A hundred years, give or take," said Alec. "It was a hunting and fishing lodge initially, started by Grey Talbott and Buck Mercer, my great-grandfather. Eventually, they went their separate ways, and Buck built a full-service hotel for families. We're still running the same business today." He looked at his phone. "What did you want to know about the Playhouse?"

I pulled out my phone. "Do you mind if I record this?"

"Go ahead."

"What can we expect from the rest of the Playhouse season, now that Eliot Fraser is gone?"

"You can expect an exceptional theatre experience, with two major stars in Declan Chen-Martin and Jonah Tiller. A company like ours prepares for the worst, and we have swings and understudies ready to go. Declan is stepping into Eliot's principal roles and I can tell you that he's up to it. Audiences will not be disappointed in the quality of the performances."

His enthusiasm seemed genuine, even if the words sounded like a PR statement.

"Rumour has it that there was some conflict in the cast before Eliot's death. Can you comment?"

Alec sighed. "Actors have egos and sometimes they rub each other the wrong way. It was my job to keep everyone on an even keel, and I did. The atmosphere backstage was civil and professional, and anyone who says otherwise is misinformed."

"I have two sources who tell me that Jonah and Eliot were at each other's throats."

Alec's smile cooled. "I'm not going to be the third. Let's move on."

"What was your reaction when you learned that Eliot had been murdered?"

"Disbelief. I still struggle to accept it. I knew him both personally and professionally and I respected him hugely. So did everyone in the cast, whatever their minor disagreements." He stood. "You're barking up the wrong tree if you think someone at the Playhouse did away with Eliot Fraser. It's simply not possible." He signalled a server. "I have to get back for rehearsal. Drinks are on the house."

"I can't let him pay," I said to Bruce, as Alec walked away.

"I don't see why not," said Bruce. "He didn't give you a lick of useful information." He gestured at the walls. "Buck Mercer forced Grey Talbott out of the hotel business and then torched Grey's hunting camp to eliminate the competition. That's the real history of this place." He drained his beer. "My advice? If a Mercer says it, it's fifty percent bullshit and fifty percent horseshit."

CHAPTER 9

THE SECURITY GUARD at the backstage door was giving me the hairy eyeball. Clearly he remembered me as the last person who'd laid hands on Eliot Fraser. And had failed to save him.

"I'm here to see Jonah Tiller," I said. "I've got an appointment at ten. Cat Con—"

"I know who you are," said the guard in a voice that suggested I'd stolen his sandwich. He consulted his screen and wordlessly slid a binder toward me. I signed it, and he clipped a visitor's badge onto a lanyard. "You know the way, right?"

He clicked open the door to the authorized personnel area. A web of hallways, narrow and dim, led off in three directions; I took the one on the right and hoped it would eventually take me where I wanted to go. It was creepy as hell backstage, and not just because the last time I'd been there a man lay gasping his last breaths at my feet. I shut my eyes, willing my brain to erase the image of Eliot's tortured face. When I opened them, I realized with a stab of horror that I was *still* staring at Eliot's face.

Young Eliot.

I moved closer to the framed photo on the wall. Pictures from the Playhouse's early seasons hung along the corridor, although they apparently had not been introduced to a feather duster in four decades. I crept closer to Eliot, who was dressed in medieval armour as Shakespeare's wayward prince—

"Holy shit!" The words shot from my mouth as a body barrelled into mine. I staggered into the wall. If people in this town kept sneaking up on me, my corpse would keep Eliot's company in the morgue.

"Cat?" said a voice I recognized. "I'm so sorry. I wasn't paying attention."

"Glenda? What are you doing here?"

"Meeting a few friends for coffee," she said. "I'm part of this old-style consciousness-raising group, like they used to have in the seventies, you know? We use one of the practice rooms here. We sit in a circle and take turns talking about issues that affect us as women."

"Like how you should be allowed to have orgasms and jobs?"

Glenda frowned. "It's not a joke, Cat. Women still have to put up with a lot of shit. We haven't made as much progress as people think."

"Undoubtedly," I said. She had obviously missed my half-second of fame as a local shero when I busted the heckler. "Listen, how are you doing? Have you heard anything further from the police?"

"They told me not to leave town." She looked bitter. "As if I have somewhere else to go. This is my home. My lawyer says I should keep my head down and try not to think too much about it. My friends have been really supportive, so at least I have that."

"Maybe I could join your group sometime?" I said. Port Ellis hadn't struck me as a hotbed of feminism so far, but it hadn't struck me as a murder capital either. For a small town, it had a complicated identity.

"Maybe," she said. "It's by invitation only, though. We want members to be serious about creating change. Let me think about it, okay?"

"No big," I said. "Really."

"I've gotta run, Cat. The lunch rush starts at eleven." She raced off, leaving me to ponder the fact that I didn't qualify for automatic membership in Port Ellis's feminist underground, while Glenda Gillis did.

I continued down the hallway, recognizing a tear in the floor's linoleum that had nearly tripped me as I raced backstage the night Eliot collapsed. Eliot's dressing room was on my right, its door shut. I hurried past.

Suddenly I heard a voice, a rich and carrying baritone reciting Shakespeare. "What, my dear Lady Disdain? Are you yet living?"

Jonah's dressing room was only a few metres down the corridor. He would have had access on opening night. He could easily have slipped into Eliot's while everyone was taking their seats and Eliot was gladhanding outside. There would have been time for him to poison Eliot's cocktail. If indeed it had been poison. I made a mental note to call Cheryl Bell to see if there'd been any progress on the toxicology report.

I poked my head in the dressing room and saw Jonah, seated before his mirror, eyes closed. Here was a chance for a high-risk opening. I wasn't a high-risk kind of person, but I leapt anyway. I said, "Is it possible disdain should die while she hath such food to feed it as Signior Benedick?"

Jonah's eyes snapped open. "Such *meet* food," he said, correcting me.

"I think you can stop running lines now," I said lightly. "You know your part and Beatrice's." I thought this might make him chuckle, but he only harrumphed at me. He had his script in one hand, and with the other he pointed to a chair, piled high with books.

"I love Beatrice," I said, moving the pile onto an empty space on his dressing table. "She's my favourite character in all of Shakespeare. And *Much Ado* is my favourite play."

Jonah watched me in the mirror, giving away nothing. He looked exhausted, which was hardly surprising. His co-star was dead, and he must know that everyone in the cast of *Inherit the Wind* was a suspect. Especially the one who'd had a decades-long feud with the deceased. Oddly, haggardness suited him, giving his chiselled features added depth. And it suited Alec's vision for *Much Ado About Nothing*: Beatrice and Benedick at the end of their lives, would-be lovers who had failed at love, grasping one last chance.

Unlike Eliot, Jonah had no interest in filling the silence with the joys of his own voice. I waited for him to ask me about what I knew about Eliot's death, considering I'd been one of the last ones to see him, but he said nothing. I ventured, "Is it a relief to have a comedy to rehearse? It's such a funny play."

He regarded me balefully. "Nothing says laugh-riot like a corpse backstage."

"Better than corpsing onstage," I said, and Jonah let out a completely unexpected belly laugh. *Corpsing* was the theatrical term for inappropriate laughter onstage. Cracking up when you shouldn't, essentially.

"So you know about that, huh?" He shut the script and turned to me. "Happened to me once. I was Laertes, stone dead, and Hamlet sneezed while he was supposed to be cradling my limp body. I thought I'd have a heart attack trying to keep the giggles in."

As he rubbed his bearded chin, reminiscing, I tried

to imagine hard-ass Jonah Tiller rolling on the floor laughing. I said, "But that wasn't the production where you were supposed to play Hamlet, was it? The one that Eliot stole from you."

His eyes were cool again. "*Stole* is quite a loaded word."

"But he did, didn't he? That's what everyone said at the time. He convinced the producers not to take the risk." I kicked myself for using such a dumb euphemism. *Not taking the risk* really meant not hiring a Black actor to play Hamlet. The production, a live broadcast in prime time, had catapulted Eliot from handsome Hollywood bit player to serious actor, all in the space of four electrifying hours.

How electrifying would it have been for Jonah to play the role? We'd never know. By the time his talent was recognized and he was headlining productions as Othello and Macbeth and Prospero, he was too old for Hamlet. That ship had sailed, thanks to Eliot Fraser.

"It's so far in the past that it feels like a different lifetime," Jonah said. One of the books from the stack toppled and fell, and he glared at me. "Are you here to stir up trouble? Because I figure I'm going to have enough of that from the police. I don't need the local press on my backside as well."

"I only want to hear your side of things," I said as I leaned down to pick up the book. "How Eliot's death affected you and the other members of the cast. That's the story I'd like to tell." I told myself this was a white lie, at worst beige. The company's reaction was *a* story I wanted to tell. It just wasn't *the* story.

I looked at the cover of the book, which showed a Black man in old-fashioned costume. "Ira Aldridge," I said. "Did you know the King of Prussia thought he was such a brilliant actor that he gave him a gold medal?"

Jonah took the book from my hand. "You know about Aldridge?"

"I've been a theatre geek for as long as I can remember," I said. My middle-school library had a book about Aldridge, the great Victorian tragedian who fled America for the stages of Europe, which were much more welcoming to Black actors at the time.

"He was a genius. I'd have given anything to see him onstage. Some people just have the spark, you know?" Jonah's hand mimed an explosion. "Like our young Declan."

I thought of Declan on opening night. Even though he hadn't spoken a word, the audience had been riveted.

"He looked strong in those first few minutes," I said. I tapped my pen on my pad. There was something I wanted to know, but it was sensitive. "So Declan hasn't fallen off the wagon?"

Jonah scowled at my brusque words, and I thought for a second the interview was over. "Declan lives very seriously in his sobriety," he said sternly. "It's obvious in his focus. You just cannot take your eyes off him. Even in rehearsal, you could see it. Alec could see it. Eliot too, unfortunately." He shut his mouth with a snap.

"So," I said, feigning a casual tone as I paged through my notebook. "Eliot was jealous of Declan?"

Jonah placed the Aldridge book carefully on top of the teetering pile. "Has there ever been a theatre company that didn't run on envy?"

"I don't know," I said. "We should ask Euripides."

Once again he forgave me with a laugh. "Maybe you should be writing the book."

"What book?" I asked.

"Eliot's memoir." He gave the word a theatrical French pronunciation and looked at me speculatively. "You could finish the collaboration. You can write a sentence, and you know something about theatre. You should drop a line to his widow. I imagine she'd welcome the opportunity to kick Ms. Hussein to the curb."

Now I was completely confused. Perhaps Glenda had given me a concussion when she'd sent me flying into the wall. Jonah finally took pity on me. "You didn't know? Maybe it wasn't as obvious as I thought. Let's put it this way: Hadiya wasn't only helping Eliot between the book covers." He peered at me meaningfully. "She'd been on the scene for a while. And

Eliot liked his concubines fresh." Eww. I imagined the steam that would have come out of Hadiya's ears if she'd known Jonah thought of her as a "concubine." We could power the Port Ellis grid for years. Had she and Eliot really been an item? It seemed unlikely, but not impossible. I sat back, remembering Hadiya's hostile glances the first time I met Eliot. The bitchy comment that had come out of nowhere on opening night.

"Do you think—" I started. "Was Eliot planning on firing her?"

Jonah shrugged. He'd picked up his script again.

"You can't just fire somebody like that," I said. "I mean, she must have a contract."

His expression was cool and slightly terrifying. "Any problem can be solved," he said. "If you've got the will to do it."

A HALF-HOUR LATER I was unlocking my bike in front of the Playhouse. Jonah had frustrated my every attempt to dig into his relationship with Eliot, but my notebook was bristling with leads to follow. He'd sent me on my way with an ominous "I'll be in touch."

The day was gorgeous, bright and fair. From the hill the theatre stood on, I could see that the lake was alive with sailors and kayakers. A jet ski sliced across its calm surface, the roar of its engine reaching me even this far away. To the old-school cottagers, jet skis were Satan's playthings, a vile sign of the shadow falling across their paradise.

My phone beeped and I saw a text from Kaydence, inviting me to lunch at Glenda's. I tapped out a quick *see you there* and then opened my bookmarks on Twitter to find the tweet calling Eliot an old goat. The account belonged to somebody called SunneeDaze29, whose bio described her as "living the dream on the edge of the world." Fortunately, her DMs were open, and I sent her a quick message asking if I could talk to her about her Eliot Fraser tweet. I didn't have a huge amount of hope, to be honest: three-quarters of journalism involved sending ever-more-desperate queries into an echoing void.

Kaydence and Dorothy were seated in the centre of the café, at the table reserved for Port Ellis's A-list. Kaydence shoved the specials menu across at me. Her earrings were lemons and her skirt was printed with watermelon slices and suddenly I had a craving for fruit salad. Across the table, Dorothy was squinting at the menu. "Does this say 'quip'? What in god's name is a kale quip?"

"Quiche," Kaydence said patiently. "It's kale quiche. It's actually pretty tasty, Dorothy."

"I just want a damn BLT," Dorothy grumbled. "Is that too much to ask?"

They continued to bicker, their conversation eventually leading to gluten intolerance (a completely artificial panic, Dorothy contended, to rival the Salem witch trials). I watched them, amazed at their ease with each other, the lightness of their conversation. We had an unidentified killer in our midst, and Dorothy's newspaper teetered on the brink of insolvency, but they acted like they were on a vaudeville stage.

Maybe I could learn to like this town.

The fleeting thought was gone by the time Glenda arrived at our table, pen in hand, to take our orders. At the sight of Kaydence's sympathetic face, Glenda crumpled.

"Was it bad?" Kaydence touched Glenda's arm, and the café owner nodded, sniffing.

"They wanted to know everything that happened on the baking show. Did Eliot grope me? Was I just imagining it? Had I harboured a grudge all this time? Then they asked if I'd ever worked with toxic or noxious substances."

"Does the coffee count?" Dorothy asked, and then she put up an apologetic hand as Glenda glared at her. "Sorry. Not the time for levity, obviously."

Tight-lipped, Glenda took our order. When Dorothy asked for a strawberry cheesecake bar, Glenda sniffed. "Fine, but they may be a bit salty. Some tears might have fallen in the batter when I made it this morning."

"You're a bit salty," Kaydence muttered to Dorothy after Glenda had left. Dorothy squinted innocently into the distance, as if she had no idea what her marketing manager was talking about.

The crowd had thinned a bit by the time we'd finished lunch. I'd offered to get this one and was at the counter paying when the café door was yanked open to a great clamour of chimes. I turned to see a Porsche Cayenne double-parked outside, hulking over the smaller car next to it like an elephant overshadowing a gazelle at a watering hole.

A heavy floral scent hit my nose even before I registered that Martha Mercer was looming over our table, yesterday's copy of the *Quill & Packet* dangling from her talons. Every hair of her perfect blowout seemed to bristle with rage.

"What the hell does this mean?" Martha hissed. "'Town council should think seriously about whether the Bella Vista retirement complex can add anything useful to this community, or if it will merely be another drain on the already strained infrastructure that undergirds Port Ellis.'" She didn't need to consult the actual paper, which meant she'd memorized the editorial. It was unsigned, but Amir had written it in the cool, biting style I admired.

Clearly I was alone in this.

Martha Mercer was shaking with fury. The paper dropped from her fingers onto the table. Kaydence looked over at me, her eyes wide with delight, and mouthed "cat fight."

Dorothy picked up the newspaper and slowly folded it back into shape. "You might want to watch out, Martha. There's only one person here who knows CPR, and she's not exactly good at it."

I marvelled at the deftness of this insult, which managed to skewer both me and Martha at the same time.

"You think you'll ruin us with your ridiculous crusades, Dorothy Talbott. As if you and your family are so lily-pure." She leaned closer, but Dorothy didn't flinch. Was she really such a stone-cold badass, or was she just blind? "But we know the truth, don't we? You could put Calvin under Niagara Falls and he still wouldn't come clean."

She straightened, bony hands on hips. "We'll be here long after you're gone. You and your ... your"—the venom seemed to spit from her mouth—"idiotic rag. If you dare publish unsubstantiated garbage like this again, you'll be receiving a libel notice from my lawyers. I'd probably be doing you a favour by taking the stupid thing off life support."

A silence had descended over the café. Even Glenda stood open-mouthed, coffee carafe in one hand. Martha seemed to gather herself, as if she felt every eye in the place on her. Without another word, she turned on one Tod's loafer and strode out the door.

I took my seat again, my mind racing. "Is she always like that?"

"You mean, flouncing around in an imperious rage if the town peons don't behave exactly the way she wants?" Dorothy took a sip of coffee. If she was upset by Martha's threats, she wasn't about it to show it. "I'm a bit surprised, to tell the truth. She's become much better at controlling her temper in recent years, to get what she wants. There was a time when she was actually dangerous."

Now my ears were pricked. "What do you mean?"

"You'd hear stories. You'd hear the fights, come to think of it. When she and Eliot were first married and she found out he was catting around. Ashtrays flying through the air. And we had serious ashtrays in those days."

"Things were that bad between them?"

Dorothy gathered her giant NPR tote bag. "We all thought she'd kill him before she'd let him go," she said, standing to leave. "But she bounced back more quickly than anyone expected. Rod Mercer may not have been famous, but his wallet was fat enough." She rubbed the small of her back. "It seemed like Martha and Eliot were getting on better when he arrived this summer. She got him to come back here to star in the play. She convinced him to shill for her damn retirement village."

"Wait a second," I said. "I don't remember Eliot giving an endorsement for the retirement village."

Dorothy gave me a chilling little smile, and I

suddenly remembered that there were two sides to the Mercer-Talbott feud.

"Exactly," she said. "He wouldn't do her bidding, at the end. And what do queens do with disloyal subjects?"

She left, leaving a gape-jawed crowd in her wake. It was only after she'd gone that I remembered that Martha had also landed punches. *You could put Calvin under Niagara Falls and he still wouldn't come clean.*

Calvin, Dorothy's husband.

CHAPTER 10

I WAS STILL thinking about Dorothy and Martha's seniors cage match when I got back to the newsroom. Dorothy had gone home to contemplate the picked-over bones of her enemy. Kaydence was visiting a chocolate store that had just opened, hoping she could convince the owners to buy an ad or two in the *Quill*.

She was certain to come back with some chocolate at the very least—single estate and fair trade, judging by the other shops that were opening in town. You could still find a KitKat in Port Ellis, but you had to brave the fumes of the gas station to get it. I tried not to be too sad about the candy store I used to visit with my grandparents—Mr. Legarde's Ju-cee Emporium, with its mountains of sour chews and gumballs. Not one of them single estate or fair trade. It was a ridiculous thing to get hung up on. If I wasn't careful, I'd only be looking at my life through the rear-view mirror.

Crack. The sound nearly made me jump out of my skin.

"Sorry," Bruce said, holding up a snapped bread-stick with a guilty look.

"It's okay," I said, sliding behind my desk. "No worries."

It was a three-bag day for Bruce: carrots, bread-sticks, and something unfortunately pungent that he ate with a spoon. Like me, Bruce was a stress eater. Unlike me, his stress eating did not involve a delicious marriage of carbs and fats.

With a push against his desk, he propelled his chair across the floor toward me. It was a beautiful thing, no wasted movement. He stopped himself by clutch-ing the arm of my chair. "I've got something," he said quietly.

"Is it something you should see a doctor about?"

He snickered. "I've got a friend at a cop shop nearby," he said. "And this friend just happened to have seen a report that was not intended for his eyes. A preliminary report from the medical examiner."

I sat bolt upright. "Eliot Fraser?"

Bruce nodded. "Now take this with a grain of salt. And obviously get it confirmed elsewhere. But my friend said that one of the things he saw—and he only got a quick glance—was that Eliot was presenting with cyanosis."

"With what?"

"Cyanosis. I looked it up. It means you turn blue. Basically you turn into a Smurf, and then the doctors save you. Or you go to the big Smurf Village in the sky."

Eliot's ghastly, gasping face flashed in front of me. The weird tinge of his skin. At first I'd thought it was just his stage makeup, but it had looked blue.

"And what causes cyanosis?" I asked Bruce.

He shrugged. "Just because I took a lot of acid in university doesn't make me a chemist. But the only other thing my source mentioned was that he saw the word *nitrate* mentioned a few times in the report."

I slapped Bruce on the arm and told him he was a god of reporting. He blushed, but it was true; he was keeping the paper afloat. Since Amir had put me on the Eliot Fraser beat, Bruce had had to shoulder every boring story that filled a regular issue of the *Quill & Packet*. He was currently juggling a piece about a Go Fund Me for a centenarian's dental surgery, and another on a meeting of the town council about whether to install a traffic light at the corner of Superior and Huron.

Now he'd given me my first solid lead. If it panned out, I was going to Bulk Heaven to buy him a kilo of trail mix.

"Thank you," I said as he waved me away, embarrassed, and rolled his chair back to his desk.

So they had the toxicology report, even if they weren't willing to share it. I fished my phone out of my backpack and called Detective Hayward. He seemed like a softer touch, and measurably less busy, than his boss Inspector Bell. He picked up on the third ring, and I could tell from his voice that he would rather have had a call from his doctor reminding him about his colonoscopy.

"What can I do for you, Ms. Conway?"

"I'm just wondering about the medical examiner's report into Eliot Fraser's death. Is it ready for release yet?"

"When it is, you'll be the first person on my speed-dial."

"Right. Okay. It's just that I hear you might be investigating nitrate poisoning as a cause of death."

If I'd hoped to startle him into a confession, I was destined to be disappointed. "Is that what you hear? I'm glad you shared that with me. When we have a release ready, it will land in your inbox."

"Are you saying—"

"I'm saying goodbye, Ms. Conway."

And then he was gone. I stared at the phone. He hadn't confirmed Bruce's tip, but he hadn't denied it either. It was a start, but not enough to run a story yet.

There was only one thing to do in a case like this: consult Dr. Google. An hour later, my head swam with information about nitrates and nitrites, organic compounds used in food preservation as well as some performance-enhancing drugs and heart medications. Nitrate poisoning was rare, but it happened. Had Eliot accidentally taken the wrong dose of a medication prescribed to him? Or had someone slipped him a lethal cocktail? I fired off queries to two academics I found on the web: a toxicologist and a professor of chemistry.

A Twitter message notification caught my eye. I was in luck—SunneeDaze29 had responded. *Tied up at the moment*, she'd written, *but send your questions and I'll see what I can do.* And then she'd typed, *I loved what you did to that dick on the street.*

The upside of being fired, if there was one, was that my full meltdown had sparked something in a certain group of women. Young women who were still in their prime harassment years. They'd reach out periodically, find me online, even though I'd gone back to my maiden name. I was their fuck-you mascot.

I began to type rapidly. *Thanks for getting back to me*, I wrote. *I'm glad my freakout had an impact! So how did you know Eliot Fraser? Can you tell me what you meant by the comment you posted? Did these incidents happen to you, or to someone you know?* I added my email address and phone number, and hit Send.

Before I could put the phone down, it rang. I glanced at the number, but it was private. When I answered, the voice on the other end was cool, clipped, and in no mood for small talk.

"Is this Cat Conway? I need to speak with you."

"Okay," I said slowly. "I'm happy to, but first you'll have to tell me who I'm speaking with."

"It's Hadiya Hussein. And it's important."

WHEN I GOT to Centennial Park, Hadiya was sitting on a bench with the breeze ruffling her hair. She was wearing yoga clothes today, with a flowing cardigan overtop. She looked sleek and casually fabulous. I glanced down at myself: a tiny bit of lunch clung to the left leg of my jeans, and the Velcro on my right sandal had given up the fight. My hair stood in a giant Art Garfunkel nimbus. I wasn't usually big on comparisons, but I couldn't deny that we looked like the before and after pictures of an electrocution.

She raised an elegant hand in greeting. "Thank you for meeting me," she said, sliding along the bench to make room. "I wanted to follow up on our conversation at the theatre and see if you were interested in a collaboration. I'll tell you what was going on backstage in exchange for any juicy details you learn about Eliot that might help with my book."

"I thought you were ghostwriting a memoir," I said.

"I'm turning it into an authorized biography, assuming the latest Mrs. Fraser agrees," she said. "I want my name on it, seeing as I did all the work, and Eliot isn't here to pretend to finish the job. So? What do you say?"

"Maybe," I said, noncommittally. "That depends on what you're offering." I was dodging requests from Claire Silverberg and Nick Dhalla, so Hadiya Hussein was going to have to show me hers first. Journalism was a game for the scrappiest misfits in the schoolyard, and you had to fight hard to earn your spot. That was how it had worked since time immemorial. I had twenty years in the profession on Hadiya; I took my notebook out of my backpack and waited for her to start.

But Hadiya wasn't playing. "In case you hadn't noticed, you're not exactly Ronan Farrow these days," she said coolly. "You might want to think about that before you pull rank on me or try to steal my job." Her mouth was set in a thin, angry line. I stared at her, shocked, but before I could say anything, she erupted, shaking her finger at me. "I know Jonah's been bad-mouthing me, saying I don't know anything about theatre. Which is bullshit, by the way. I do my research. Jonah thinks he's enlightened, but he's ageist and sexist and a theatre snob."

Another one of the cardinal rules of interviewing: when someone loses their cool, don't interrupt the flow. Hadiya was on a roll. "I'm young and pretty, so obviously I must be fucking Eliot. I know what people say about me. They see me fetching his coffee, listening to his endless, self-involved stories with a smile. Taking his suits to the cleaners. Picking up his Viagra prescription at the drugstore. They don't see the second shift at the computer."

Hadiya was right. And as bitter as could be, which was my good luck. "Believe me, I know how frustrating it is to have to fight for respect, Hadiya," I said, injecting motherly warmth into my voice. "But Eliot had the reputation he had for a reason. He was promiscuous and self-obsessed. He could be disloyal, even cruel, to colleagues and to wives. And some say he was a sexual predator. I'd love to know what you have to say about that." I raised my eyebrow at her expectantly, my notebook open in my lap.

She stared at me for a minute and then laughed. "Jonah really does run his mouth. Did he tell you that I was some little bunny caught in Eliot's trap? You can close the notebook, by the way. I'm not trading today." She shook her head. "I'm disappointed in you, Cat Conway. I saw that video of you and I thought, *there's a woman who does things differently*. But you're living in the past, like the rest of the newspaper business. If you can even call it that. Businesses tend to make money."

I SAT FOR a few minutes on the bench, after she'd flounced off, scribbling notes next to a list of suspects. Beside Hadiya's name, I wrote *I disappoint her*. Who else had been on the receiving end of Hadiya's contempt and fury? Presumably Eliot Fraser, for one; if Jonah was to be believed, he'd planned on firing her from his book and his bed. Hadiya had picked up his prescriptions. How easy would it have been to give the vain old satyr the wrong pills?

Across the lake, I could see the *Old Maid*, her paddlewheel churning. The guide on board would be pointing out the most glamorous compounds, the helipads and the boathouses that slept twelve.

Hadiya wasn't wrong. I was still groping in the dark for a story. Who else had Eliot harmed in his long march to his own pleasure? What was I expected to discover under Declan's pleasant facade? Did Jonah reserve his ferocious intensity for the stage?

With a sigh, I got up and stretched. I felt closer to sixty-five than forty-five. I slung my backpack over my shoulder and pulled my shirt free of my sweaty back. The lake looked incredibly tempting, and for a minute I considered getting my swimsuit and jumping in. But Hadiya's bitter jibes had settled under my skin. I needed to get back to work. If I left now, I might still be able to find Declan and Jonah at the Playhouse.

On Lakeshore, I stepped into the road to avoid a TV crew interviewing shoppers outside the Harvest Table. I wondered if any journalists had tried talking to Glenda, and if so, how many bites she would take to devour their heads. I was still laughing to myself when

I entered the laneway that ran behind the Second Act, where I'd left my car.

I stopped short with a jerk, as if a giant hand had grabbed my shoulder. A squeak left my mouth, shockingly loud in the silent alley. There was a brittle grating under my foot as I stepped closer, and I looked down: a spray of tiny, glittering cubes littered the ground. Shattered glass. I looked at my car, or at least what was left of my car. Where there had once been a windshield there was now just a gaping hole.

My pulse thudded in my throat, in my temples. A loud clang of metal behind me and I whirled, ready to run. Someone from the coffee shop down the laneway was tossing a bag of garbage into a dumpster. Otherwise I was alone. I rubbed my chest, trying to still my galloping heart. Whoever had smashed my windshield was gone.

"Hey," I called to the guy who'd thrown the bag of garbage. My voice screeched like a badly tuned violin. "I think somebody smashed my window. Did you see anything?"

He ambled over, wiping his hands on his apron. I couldn't tell the baristas apart; this one had floppy hair and full-sleeve tattoos, like the others. He shook his head. "I've been inside all day. It's crazy busy." He peered at my poor, abused car. "That sucks, bruh. What's happening to this town? It's like fuckin' Detroit around here."

I DROVE VERY carefully to Harold's Motors, the garage my grandfather had always used to service his succession of Chevy Impalas. Harold's son—grandson, possibly—let out a low whistle when he saw the wreckage of my window. "You hit a deer?"

"Nobody dear," I said. "Just the opposite."

The mechanic gave me a puzzled look. I wanted to tell him that nerves were making me babble. My heart had pretty much slowed to a normal pace, but my thoughts were doing Indy 500 laps. Who wanted to smash my window? Was it a dumb, random act of vandalism, or was somebody sending me a message? A message with a rock attached? I didn't even know if it had been a rock. I'd swept the glass off the seat so I could drive, but I hadn't found anything incriminating. No rock, no crowbar, no note. Nothing.

I stood in the relative cool of the garage and drank a Diet Coke I bought from the vending machine. My hands had stopped shaking, at least until Harold's grandson showed me the estimate to replace my window. When I looked up from the paper my face must have told a story, because he gave me a sheepish smile. His mouth said, "I'll be in touch when it's ready," but his eyes said, *Maybe you should have been a mechanic instead of a journalist.*

I thanked him and stuffed the estimate into my bag. He walked over to peer into my car, and I slumped into a chair by the front door. The plastic seat burned, and I wondered for a moment if I could just sit there and melt into a puddle and be mopped up around Labour Day.

These pleasant thoughts were interrupted by the beep of an arriving text. I took my phone from my bag and thumb-swiped in. It was not, unfortunately, a message from the tax department telling me I was owed a million-dollar refund. Instead, my mother had sent me a posting for a journalism job. *The Guardian*, she'd written, *could use a smart and experienced voice like yours. Time to raise your sights, honey.*

She'd also helpfully included *Publishers Weekly*'s review of her latest book, *Grit and Gumption: A Warrior Woman's Guide to Finding Inner Strength. Publishers Weekly*, perhaps not knowing that my mother's warfare consisted of battling crowds at the farmers' market, had given it a starred review.

I rubbed my sore neck. No other hand had touched my neck, or indeed any part of my body, in longer than I could remember. Our health plan at the *Quill & Packet* did not extend to massage therapy. And now I needed a windshield replaced. In theory, I could ask my mother for the money. Or I could sell a kidney on the black market. Only one of those options was appealing, and it wasn't the one involving my mother.

I suddenly felt the pressing need for a win. Or, failing that, a friend. I found the number in my contacts and hit Call.

THE UBER DRIVER stopped to let me out, giving me a look over his shoulder that said, *You sure about this?* I was sure—mostly. The Swiss Motel sat on a sideroad to the north of town, on the unfashionable outskirts where car dealerships encroached on family farms. All the cars in the parking lot were caked with dust, and one had duct tape holding the passenger door closed. For the first time that day, I began to relax.

At the reception desk, a girl sat pecking at her phone under a mural of an alpine paradise. She didn't look up as I walked past into the dim bar. Apart from the cowbells that hung from the walls, it was un-Swiss in every way. Unless Zurich had been overtaken by bikers and day drunks when I wasn't looking.

The bartender ambled over and I ordered a beer with a shot of Teacher's on the side. It gave me an illicit thrill, drinking in the afternoon. Drinking on the company dime. The sudden violence of the smashed windshield had made my cortisol spike; my skin felt weirdly alive. Even the little scurf of filth on my table seemed dangerous and new. The lanky German journalist I'd sparred with at the press conference sat at the bar, morosely fishing something out of his pint glass. Stuck in a crappy motel, drinking fly-dappled beer: there was probably a word for that in German.

When Nick Dhalla walked in, he was on the phone. Working his Eliot Fraser contacts, most likely. It seemed he never slept and rarely ate and considered shaving a waste of time that could be better spent on digging or drinking. This might have explained the departure of three wives, though not the imminent arrival of wife number four.

Despite all of it, he was still the most honest, decent, and straight-shooting person I'd ever worked with. And I'd always felt oddly attracted to his dishevelment, which was so opposite to what I'd known during my marriage. He was the anti-Mark, and at the moment I was pro anything that was anti-Mark.

He ended his call and gestured to the drinks on my table. "I guess you don't need anything," he said, and went to order. When he slid into his seat with a pint of his own, he nodded at my phone. "I see you're back on Twitter," he said. "Nobody leaves that hell-site for very long." He took a long swig of his drink. "At least no one can actually punch you through the screen."

I threw back my Teacher's in one quick swig. It went down like honey-dipped barbed wire. Not a bad thing. Was I going to tell Nick about my car? If I did, what was there to tell? The windshield was smashed, possibly by a bored kid with a rock. Or possibly by someone who thought I was sticking my nose where it shouldn't be. Without more evidence I didn't want to give in to fear, and the last thing I needed was Nick's pity. I said nothing.

He ran his hand along his shadowed jaw and cast a glance at the slumped-over German. "Every outlet in the world's here. They're going to have to start putting up tents. I'm pretty sure I saw Waxing Wayne setting up next to the Playhouse." Waxing Wayne was one of the star reporters at the network that once employed me, a man so perfectly put together he seemed to travel with a personal aesthetician.

"That guy doesn't age," I said. "The miracles of modern chemistry."

"That's one of the reasons I couldn't understand when you went to the dark side. All that bullshit about how you look all the time."

"Is that your way of telling me I'm too scruffy for TV?"

He smiled at me slowly. I wished he wouldn't. Most of me wished it, anyway. "I would not call you scruffy, no. But I do think your brilliance was kinda wasted."

I snorted. "Brilliance." Secretly, of course, I was pleased. The last time I'd been called brilliant it was a sarcastic jab by my teenaged son.

"I could use some of that right now. Your contacts in the town. Your eye for the things that don't measure up. You know Claire would pay top dollar if you wanted to freelance. You could write your own cheque. You and me, teaming up again."

He cocked his head at me and said nothing else. So he was using his little silence trap on me. Clever. My fingers shredded my beer coaster, leaving a pile of wet pellets on the table. No one in the Swiss Motel gave a damn about my dilemma. The slumbering drunks continued to slumber. On the sound system, Tim McGraw was asking God not to take his girl.

"It would not be very cool for me to become your sidekick," I said. "Amir took a chance on me. I'm not sure he'd appreciate it if I abandoned him now."

Nick pushed aside his beer and thunked his elbows on the table.

"Look," he said. "I'm glad you landed butter-side up. You've got a job, you're still a journalist. That's a good thing. But this town is where you want to be at the end, not now. You get me? You've still got too much juice in your tank."

One of the patrons at a nearby table roused himself from his beer coma long enough to let out a long, rumbling fart. No one seemed to notice except Nick, who closed his eyes. "I rest my case," he said. "Now go and call Claire and tell her you'll work with me on this Fraser story. One major scoop and you ride out of here on a wave of glory."

I'd settle for a wave of adequacy, but I didn't tell him that. I drank my beer and pondered his offer. Was he offering me a road to salvation or another dead end?

CHAPTER 11

WHEN HAD I stopped sleeping? It had got dramatically worse after Mark walked out, for sure, but it had been erratic before that. I'd tried supplements and pillow props, teas and meditation apps, and still, sleep felt like the mirage glittering on the horizon, holding out the promise of relief but never delivering it. Every morning, three o'clock found me staring at the ceiling, playing Pick-a-Regret. Today's choice: To work with Nick Dhalla, or not to work with Nick Dhalla? Which option would make it easier to pay for my windshield? After hours of pointless rumination, I was no closer to a decision.

At the *Quill*, I poured a mug of the coffee Bruce had made and sat down at my desk. Having an assigned spot in the newsroom was one of the privileges of a small-town paper with a handful of full-time employees. Only slightly less ancient than the chairs in the microfiche room, my desk was vintage IKEA from the 1990s, the faux wood shredding at every corner.

I booted up my laptop and checked my social media feeds and comments. They'd been practically dormant since I'd moved to Port Ellis, a source of both relief and anxiety. It was the journalistic equivalent of the tree falling in the forest: if your stories didn't attract public attention, did they have any value at all? But since my interview with Eliot had become the last public words of a great man, I'd experienced a turnaround. Granted, most of the comments consisted of hearts and crying-face emojis. But the trolls were out too, some baying for my blood (*disrespectful bitch*) and some for Eliot's (*nasty old boozehound*).

I scrolled through, looking for leads. If Eliot had hurt as many people as I suspected, SunneeDaze29 wasn't the only person out there devouring accounts of his death and savouring that tantalizing Teutonic dish, schadenfreude.

"You've got mail," said Kaydence, dropping a white envelope on my desk. My name was printed on the front with no address.

"Where did this come from?" I asked warily. There had been a spate of envelopes like this at my last paper, filled with white powder that had necessitated calls to emergency services and the deployment of the haz-mat unit and brought the newsroom to a grinding halt. Laundry detergent, not ricin, as it turned out, but still wildly disruptive and more than a little embarrassing for the recipient at the centre of the drama. I held the envelope close to my ear and shook gently, listening for the telltale rustle of powder. Nothing.

"It was lying inside the front door when I got here," Kaydence said. "Are you going to open it?"

I slid my thumb under the flap and ripped it open. Inside was a single sheet of plain white paper printed with one sentence: *Mind your own business or you'll get more than a smashed windshield.*

My skin prickled and I felt my ribs contract as if I'd been kicked. Wordlessly, I tucked the sheet of paper under the keyboard, my thoughts tumbling and tangled like clothes in a dryer. Was this a message from Eliot's killer? Or had I trampled some unspoken norm with my clumsy outsider's feet?

"You look like you're going to throw up," said Kaydence. "What does it say?"

Before I could answer, Amir was at my elbow. "In my office, please."

I got up and followed him. He closed the door and we faced each other over his battered desk. "Tell me everything," he said.

So I did. I told him about my poor abused car, the various conversations I'd had with Port Ellis residents over the past twenty-four hours—at least a couple of whom had seemed angry and dysregulated enough to take their feelings out on my windshield—and the note I'd received just now. He listened without interrupting. "The paper will cover the cost of the repair," he said when I finished speaking. "The note makes it clear that you were targeted because of your reporting."

I felt a rush of gratitude. In principle, I accepted that the change in my financial circumstances was the cost of freedom from a bad relationship and one worth paying. But the reality of having to worry so much about daily expenses eroded my sense of competence and dignity and often frightened me. "Thank you," I said.

"And we have to call the police." He held up a hand to prevent any protest I might think of making. "The car was near your apartment. This is serious, Cat. Is there somewhere you can stay for a few days?"

"I'm not leaving my home," I said.

Amir grumbled something about stubbornness (mine) while he searched his phone, tapped it, and placed it between us on speaker. Perhaps he didn't trust me to make the report without supervision. Detective Hayward listened politely as I told my story for the second time and then asked me to run over to the detachment office with the note and sign a statement about the incident. I agreed that I would but not until tomorrow. I wouldn't want to give my harasser the satisfaction of derailing my investigation, would I? Amir sighed, and I thought I could hear Detective Hayward gritting his teeth through the phone.

Smiling to myself, I returned to my desk and opened my email. There was a response from Dr. Yvonne Chukwu, the toxicologist I'd reached out to the day before. She seemed keen to connect and had provided both her office and her cell numbers. I dialed her cell and she picked up right away, sounding genuinely delighted to hear from me. I was deliberately vague about my reasons for being interested in nitrates, but she didn't seem to care. Apparently, she didn't get a lot of requests from the media to talk about her favourite subject.

"We do see nitrate poisoning in large mammals, like cattle," she said. "Usually because of fertilizer." I heard typing on her end. "Nitrates and nitrites are related compounds. You tend to hear about sodium nitrite poisoning in humans, less so with nitrates—but you need to treat both these chemicals with care."

I asked her a few more questions, feeling increasingly like I was back in grade eleven chemistry and was about to flunk the final exam. I thanked Dr. Chukwu for her time and told her I'd call her back if I had any further questions.

I got up from my desk and wandered back into the kitchen. Had Eliot inadvertently taken a medication he shouldn't? It seemed unlikely. The fertilizer connection didn't make sense, either. Eliot might have been good at spreading it, but I couldn't see him accidentally eating a bowl of Miracle-Gro.

Bruce was in the kitchen, rooting around in his empire of half-filled Tupperware. He opened one and stuck it under my nose. "Mango guacamole?"

"You should be arrested for possessing that," I said. "Those flavours do not go together." As the words left my mouth, I felt a sharp, electric pang. Some things did not go together: they were fine on their own but fatal in combination. I ran back to my desk, leaving Bruce slack-jawed, holding his foul dip.

Dr. Chukwu was every bit as friendly the second time, although I barely said hello to her in my hurry to get out my question: Which drugs interacted badly with nitrates?

"Well, this isn't my field of expertise necessarily," she said as I bit my lip. Professional eggheads liked to be certain in their pronouncements. It took patience to get them to make bold leaps, like two plus two equals four. I waited, hoping she'd fill in the silence.

She did. "The thing you really have to worry about is the interaction with PDE5 inhibitors."

I bit back my impatience. "Sorry, can you explain that?"

There was an awkward pause on the other end of the line, a stifled giggle. Was Dr. Chukwu embarrassed? She said, "You know, that group of vaso-dilators. Erectile dysfunction drugs."

After I hung up the phone, I stared into space. I heard Hadiya's furious voice as she'd sat on the bench. She'd had to pick up Eliot's prescription at the drugstore. Had Eliot's boner medication been his downfall? The irony was almost too painful. Hadiya knew he was taking it. She'd certainly had access to him. Had she arranged for Eliot's toxic cocktail?

I made a note to talk to her about it, and to make a list of anyone else who might have been close enough to Eliot to slip him a dangerous chemical. But right now I had another deadline looming: my profile of Jonah Tiller.

It should have been easy to write—he was a lively interview—but by midafternoon, the piece still felt fuzzy to me. Jonah was a public figure with a profile like a comet: periods of intense, blazing, attention-commanding presence interspersed with mysterious and lengthy trips to outer space. Some of those disappearances, following on the heels of well-reported struggles with alcohol and drugs, made sense. But other gaps in his history were puzzling. At twenty-five, he'd burst onto the theatre scene in New York, playing Mercutio in an experimental production of *Romeo and Juliet* with an all-Black cast. But before that? I'd spent the day reading all the major interviews he'd ever given, as well as most of the minor ones, and I'd learned only three facts about his origin story: he'd grown up in the New York City area, his parents were deceased, and he'd discovered his talent for acting in a youth Shakespeare company.

Jonah might hate talking about his family—lots of actors did—but surely he'd be willing to answer a few follow-up questions about his theatre training. In any event, I was restless and in need of some fresh air, so even if he wasn't available, it wouldn't be a wasted trip.

I hopped on my bike and headed over to the Playhouse. The security guard chucked a visitor's pass at me and waved me through, busy with more pressing concerns. The staff were trickling back into the building; police tape was being rolled up and discarded. It was cheering to hear the buzz of theatre life reasserting itself. I was smiling when I knocked on Jonah's door.

It flew open so quickly that I had to jump to avoid it. Jonah stood in the frame, bristling. "What the hell do you want?" he said.

"I ... had a few more questions for you. For the profile." Jonah was a big man, and the hallway felt suddenly tiny. I took a step backwards and hit the wall. "I should have called first. I'm sorry."

"You should have. Because I would have told you not to bother."

"I ..." I was floored. This was an entirely different Jonah Tiller, and I had no idea what I'd done to merit his ire. Hadiya was right—there was more to him than I'd imagined. "You seem to be upset with me, Jonah. Have I offended you in some way?"

"Like you don't know. What have you been saying to the police about me? I'm their favourite suspect these days, thanks to whatever information you've been trading. I hope you got something useful in return."

"I haven't said a word to them about you," I protested. "They haven't talked to me at all, about anyone. They've refused an interview with the paper." I held my hands out in a time-honoured gesture of peace. "But even if they did, I wouldn't reveal anything that you'd told me. I don't do the cops' jobs for them, Jonah. They don't need me to help them stack the deck."

He seemed to shrink down to a normal size as he exhaled. "You swear? You haven't fed them information about my relationship with Eliot?"

"I swear," I said. I could feel a damp spot on the back of my shirt sticking to my skin as I eased off the wall.

"I believe you," he said. "And I apologize for yelling at you."

"That's okay," I said. It wasn't, but I could handle it.

"I've had a few conversations with the police," he said. "More than other folks around here have. Eliot made all kinds of enemies in his life, but I'll tell you what: there's no one more interesting to a cop than whatever Black man happens to be nearby. I might have hoped for better with a Black woman in charge of the investigation, but no such luck."

Racial profiling definitely explained why Jonah was spitting mad. In his shoes, I'd be furious too. Unless, of course, I'd had a hand in the murder. Had Jonah? It seemed possible, although I felt guilty for thinking so. "I'd like to know more about your experiences with racism, Jonah. Both inside the theatre and out. Actually, that's one of the things I wanted to talk to you about today."

"Flavour of the times, is it?" He rolled his eyes. "I guess we should be grateful that people want to hear about racism—not that it makes a goddamn bit of difference on the ground. You can run a front-page story about my 'experiences with racism,' Cat, and I'll still have the cops breathing down my neck. And even though I had nothing to do with Eliot's death, people on Broadway and in Hollywood will hear that the cops were sniffing around me. Some will even think I did it, not that they'll ever say so out loud. No, they'll just find reasons not to hire me. And then I'll spend a few more years wondering why my agent never calls."

He wasn't wrong, and I knew it. "Look, I want to help. Honestly. What if we used this profile to talk about some of the unique challenges you faced as a Black actor, right from the beginning? There isn't much out there about your childhood, your early influences, how you fell in love with acting. It's a great opportunity to give your fans a fuller picture of your life and career."

Jonah's expression shuttered. "Let me think on that." He looked at his watch. "Today isn't great for me, anyway. We're supposed to open *Inherit the Wind* with the new cast next week, and I don't mind telling you, it's a big adjustment. Eliot was a prick, but he was a pro onstage. You have a deadline, I get it, but give me a couple of days to focus on the play."

"Sure," I said. I didn't mind deferring the interview. At this moment, I didn't relish the prospect of sitting alone with Jonah in his dressing room. Next time, I might find a reason to bring Bruce along for the ride. "I'll email you ahead of time and set up an appointment."

"Thanks for understanding," he said, and clapped me on the shoulder. I caught myself before I recoiled, but I left quickly afterwards.

As I cycled to the office, I tried to shake off the creeping sense that I was getting worse at my job. Journalists relied on their instincts, and today mine had sucked. I'd expected a warm welcome and I'd been dead wrong. But I reminded myself that I'd gone out to the Playhouse in search of information about Jonah's past, and, after today's encounter, I was inclined to believe there was a story worth pursuing there.

Back at my desk, I opened my browser and searched

for youth Shakespeare companies in the state of New York. It was a manageable number, and I opened the sites one by one. I wasn't sure exactly what I was looking for, but I felt sure I'd know it when I saw it. I hit pay dirt on the third attempt: Jonah Tiller was a top-level donor to Shakespeare Heals, a rehabilitation program operating in two juvenile detention centres in New York State. The program was designed to improve literacy and communication skills, self-esteem, and personal responsibility, and to lower recidivism rates among post-incarcerated youth. Laudable goals, for sure, but I wondered if Jonah's interest was more personal. There was more to learn here, and after today's outburst, I wanted to be on firmer footing before I questioned Jonah about it. I composed a message to the current director of the program, asking for a phone meeting, and closed my laptop for the day.

"Cat! Let's go!" Amir called from the front door.

"Where are we going?"

"The Second Act. Staff drinks. No stragglers."

There wasn't much point in telling Amir that he didn't need to run happy hour like boot camp. Not for the first time, I noted that my old friend was wound pretty tight. It was a rare occasion when he came out for drinks after work, and I wasn't sure he'd initiated them before today. Maybe one of his management courses had advised him to participate in social events with his employees. I imagined his to-do list, a check mark beside "Staff Engagement." On the other hand, what was on my to-do list today? Finish writing profile of Jonah Tiller? No check. Botch follow-up interview? Check. Think bitchy thoughts about well-meaning colleague? Check. *Do better, Cat*, I thought. *Be better.*

WE WERE AN odd company, the staff of the *Quill & Packet*, and our drink selections reflected it. Bruce quaffed a local craft beer. Amir had a G&T. Kaydence had the Othello, which was Adeline's version of a Dark and Stormy, and I had the Rosalind, a luscious concoction of elderflower, Prosecco, lavender syrup, and gin. The drinks were, as usual, excellent, and I felt the stress of the day recede.

"Another round?" asked Adeline, stopping at our table.

"Yes, please," said Amir, and Kaydence and I raised our hands to be counted in.

"Not for me," said Bruce, pushing back his chair. "I've got a date tonight."

"You do?" I asked. "A *date*-date?"

Bruce laughed. "Surprised, are we? Careful your chin doesn't hit the table there, Cat."

"Did you find her through Beach Buddies?" Kaydence seemed to be stifling a laugh, which caused her to choke on a peanut. I thumped her on the back.

"Oh, extremely funny, Joan Rivers," Bruce said. Even Amir was grinning, and I looked at them, mystified.

"A million years ago, Bruce founded this alternative weekly for the tri-lake area," Kaydence explained to me. "Beach Buddies was the dating column. He told me about it when we were out for a beer."

"Only nine hundred thousand years," Bruce said. "And *The Rambler* was exactly what these rich stiffs needed. We covered the important stuff no one else wanted to write about. And we had a blast. Is it my fault that no one appreciates quality?"

Amir quickly smoothed things over. "It lasted only a few years, right, Bruce?"

"Three of the best years of my life," Bruce said. "Goodnight all." He stood and saluted us. I raised my glass to him and drained it.

"Hey," I said to Amir. "I didn't tell you about my run-in with Jonah Tiller today. He lost it on me." I filled in the details of Jonah's tantrum and my preliminary research into his past. "I hate to say it, but he could definitely be a suspect."

"There's a story there, for sure," said Amir, his expression softening. "And as your editor, I admire your instincts. But at the same time, Cat, you need to take some precautions. There's most likely a murderer in town, and you shouldn't head off on your own without at least telling someone where you're going."

"Okay, boss," I said.

"He's right, Cat," said Kaydence. "You could have been hurt today. Leaving murder aside, the Playhouse has a history. You're not the first woman to get a scare backstage. It's all blind corners and dark hallways. My aunt worked there in the early years, and she said it was wild. Dangerous, even."

Adeline put a fresh drink in front of me. It landed a bit too firmly, liquid sloshing over the rim. She forced a smile. "I'm a better bartender than server," she said. "Sorry, Cat. I'll get you another." She set the other two drinks down without further mishap.

"Don't be silly," I said. "No harm done. Why don't you sit down for a minute and join us?" I looked more closely at Adeline, realizing that she seemed worn out. It was hardly surprising: she was running a business on her own, a year after a divorce, and her precious son had been onstage when a fellow actor was murdered. Honestly, Adeline raised "getting on with it" to a high art.

"Just for a minute," she said, gesturing to the bartender.

"Excellent," said Kaydence. "I want to pick your brain about that delicious son of yours. Is he dating anyone? And if not, how do I sign up?"

Adeline's face brightened. "He says he doesn't have time to date." She leaned in, conspiratorially. "But I think it would be healthy for him to expand his social circle. A nice girl like you would do him good,

Kaydence. The only people he wants to talk about are Alec Mercer and Jonah Tiller. If he's not careful, he'll take after his mother. I want him to have a life outside of work."

"Is that ever true," said Amir, surprising all of us. This evening's two-drink bacchanal notwithstanding, Amir wasn't exactly setting Port Ellis on fire in his off-hours. "I wish my parents had taken that advice."

His parents. Now I understood. Amir's parents were facing eviction from their cabin on the Raven-head property, and I knew it weighed on him. His mom had been one of the camp cooks, always slipping extra cookies to us during late-night snack time. His dad was a gardener with a rare talent for coaxing vegetables from the rocky soil. Since the camp had ceased operations, they'd stayed on as caretakers, but that arrangement was coming to an end. "I've been meaning to ask, how are your parents doing? Will they be able to stay on after construction?"

"They'd love to, but that won't be an option, unfortunately," he said. "They don't own the house they live in. It's part of their arrangement with the Mercers. Martha has made it clear that she'll be using a professional property manager for the new development, so they'll be out of a job and a home. They've been there for forty years. No pension, and barely any savings. The price point for the smallest house on the new plan is completely out of reach for them."

"Oh," I said, inadequately. "They must be upset."

"They're resigned. They haven't been in the habit of expecting much from life. I, on the other hand, am very upset. I have to figure out how to house and support my parents on my princely earnings from the *Quill & Packet*." He blushed. "I'm sorry, everyone. That was inappropriate of me to say."

"No," I said. "Not a bit." Kaydence and Adeline made encouraging noises while finding themselves in a sudden hurry to leave.

Amir gave me a wry smile as our companions retreated. "God. This is why I don't drink. How mortifying."

"You're human," I said. "And I personally enjoy the reminder once in a while. You have a lot on your shoulders."

He looked me straight in the eye. "I know this isn't your dream job, Cat. How could it be? But I'm asking you as a friend: please stick around for a while. I need to grow this paper. I need to succeed here, not just for myself but for my parents. And I can't pull it off without you. Give me at least a year, okay?"

"Where would I go?" I said, and I saw his face fall at my non-answer.

I didn't know what else to tell him, or what to tell Nick, for that matter. All I knew was I'd have a lot to mull over when three a.m. rolled around.

CHAPTER 12

"I'VE SEEN ELIOT FRASER die two hundred times by now," Kaydence said. We were at the morning story meeting. I had just returned from giving my statement to the cops. Kaydence had put out a call for videos and photos from the gala and she'd been inundated. "It's all the same footage from different angles. What are we looking for exactly?"

It was a fair question. "Set aside all the footage from inside the theatre," I told her. "We can come back to it. I want to know if there's anything from backstage, anything from someone in the cast or crew. A perspective that we might not otherwise have access to."

"Got it," said Kaydence. "You owe me lunch, though."

"How about you, Cat?" asked Amir. "What's the status on your Tiller piece?"

I felt Bruce giving me the side-eye as I reported on my progress, which was not, admittedly, stellar. At this rate, he'd be writing the whole paper. I'd hoped to have Jonah's profile finished by now, but I wanted to close the loop on his history.

Amir wasn't having it. "We need to print something," he said. "Call it part one, if you must. But I want a picture of Jonah Tiller on the front page with at least fifteen hundred words for the next edition. Don't make the perfect the enemy of the good."

"I hate that expression," I said. "But I take your point."

"Anything else?"

"I want to try another angle on the Eliot Fraser murder," I said. "A darker piece on the history of the Playhouse. I'm hearing stories about historical sexual assaults going back to Eliot's first season here. He must have had long-standing enemies in the community, but the police aren't working that angle. I've got a lead on a witness with some information, and I want to pursue it. Assuming you're willing to publish it if it pans out."

"I'm not," said Dorothy, giving me a stern look from behind her glasses. Her gigantic, magnified eyes unsettled me. "You'll upset people, and for what? There's no connection. Let sleeping dogs lie."

"I have to disagree with you there, Dorothy," said

Amir. "If the police are neglecting Eliot's history with this town, it's our role to step into the breach. As far as I can tell, they're no closer to figuring it out, and the town is in limbo until they do. We have a duty."

"Spare me," said Dorothy, her tone dismissive. "You want to sell papers. Obviously, I want to sell them too. But not that way. Not with scurrilous gossip and insinuations."

"Unless it's about the Mercers," I said, wincing as soon as I heard the words outside my own head. Amir mouthed "not helpful," which struck me as broadly applicable.

"Right then," said Amir. "Meeting's over, people. Dorothy and I will meet privately about this issue and I'll let you know our decision, Cat. In the meantime, put your head down and get that Tiller article done, please. Along with a piece on Eliot's memorial service—who was there, quotes from the eulogy, you know the drill. Bruce, you'll take photos?"

"That's the plan," said Bruce. "Anyone else heading out there besides me and Cat?"

"Obviously," said Kaydence. "Everyone I know is going. No one wants to miss it."

It was true: in Port Ellis, you generally needed a ticket for theatre on this scale. This wouldn't be Eliot's official memorial service—his latest wife would cremate him when the body was released, and inter his remains at Forest Lawn Memorial Park in Hollywood—but the police and the international press would be there, automatically bestowing upon the event the title of Port Ellis's Most Gossip-Worthy Send-Off. I spent the next forty-five minutes editing my piece on Jonah by removing all the juicy unanswered questions and pasting them into a new document to revisit later. What was left was a perfectly readable profile matching Amir's specifications. If there was another side to Jonah Tiller, and I was sure there was, the readers of the *Quill & Packet* wouldn't be hearing about it just yet.

The door to Amir's office opened, and I watched him escort Dorothy out into the hallway. He returned to find me sitting in a chair across from his desk.

I passed him the printout of the Tiller piece. "She looked pissed," I said.

"I don't know if *pissed* is the right word," he said, taking the paper from me. "She's conflicted about what she wants the paper to be. We have the same conversation every few months. She knows we need to modernize, which is what she hired me to do. What I hired you to help me do." He gave me a hard look that told me he wasn't over last night's disappointment. "But change is hard, especially when you're Dorothy's age. She takes it personally." He shook his head. "Anyway, thanks for this. I'll look at it now."

"Listen, I have another idea for my next story," I said. "I have a lead." I told him about Dr. Chukwu and what she'd told me about the potentially lethal combination of nitrates and erectile dysfunction drugs.

"Interesting," he said. He tilted back in his chair, wearing his thinking face. "I agree, there's something there. Keep at it."

"You might want to be careful," I told him. "That chair isn't much younger than the ones in the basement. They can be unpredictable."

He shifted his weight and the chair whipped upright, almost launching him across the room. He steadied himself, gripping the edge of the desk, his cheeks flushed. He cleared his throat. I stared determinedly at a patch of sunlight on the frayed industrial carpet. "I told Dorothy that I want you on the Eliot Fraser beat exclusively until the police name a suspect," he said.

The urge to giggle passed, and I looked back up at him. "She must have loved that."

"Let me worry about Dorothy. I want you to focus on the investigation into Eliot's death, starting with your lead. And you have my blessing to pursue the historical sexual assault angle. We can't let the reporters from the city bigfoot all over this, Cat. Give Nick Dhalla a run for his money."

"Nick Dhalla?"

The sharp glint in his eye was back. "It's hard to keep a secret in Port Ellis. But you're in a position to make that fact work for you. If you want my advice, start using your local advantage to break some news."

It was a comment with layers to it, and I wasn't keen to peel them back. Fundamentally, though, Amir wasn't wrong: I needed to focus on digging and writing. I spent the rest of the day pulling together background research on murder by poison and drafting a fairly purple opening paragraph that I was certain would kill with the Bakehouse set.

But late in the afternoon—the best time of day for burying secrets—a terse press release hit my inbox, saying that Eliot Fraser's toxicology report had arrived. Buried in the bureaucratic jargon were the words I was looking for: *nitrates* and *sildenafil*. At the time of his passing, Eliot had also been full of booze and codeine. Old-school to the end. He was consistent, I had to give it to him.

And so was I: consistently on the back foot. I gritted my teeth and wrote up a quick piece on the tox report to post online. Then I called Detective Hayward for a comment. If the speed with which he hung up on me was any indication, the cops felt I'd forced their hand, and they weren't happy. So much for milking my local connections.

By the end of the day, I was ready to hit the open bar at Eliot's memorial.

THE CROWD LINED up at the Playhouse bar were a bit jolly for a wake. Free drinks tended to do that, though. I stared at the rows of bottles. What was it he'd consumed with Jason Robards at Sardi's? I queued up with Kaydence, Bruce, and the other rubberneckers, true mourners being thin on the ground. I ordered a whisky, neat, and raised my glass in tribute. "It was a slice, Eliot," I said aloud, and took a slug.

"Cheers," said a portly man with bushy ears, clinking my glass. "A slice, indeed. To Eliot Fraser, friend, comrade, thespian, swordsman without equal."

Eww, I thought.

"George Weatherbottom," he introduced himself. "I'm the town lawyer. Well, one of two, if you count that girl who does divorces."

"Why would you count her?" I said. God, I was tired.

He chortled. "Why indeed? Eliot would have liked you, my dear. He said a woman with a sense of humour was as rare as a woman who wouldn't pester you the next day."

"That Eliot," I said. "He was a naughty one."

George's eyes glittered. "Were you …?"

"No, absolutely not," I said. "I was writing an article about him. I'm with the *Quill & Packet*."

"Then perhaps you'd like to join me? I'm on my own today."

"So am I, but I'm on the clock, I'm afraid." His

moustache drooped in disappointment, and I put a conciliatory hand on his arm. His potential as a source was great, even if his potential as a human being existed in negative integers. "I'd love to chat with you later."

I tipped my glass to him and caught up with Kaydence and Bruce, who had snagged a standing bar table. "Any gossip so far?" I asked.

"Alec Mercer and Declan were having some kind of drama," said Kaydence. "We tried to take their picture and Alec said it was an inappropriate time to bother them and then they went out the emergency exit door." She pointed to a grey metal door beside a raised platform with a podium. "Any idea what they'd be arguing about?"

"Declan thinks Alec is making them return to performances too quickly." I shrugged. "People go uncensored in a big way at funerals. Maybe Declan decided to speak his truth." I turned to Bruce. "I'm heading over to Martha. Make sure you get some shots of her, okay?"

Eliot had no immediate family in Port Ellis, and the Mercers had stepped in to host the memorial. Martha's outfit screamed *dancing on your grave*: diamond rings stacked three deep, teardrop earrings that cast rainbows of fractured light around the room whenever she moved her head, and a diamond sunburst pendant at her throat large enough to make you wonder if it was real. She wasn't wearing a red dress, but she might as well have been.

She was surrounded by a phalanx of similarly bedazzled women, evidently the seasonal golf-clubbers who owned the massive piles around the Pinerock. I took up a spot nearby, perfect for recreational eavesdropping.

"Fractional ownership in our bay? Can you imagine? Jared says we'll fight it tooth and nail," said one. "We'll be overtaken by pontoon boats and jet skis before you know it."

"Why can't the other developers be like you, Martha?" asked another. "You'd never construct a monstrosity on Jane. It's a different class of cottagers on Marjorie, with the small lots and the rentals. No one objects to a development there." Clearly Martha's pals weren't regular readers of the *Quill & Packet*.

"Alec is waving me over, darlings," said Martha. Was it my imagination, or was she slurring her words ever so slightly? "It's time. You'll come by the house after, yes?" She separated from her pack in a flurry of air kisses and tottered toward the dais, where Alec helped her ascend.

The microphone crackled to life. "Thank you all for coming," she said. "Eliot's third wife sends her regards and regrets that she is not able to be with us today." She paused, choosing her words with the care of the inebriated. "Obviously that is not true, but I suppose it's what you say when your murdered husband's first wife writes to tell you she's hosting a memorial service." Alec handed his mother a glass of water, and she took a drink. "I did not expect to be here, although I expected to outlive Eliot. He drank too much, smoked too much, and screwed around too much—everything that moved, as long as it had breasts and was half his age. He should have died twenty times over from drunk driving, lung cancer, and VD." She paused. "What do you call those nasty diseases now?" She looked at Alec and he whispered to her, his expression pained. "Anyway, he got murdered instead. Poisoned. Because of his Viagra!"

Martha continued, swaying to her own internal hurricane on stilt-like Louboutins. "He would have hated you knowing that he took Viagra. He took pride in being ... active. It makes you wonder if he burned out that motor through overuse." She staggered slightly, and Alec grabbed her elbow. She shook him off. "What else to say about Eliot? He was a natural performer, but that's not what you came to hear. You want a personal insight? A fatal flaw? Eliot knew how to act, but he didn't know how to stop. You could say he was a born liar. You couldn't trust him, not for one second. He cared about one person, and that person was Eliot Fraser. He wasn't a nice man, and he wasn't a good man, but he had talent. Unbelievable talent. So, let's raise a glass to that." She held the water glass in the air. "To talent," she said, and the room followed suit.

Alec helped his mother down the stairs and returned to the mic. "Thank you, Mother. At this time, we invite anyone who'd like to share some *appropriate* thoughts or memories of Eliot to do so. Maybe some of his acting colleagues would like to make a start?" Alec stared meaningfully into the audience, and I followed his gaze to where it landed—on Jonah Tiller, a head taller than anyone around him.

Jonah muttered—it might have been a curse, but I was too far away to make it out—and then moved toward the dais as the crowd parted around him.

"Thank you, Alec," he said in his honeyed voice, "for this opportunity to remember Eliot Fraser, a brilliant actor and a terrible man. His technical skills as an actor were exceptional, although in my opinion he lacked sensitivity. But who am I to comment?" He looked up meaningfully. There was a nervous titter from the cluster of golf-club gals. "You didn't have to know Eliot well to know how ruthless he was when it came to his career. It's no secret that he stole a role from me, or should I say it's no secret to our local police force, which has asked me about it on three separate occasions."

Jonah saluted Inspector Bell, who was standing with her back to the far wall, and who did not smile back. "Of course, that wasn't unusual behaviour for Eliot. He was a famously ungenerous colleague. He loved nothing better than exerting power over others, undermining their confidence, making them doubt their own talent. Women were objects to him, and it was a miracle that MeToo hadn't caught up with him yet. Just one more way in which he was lucky in life." Now Jonah raised a glass, and the audience, confused, followed suit. "Bon voyage, Eliot. Enjoy the toasty weather down there."

For the second time today, I was in serious danger of collapsing into a fit of giggles. I scanned the crowd for Kaydence but instead caught sight of Declan. He was standing against a wall, looking genuinely ill. Whether or not he'd liked Eliot, I realized, Declan had been subjected to a tremendous shock, cheated of his chance to perform alongside one of his professional heroes, and then asked to step into a marquee role in Eliot's place. For someone with Eliot's temperament, it would have been the opportunity of a lifetime; for Declan, I suspected, it was overwhelming. I made a mental note to ask Adeline how he was doing.

Alec stepped up onto the dais and took the microphone. He had the glazed look of a soldier stumbling off a battlefield. "Thank you for coming, everyone," he said. "That concludes the formal portion of our event. Please remember to pick up a ticket for the boat cruise and silent auction on your way out. We encourage you to remember Eliot by supporting the Playhouse that was instrumental in his career. The bar will be open for another thirty minutes. Please stay and share your memories of Eliot with each other."

"Damn," said Nick Dhalla, who had come up beside me, silent as an adder. "I fucking love funerals." Nick put a hand on my elbow. "Come on, I'll buy you a free drink."

I forced a smile, not wanting to let on that he'd interrupted some quality intelligence-gathering. "You're on," I said. We joined the line, behind a familiar figure.

"We meet again, young lady," said George Weatherbottom. "And this gentlemen is …?"

"Nick Dhalla," I told him. "Former colleague. I told you, I'm a free agent, George."

"Ha!" he said. "That was how we played it too, when we were young. Those were the days."

"You and Eliot?" said Nick. His voice was mild.

"And others too. We were a merry band, oh yes."

"Ah, youth," said Nick, and I restrained myself from rolling my eyes. Poor George had no idea who he was dealing with. "I got up to some crazy stuff myself."

George nodded approvingly. "I don't doubt it, my friend."

I leaned in. "I had a question, George, that I thought you might be able to help with."

"Oh?"

I put my hand on his arm for the second time that

evening. "The thing is, we heard that there were some young women who complained about Eliot back in the day. I thought you might know what that was about? Sour grapes, maybe?" The words tasted as unpleasant as they sounded.

His expression darkened. "Ridiculous!" he said. "A tempest in a teapot. It's not as though they weren't paid for their trouble."

"What trouble, exactly?" I asked, as Nick said, at the same moment, "Paid?"

Comprehension had been slow to dawn, but now I saw it pass across George's florid face. He stepped out of the drinks line. "I should be going," he said.

"Do you have to?" I said, pouting a little. "I was hoping to talk for longer."

He shook his head, as if clearing it. "No," he said. "I'm not talking to you anymore. Eliot was my friend. That might not mean much to you, but it means something to me. And I don't snitch on my friends."

CHAPTER 13

I GAVE NICK a ride back downtown after the memorial in my freshly de-vandalized car. Somehow we had silently agreed that we were going for a drink together. He slouched in the passenger seat, window down, blowing smoke into the night air. "This town," he said. "It's like *Succession* meets *Green Acres*."

I parked in my spot behind the Second Act. We walked down the alley and came onto Lakeshore, and I noticed that the street was quiet. The news crews had packed up for the day.

Nick held the door of the Second Act open with one hand and tossed away his cigarette butt with the other. Inside, once we'd slid the velvet curtain aside, it was quiet. There was no sign of the crowds that had filled the restaurant since Eliot's death. Even for a normal summer night, it was weirdly empty.

"It's dead in here," I said, and then felt a pang of remorse. "I mean quiet."

Nick laughed. "Let's go get a stiff one."

We'd started to weave through the tables when I stopped short. Nick bumped into my back. The lack of diners wasn't the only weird thing. Adeline was perched at the bar, a place she never sat. In fact, she was rarely still. She was always mixing, pouring, greeting, waving goodbye. She had a nuclear reactor inside her five-foot frame.

But now she was sitting beside Declan, their heads together. Declan's hung low, and I wondered if he was telling his mother about having an argument with his director at Eliot's memorial. I made a mental note to ask him about it later.

They were speaking in quiet, intense tones and I couldn't hear what they were saying. Adeline's hand snaked out and took Declan's glass and, with one quick movement, reached over the bar and dumped it down the sink. He said something sharp to her. I felt my heart twist for Adeline.

I whispered to Nick, "Let's get out of here," but before we could turn around Adeline had spotted us. She waved. Declan turned to look at us over his shoulder, and I was shocked to see how lousy he looked. He had practically fallen into mortal man territory.

Reluctantly, I brought Nick over to the bar. "Adeline," I said, "this is my old friend Nick Dhalla. Nick, meet Adeline Chen and her son, Declan Chen-Martin."

Nick shook Adeline's hand, then held his out to Declan. "I loved you in *Special Forces*. Especially that episode where you busted the acrobat smuggling ring."

Declan stared at Nick's hand and made a sound like a growl. Without a word, he heaved off the bar stool and pushed past us into the night.

I didn't even want to look at Adeline's face. I was used to having a rude son, but mine was fifteen. And he didn't have a drinking problem, at least not yet. I knocked quietly on the wooden surface of the bar.

Nick, to his credit, took it smoothly. He dropped onto the stool next to Adeline's. "I love your place," he said. "I feel like I could actually live in this town if I had a place like this to drink."

But Adeline said nothing. She was looking at the red curtain at the door, still waving from Declan's dramatic departure. After a moment, she asked Nick, "Do you have any kids?"

"Two," he said. "As far as I know."

"Then you know what it feels like. You know why Shakespeare wrote 'How sharper than a serpent's tooth it is—'"

"'—to have a thankless child,'" Nick finished. "Yes,

I do. I'm not sure why we have them, except that we live in hope they'll wipe our asses when we get old."

"Good luck with that," I said. "They're going to put us in some old-people warehouse and shut off their phones."

"Drink?" asked Adeline.

"Hell, yes," I said. She slipped around to the business side of the bar and gently nudged aside Tara, the bartender who spent most of her shifts with one eye on her biology textbooks. Tara gave up without a fight and moved off to polish glasses. "Surprise us," I told her. "We'll be at fifteen." I took Nick's elbow and guided him over to a prime two-top overlooking the lake.

"I love it when you're forceful," he said. That smile again. It really undid all my locks. *Don't be such an idiot*, my wise inner voice warned. But was it so wise, really? I'd done everything I was supposed to do: school, marriage, kid, job. And here I was, back where I'd started. Maybe that inner voice was a fraud.

"So, you're bartending," Nick said. "I'll bet you hear the most interesting things."

"I really do. I hear about how the Prestons are having a new pizza oven brought in by helicopter. Also how the condo being built on Erie is going to bring undesirables to town. It's all extremely fascinating."

Nick stretched his legs under the table, and I felt his boot touch my ankle. A hit, a very palpable hit. Or maybe it was an accident? Nope. His foot sat gently against mine.

"Oh, I don't know," he said. "I think you've still got it. I saw you talking to our friend George at the memorial."

I sat up straighter, pulling my foot underneath me. "And?"

"I've been doing my own research. He's got his finger in all this town's pies. I figured you were trying to find out which ones." He cocked his head like a friendly puppy, and I had to remind myself that Rottweilers cocked their heads too. "Did you?"

"Did I what?"

He laughed. "You should have been in the mafia. You've got the gift for *omertà*. Remember when that lawyer was trying to get you to squeal, years ago? And you just stared him down. I could practically see his hair catching fire."

Of course I remembered. But I was flushed with warmth at the thought that he did. We'd worked on a story together at our old paper about well-connected developers illegally buying land in the Greenbelt. We'd gone to interview one of the lawyers, who'd thought he could intimidate us away from the story. When he realized he couldn't, he blustered for a bit and then agreed to an interview on background. Afterwards, we'd headed to a bar, high on our success and a bit flirty.

"You were—"

At that moment, Adeline arrived at our table. Thank god. He was what? I had no idea what I'd been about to say except that it was going to get me in trouble. Adeline took two vintage lowball glasses off her tray and placed them before us.

"My version of the Sazerac," she said. "No absinthe, unfortunately. Port Ellis isn't that fancy yet. But they're infused with my homemade dandelion bitters."

Nick lifted his glass to the light. "I'm definitely moving to this town."

Adeline turned to me and mock-whispered, "He can stay." She tucked her tray under her arm and went back to the bar.

Nick watched me in the glow of the candlelight. I hadn't been watched in such a long time. Part of me started to feel like the melting wax, warm and soft. "You've got a cozy setup here," he said. "Couple shifts in the bar when you need cash. Nice little job at the paper."

Of course he had to go and ruin it. "It's not a *little* job. It's a proper job."

Nick shrugged. "Fine. But does anyone notice anything you write? Outside of the pizza-oven people."

I felt myself bristling on behalf of Dorothy and Amir, Bruce and Kaydence. "The paper does important work. It's important to the people who live here."

Nick widened his eyes at my vehemence. "Okay! I get it. But what about now? You've got a bombshell story here. Once in a lifetime. You could blow it wide open. I know you. You've got the chops. Like the way you were working the memorial."

I stared at him, a slow suspicion rising. "You really want to know what I found out."

He leaned forward and put one of his hands over mine. "What I want is for us to work together on this thing. Get the band back together." He clinked his glass against mine and raised it in front of him in a toast. "To adventures past and future."

I lifted my glass, wondering if that was a threat or a promise.

WE HAD OUR fourth drink in my kitchen. I'd stumbled coming up the stairs and felt his hand at my waist, steadying me. It stayed there after I was steadied, and we stood for a moment on the landing outside my door, with the air charged between us.

Inside, I led him through the living room into the kitchen. The room spun around me, and not just because of the Sazeracs. I could hear him drop his jacket in the living room. He came into the kitchen, holding aloft a glass ball. It was an award I'd won for a feature about a cop who couldn't get treatment for her PTSD.

"That was a good night," he said. "The night you won this."

"Remember the summer student who got so hammered that she tried to sing with the band?"

"And you held her hair when she puked in the planter outside. You've always been a good egg, Ms. Conway."

I turned to the cabinet so he wouldn't see my face flushed with gratitude. When had I become so needy? Maybe when my husband stopped touching me. Maybe when my bosses decided I was disposable.

"I knew there was a bottle of Kahlúa here somewhere—" When I turned, he was right there in front of me. He took the bottle from me.

"Do you really want a drink?" he asked. "Because if you do I'll pour one. But if you want something else, I'm here for that too."

I felt his hands, light and unthreatening, on my hips. I took a deep breath. I wanted this. Maybe not forever, but for now. I reached up and pulled him close to me. He tasted like rye and cigarettes, like the past I'd left behind. I closed my eyes and let myself remember.

I WOKE IN the morning with the sunlight nailing my hangover right into the centre of my skull. Groaning, I reached for the blinds and tugged them down. It took a monumental effort of will to sit up.

When I did, I noticed that the other side of the bed was empty. The apartment was quiet and still.

Downstairs, I could hear the faint clank of beer kegs being delivered to the restaurant's loading door.

I could smell coffee, but I couldn't hear the burble of my coffee pot in the kitchen. I forced my gritty eyes open and looked around. There was an offering on my nightstand: a latte from Glenda's in a paper cup, and one of her maple scones. I touched the cup. Still warm.

When I lifted the coffee I noticed a slip of paper underneath, torn from a reporter's notebook. *Getting the band back together,* he'd written. *You on bass, me on drums. What do you think?*

I leaned back against the pillow and took a sip of Glenda's perfect latte. I wished I had an answer to that question.

CHAPTER 14

WHAT DID THEY call it nowadays? A vulnerability hangover? The effects of the alcohol were fading, but I still felt like one gigantic raw nerve. I'd gotten too close to Nick Dhalla last night, and I could feel the regret seeping out of my pores already. As much as I might have wanted to be, I'd never been great at casual sex. I'd have loved to play bass in whatever band Nick imagined we'd had, striding through the world with raunchy abandon. But in truth, I felt more like a doe-eyed backup singer hoping for a ray of reflected starlight from the frontman.

I propped myself up against the pillows, which still smelled faintly of Nick's cigarettes. Not so long ago, I'd lived in a house with polished slate tiles, pale, low-slung sofas, and wide-paned windows with views. I'd owned multiple sets of crisp linens and wine glasses in various shapes and sizes that corresponded with specific grapes. People had come twice a week to plump and scrub and polish, on Mark's dime. I'd slept with earplugs and an eye mask next to a man I'd recognized less with every passing year. Was my present dusty existence liberation? More shabby than chic, with few friends and fewer benefits?

Ugh. I could feel negative thoughts jockeying for position in my brain. I needed to move if I wanted to outrun them. I threw off my covers and rummaged in my dresser for some clean bike gear. A ride in the fresh country air might do the job, and if it didn't, at least I'd sweat out some of the booze.

Most of the businesses were still closed at this hour; only Glenda's was humming. I pedalled hard, clearing the downtown in a few short minutes, putting some welcome space between me and my bad decisions. Twenty minutes later, I was at the Playhouse. I locked my bike in the parking lot and wandered out onto the lawn, which was still wet with dew. There were a few footprints but no visible signs of life; I'd arrived after the birdwatchers but before the picnickers. Which meant there was no one to see how hard I was panting after some moderate physical exertion.

I stopped at the fountain to splash some water on my face and then turned to look at the Playhouse. The brick glowed rosily in the morning light. A sparrow landed on the grass near me, teasing the ground with its beak. A light breeze rustled through the perennial gardens. I could sit here for a minute or two, I thought. I could just be, and not do. I could empty my mind. There was a bench in a patch of sunlight nearby and I claimed it. But serenity proved once again out of reach. As I took my seat and closed my eyes, imagining roots extending from my feet into the earth and grounding me like a great tree, a sound startled me. A strange, keening sound. I bolted back to my feet. Something close by was in pain. A human? An animal? I couldn't tell. I scanned the lawn around me but saw nothing out of the ordinary. There was only the green silence of the park.

My brain had obviously stepped up its resistance to meditation and was now inventing distractions. I sat again and closed my eyes, envisioning my troubles as nothing more than weather moving through the branches of my tree.

Another moan, definitely not imaginary. "What the hell," I said aloud, rattled. I picked up a stick and poked gingerly at the dense shrubs in a nearby flower bed, half expecting an injured animal to lunge out at me, relieved to find nothing there. I kept my stick with me as I circled around to the other side of the fountain, wondering if a creature could be sheltering under the ledge.

A rustle of leaves behind me made me turn, startled—and I nearly screamed as my toe caught on something solid and unmoving: a man, crumpled on the ground, with my foot wedged under his shoulder. Time folded as I dropped to my knees beside him and rolled him toward me, grappling with his weight through damp clothing.

It was Alec Mercer.

His skin was cool to the touch, and I thought I felt a faint pulse, although it was hard to tell with my own blood thumping loud and fast. I stood, cupping my hands around my mouth and drawing as much air into my lungs as they could hold. "Help!" I yelled in the direction of the building. "Call 911! Someone help!" I saw a door open and shouted again, waving my arms as I did: "I'm at the fountain! Hurry!"

I dropped back to the ground. "Alec," I said, "can you hear me? I've got you. You're going to be okay." There was no response. I could see blood matting his hair on one side of his skull, dribbling across his forehead and down one cheek. Lying on his back, with his head lolling to the side, he looked far from alive. I felt myself start to panic—*please, please, please not again*—until I saw his chest rise and fall, almost imperceptibly. I held his hand, squeezed. "Stay with us," I murmured.

"Alec! Alec, oh my god!" Declan landed beside me, clutching at Alec's shirt.

"We need an ambulance," I told him.

"It's on the way," said Hadiya, who was now standing at Alec's feet. "How can I help?"

"Get Declan off him," I said. Declan was hyperventilating, his ear bent toward Alec's chest. Hadiya grabbed Declan around the waist and tugged with surprising strength until he fell backwards, where he curled up in the fetal position. Hadiya took his place next to me.

"Can you hear that?" she asked, tilting her head. Sirens.

"Thank god," I said.

She wet her hand in the pool and held it under his nose. "He's breathing," she said. She stood up on her knees and looked toward the parking lot. "Just a minute more. They're here."

I could hear a gurney clanking and rattling across the lawn, and then, for the second time in a few short weeks, felt the liberating power of the words "we'll take it from here, ma'am." I stood, staggering on stiff legs, and Hadiya held out a hand to steady me. "Thank you," I told her.

"Is he alive?" Declan had roused himself and was hovering beside the paramedics as they moved Alec onto the gurney and placed an oxygen mask over his face. One of them had sprinted to the rig and driven it down to the fountain, destroying a bed of black-eyed Susans and defacing the lawn with tire tracks in the process. The next garden club meeting was going to be a rager.

"They need to get him to the hospital now." The local constabulary had arrived. Dick Friesen, portly and sweet-tempered, put a hand on Declan's arm. "Let's step over here while the paramedics work, all right? It's what your friend needs."

"I want to go with him," Declan said. His voice wobbled on the edge of tears.

"Are you family?" asked Ele James, Dick's constable. She pulled out her notebook with a sober look that belied the spark of excitement in her eyes.

The question seemed to snap Declan back to reality. "No," he said. "Not family."

Constable James clicked her ballpoint pen. "We have a few questions for you about what happened here and then you'll be free to go to the hospital and check on your colleague. Okay?" Declan nodded. "Can you tell me what you were doing when you realized something was wrong?"

"I was running some lines at rehearsal," he said. "I heard shouting from out in the lobby, so I came out to see what was going on."

"It's nine o'clock in the morning," I said. "Who were you rehearsing with?"

"You're Ms. Conway, aren't you?" said Constable James. I acknowledged that I was. "I'd appreciate you letting me ask the questions for now ... I'll have some for you as well." Forestry ambitions notwithstanding, Ele James was all business today.

"Carry on," I said.

"I wasn't rehearsing with anyone," Declan said. "I like to work alone in the mornings when no one's around. I like to experiment with space, give my character permission to explore his physicality."

"Okay," said Constable James. "And while you were … exploring, you heard shouting?"

"Exactly," said Declan. "Shouting. Doug, the security guard, and also Hadiya, I think. Doug said he had called for an ambulance and we should go down to see if we could help. So we did."

Sergeant Friesen turned to Hadiya. "And you, Ms. Hussein? What were you doing at the theatre this morning?"

"I was writing. I've been given use of an office backstage to work on my book."

"What time did you arrive?"

"I'm not sure," said Hadiya. "I couldn't sleep, so I decided to work. There's a lot of demand for Eliot's memoir and I've set myself a very tight deadline. It was still dark. I used my passkey. You can check the security system."

"And when did you realize there was a problem outside?"

"I was taking a break, I guess around eight thirty?" Hadiya looked bewildered. I understood. It felt as though hours had passed since I'd arrived at the Playhouse. "I got a coffee in the staff kitchen, and I was planning on drinking it outside. But when I got upstairs, Doug said that someone was screaming in the park and he was calling 911. I opened the door and saw that it was Cat. I yelled to Doug that I'd go and help, and then Declan came out of the theatre and we both started running."

I realized suddenly that I was shivering, wet with spray from the fountain. That, and rescuing people was hell on the nerves. There would be time later to figure out why Hadiya and Declan had been at the Playhouse at the crack of dawn, but right now I needed to find some sun. I started walking toward a set of limestone benches around a garden that had escaped the morning's EMS landscaping project. "Ms. Conway?" Sergeant Friesen fell into step beside me. "We'll need to get a statement from you. And Detective Hayward is on his way to speak with you."

"I'll be here," I said.

"I'll wait with you," he said. "You seem a bit shaky, if you don't mind my saying. Sit over here in the sun and I'll get a blanket out of the car for you."

By the time the detective arrived, I was at least warmer and had a few more synapses firing. "Ms. Conway," said Detective Hayward. "You certainly have a nose for trouble."

It was an inauspicious beginning. "It's a public park,

Detective," I said. "I'm just a regular citizen out for some exercise." The day had barely started and I was longing for my bed. Midlife came with a long list of indignities, but what I most resented was my loss of stamina. I'd been able to pull all-nighters right through my thirties, drunk on adrenaline. No longer. "But since we're chatting, do you suspect that Alec Mercer was attacked?"

"You've spent more time with the body than I have," he said. "At this point, your guess is as good as mine. Inspector Bell asked me to convey that she hopes we can trust you not to compromise the investigation by releasing details of the incident."

"You can tell her that I have every intention of staying out of her way," I said.

He took my statement and dismissed me. "Inspector Bell may have more questions for you," he said.

"I'd be disappointed if she didn't," I told him as I headed for the Playhouse, a washroom, and a cup of coffee.

Doug stepped out of his Plexiglas cubicle to greet me. "Are you okay?" he asked. "That was a lot of drama, even for the Playhouse."

If today's events had softened Doug's opinion of me, so much the better. "Still in one piece," I told him. "But yeah, not what I was expecting when I got up this morning."

"That's quite a pair of lungs you've got," he said. "I could hear you through the doors. Lucky for him you were out there." He shook his head. "I don't know what's happening to Port Ellis. Used to be the safest place in the world. Barely a burglary a year! And now an attack on a Mercer in broad daylight? The wife wants me to hand in my notice, retire."

"How long have you been working here?"

"Since the second season," he said. "I'm the longest-serving employee, other than Natalya. She's been here from the start."

"Natalya?"

"The props mistress. Natalya Kravchuk. She's not everyone's cup of tea—kind of cranky, if you want the truth—but she's a softie when you get to know her. The actors, and most of the crew, they're only here six months of the year, May to October. But a few of us are here all year round, including Natalya. She bakes cookies at Christmas for all the off-season folks."

"Do you know if she's here this morning?"

"Oh, definitely. I saw her come in around eight. That's normal for her these days. The police messed up her props room." He grimaced as if to say he would never have taken such liberties.

"Could I talk to her?"

"I can ask." Doug picked up the phone, uttered a few crisp words, and hung up. "She says you can talk to her while she works. She wanted me to be sure you understand you can't touch anything."

"Understood."

"What the hell is going on up here?" Jonah Tiller stepped through the secure door from the backstage area. "I just got a text from Declan saying there's some kind of emergency?"

"Alec Mercer was injured," I said. "The police are interviewing witnesses." I scanned the lawn and saw Inspector Bell talking to Hadiya and Declan. I was guessing she'd found their stories as peculiar as I did. "He should be up in a few minutes. What are you doing in the theatre at this hour?"

"I had a meeting with my UK agent in London," he said. "It sounded like it was going to be unpleasant, so I came here to take it. The lady who runs my B & B is sweet, but she has an eavesdropping habit." His expression darkened. "I should never have come to this godforsaken town. I was supposed to start filming a detective series in Brighton in November, and now, because of all this, they're considering a 'different direction.' Eliot Fraser: the gift that keeps on giving."

"I'm sorry," I said, inadequately.

He waved off my apology and walked to the window to check for Declan himself. "Here he comes." He opened the door to admit Declan and Hadiya.

Declan collapsed in Jonah's arms. "Can you take me to the hospital?" he said. "They wouldn't give me any information about Alec. He was so pale, and his head was bleeding. I don't know how long he was out there ..."

"Of course I'll take you." Jonah held Declan by the shoulders and seemed to examine him. "What were you doing last night? Stop. Don't answer that here. We can talk in the car." He guided the younger actor through the main doors, his hand on Declan's back.

"Protective," I said as the door swished closed behind them.

"You think?" said Hadiya. "A good journalist might be curious as to why. Just saying."

She had one perfectly groomed eyebrow raised, but her mouth was trembling. I had to remind myself that she was young, and even more of an outsider than I was. An inch of bravado covering an abyss of insecurity. I'd felt that way for most of my career, until I'd been fired—and set free. I felt a sudden surge of warmth for Hadiya Hussein.

"Can I talk to you for a minute?" I said. She looked suspicious but followed me to an alcove by the coat rack. I wasted no time. "Have the police spoken with you about Eliot yet?"

"Is this a fishing expedition?"

I sighed. "I'm just saying they might want to ask you about Eliot's medication, if you know what I mean. Just so you're prepared."

Her face relaxed slightly. "As it happens, they didn't ask about that. Maybe they think I don't know about the drugstore he carried in his suitcase."

I shrugged. "I guess they'll find out when you put

it in the book. The whole world will find out. Eliot's current wife. His kids."

Hadiya's brow wrinkled. "His kids?"

Now it was my turn to be confused. "Those cute twin girls? They're in all the photo shoots he's done in the past couple of years."

Hadiya shook her head slowly, as if wondering how someone could be so slow. "Those aren't his kids," she said. "Those are his stepkids. They were like five years old when he married their mom."

A basic detail of reporting that I should have known. I gritted my teeth against the embarrassment and said, "I guess it's a good thing you're writing the book and I'm not. I don't have a million dollars to pay a fact checker."

She laughed at that, a rare little sound of pleasure. I was about to ask her for more details about Eliot's current marriage when Doug called across to me. "A piece of advice, Ms. Conway. You don't want to keep Natalya waiting."

THE PROPS ROOM wasn't a room, as it turned out, but a vast underground bunker with rows of gunmetal grey shelving as meticulously categorized and labelled as any library system. The temperature, I learned, was carefully monitored to preserve the artifacts collected from productions past and present, and the lighting was bright but filtered to exclude harmful UV rays. The room was secured with a passcard system; only employees of the props department were issued with cards, and any visitors had to log in and be escorted by a member of staff at all times.

It was obvious that Natalya Kravchuk, a wiry woman in her sixties, had some control issues.

"So there's no way someone could have come in and messed with one of Eliot's props?" I asked after hearing a lengthy explanation of the department's security protocols that seemed more aligned with a facility designing military-grade weaponry.

"Not possible," she said. She was wearing black leggings and a long white tunic shirt. Her curly hair, black with grey streaks, was clipped in a severe ponytail. She led me to a seat at the conference table. She scowled. "Look at this mess! I can give you twenty minutes, but I need to clean while we talk."

I could see what she meant. Black fingerprint powder dusted all of the objects, including a water pitcher and two glasses, a leather satchel, and a copy of Darwin's *On the Origin of Species*. Nearby, I saw the airplane seat with the plastic tray that I'd last encountered in Eliot's dressing room. It too was covered in black powder.

"The police returned most of my props yesterday. They insisted on taking everything that Eliot Fraser touched onstage, if you can imagine. The costume people can get items dry-cleaned and deal with it that way, but with props? You're on your own." Natalya put the satchel on the table in front of her and dipped a fine paintbrush into a dish of warm, soapy water. "The hard surfaces are one thing—plastic, glass, they're fine. But paper? Cloth? Leather? Good luck to you. I use the same soap they use to clean the oil off seabirds, by the way." She stroked the liquid onto a square inch of leather and blotted it with a soft rag. "How do I know that the police wasted their time and mine?" She pointed at a laptop with her paintbrush. "I look at the security logs every single day. I'm the first one here in the morning and the last one here every night. During the theatre season, I'm here both days on the weekend. You can ask Doug if you don't believe me. So: not possible. What else do you want to know?"

"Do you know who killed Eliot Fraser?" I asked. "It seems like not much gets past you."

She hooted. "Flatterer. No. I know what happens in this department. Beyond that?" She shrugged expressively. "Not my responsibility."

"How can you be sure that none of your staff were involved?" I had no reason to suspect a props assistant, but her certainty was intriguing.

"They are all terrified of me, that's why," she said. "I have rules. My staff don't fraternize with the talent. No distractions. Keep your eyes on the job at hand. You get a reference from me, you can work at any theatre in the world. You fuck with me, you'll never work in this industry again. You fuck the talent? You're out on your ear. And that went double for Eliot Fraser."

"Why?"

"Because he was who he was. Shameless. A leopard doesn't change his spots. I told my staff, you stay away from that one or you'll answer to me."

"You were here during his first season," I said. "Is that what you mean about not changing his spots? Did you see what he got up to then? Did he bother you?"

She continued dampening and blotting the surface of the satchel, square by square. "Where I grew up, a woman learned how to defend herself. No one dares to bother me, not then, not now. My little ducklings in props? They aren't so fierce. So I protect them, for their own good."

"What about back in the early days? Who protected the ... ducklings then?"

Natalya gave me a grim smile. "You already know the answer to that. No one protected them. The leopards though, they got all the protection in the world."

I took a deep breath and spoke very carefully. Natalya knew all the Playhouse's secrets. I was sure of it. And she'd keep them in the vault unless I could persuade her to trust me. "Who protected Eliot?"

Natalya raised her eyes to the ceiling and waved her arm around her head in a gesture that seemed to include the entire theatre, the town, the world. "Who didn't?" She dabbed at the satchel again, and then put down her cloth and folded her arms across her chest. "What is it you people say? Follow the money? Silence is expensive, Ms. Conway."

"You're saying the women were paid?"

"I'm saying that balance sheets don't lie the way people do. You might want to consider that fact."

She was on the verge of shutting down. "Natalya. Tell me who he hurt back then. Please."

Her eyes were cold. "He hurt a lot of people. That's what men like him did, what they still do. I'm not surprised someone killed him. But it wasn't with one of my props."

CHAPTER 15

I LAY IN BED, staring at the knife's edge of morning sunlight slicing through the blinds. I was still no closer to understanding Eliot Fraser's murder, and now someone had nearly murdered Alec Mercer. The same someone? None of it made any sense. And Nick Dhalla had ghosted me. Again.

I'd been helping Adeline behind the bar last night, and it felt like a mule had kicked me in the back. My lumbar hurt, and my ego hurt. My eyes slid over to my phone. Still nothing. I thought about all the ways that Nick Dhalla was bad for me: Chain smoker. Workaholic. About to be married as many times as JLo, and not nearly as rich.

In the kitchen, I put a pot of coffee on and stretched

once more, listening to my spine crack like ice along the lakeshore in March. Only one thing to do about that. I pulled my yoga mat from the closet and unrolled it in the tiny space next to the couch. My laptop sat on the battered old coffee table, and I flipped it open. There was a woman in Singapore whose yoga sessions were perfect for me, just rigorous enough with not too much woo-woo about how breath is the core of life.

While I waited for the coffee I gazed at the headlines. In the absence of real news about Eliot's murder, the various outlets were filling the vacuum with any piece of fluff they could find: his widow, a former model, had announced the formation of the Eliot Fraser Foundation to bring classical theatre to underprivileged children everywhere.

I remembered, with a start, that I was supposed to be checking on Jonah Tiller's background for the second part of the profile. I picked up my phone to record a voice note, and while I was there I sent a quick message to Jake, telling him how much I loved him and how much fun we were going to have when we got together. *If we get together, you ungrateful little bastard*, I thought. I didn't send that part, though. Discretion is the better part of motherhood, a lesson they never bother to share with you at Mommy and Me.

It was certainly not a lesson my mother had ever learned. She would have scolded me for putting my coffee cup on the table without a coaster. She would have told me I was ridiculous to sit by the phone waiting for a man to call. She would have—

The phone rang. I knew, without looking, that it was her. My mother was uncanny that way. She was eighty percent Hillary Clinton, and twenty percent witch.

"Hello, honey," she said, before I could say anything. "How's Murderville?"

And ten percent Tina Fey. "It's all good, Mom. Busy, as you can imagine. I've been writing like a maniac."

"Now there's an apt choice of words. Who murders someone onstage like that? It's all very Grand Guignol." I heard the sound of a coffee grinder in the background and knew my father was hard at work preparing an espresso exactly as my mother liked it. She was often photographed in the kitchen for magazine shoots, but she treated its appliances like wild animals that might charge her if she spent too much time with them.

She was still talking, in the low and calm voice she had learned carried best across crowded auditoriums. "I think it's wise that Jake's decided to come here instead of visiting you. At least while there's a murderer wandering around."

I sat up suddenly, and my back squealed with pain. "What did you say? Jake's visiting you?"

My mother sighed. "I had a sudden opening in the calendar. I was the keynote at She Speaks in Monterey, but it was cancelled. We haven't seen Jake in ages, and you know he loves the pool."

"I haven't seen Jake in ages! And he's *my* son." I was aware that my voice had taken on a shrill edge. Somehow, whenever I talked to my mother, the decades rolled back and I was sixteen again, infuriated and powerless.

She continued in her most soothing voice, which I liked to think of as CEO Whisperer. "We'll talk to Jake about coming to see you when things aren't quite so murdery in Port Ellis. I'll make sure he texts you. Oh, and by the way, did you apply for that job I sent you?"

"I don't need a job, Mom. I have a job and—"

"Here's Dad with the coffee," she said, skating over my protests like Wayne Gretzky. "He's very keen to speak to you. Bye, sweetheart."

My dad's voice came on the line, slow and warm and infinitely comforting. "Hey kiddo, I'm glad I got you at home. What's a seven-letter word for 'left out'?"

"Um … *excluded*?"

"Too long."

I thought for a moment. My dad and I had always bonded over word games: Scrabble, Yahtzee, Words with Friends, crosswords. He was a history teacher, and he said playing with language put him in touch with his "inner poet." It also meant he always had a game to play on his phone while he was waiting in a green room for my mother to go onstage.

"Could it be *omitted*?"

"Ah, that's it. You're a genius." I heard the newspaper rustling as he filled it in. They had kept their subscription even after I'd left the paper, which I regarded as a minor betrayal. He yawned. "Speaking of which, I read that profile of Jonah Tiller you wrote. Great stuff. I loved all the detail."

"Thanks, Dad. I'm working on part two. There's lots more to say about Jonah. I'm just waiting to nail down a few things about his past."

"Speaking of the past, your old pal Nick Dhalla got quite the scoop, huh?"

Suddenly it was icy cold in the apartment. Maybe it was just a ghost walking across the grave of my dead career. Very carefully I said, "What do you mean?"

"Are you telling me you haven't read it? I only saw the story because I set up an alert for Eliot Fraser's name. I know you're going to have an amazing scoop of your own one day and I don't want to miss it—"

"Dad! What was Nick's story?"

I could hear the newspaper rustling. "It was about the stuff that Eliot Fraser got away with in Port Ellis back in the day." He muttered to himself and I bit my tongue, willing him to hurry up. "Seems like there was quite a lot of … Well, we'd call it groping but I don't think that really suffices anymore. Sexual misconduct, the story says. I guess the lawyers told them they couldn't say 'rape.'" He paused. "Are you there, honey? I can send you the link—"

"I've got to go, Dad. I'll talk to you later." Then I cut him off with an abruptness that my gentle father did not deserve.

Fuck. Fuck fuck fuck. In a second I had Nick's Twitter feed up, and there it was, the pinned tweet. *Revealed: Secret history of Eliot Fraser's backstage harassment.* He'd added the hashtag #MeToo. Of course he had.

Quickly, I skimmed the story. It was what I had suspected but not yet been able to nail down. Eliot and a few other actors had been very busy during the Playhouse's first year, most of the activity happening after the curtain came down. I wondered how they'd managed to get onstage every night when, according to Nick, they'd been conducting an unrelenting campaign of harassing and propositioning every female who worked at the Playhouse. One of their victims had been a seventeen-year-old girl working as an usher.

The story was thinly sourced on the surface, with almost no one quoted on the record. None of the women were named, and he hadn't found one to speak to him. But I knew Nick, and I knew that he and Claire would never publish anything that wasn't airtight. The newspaper's lawyers wouldn't let them.

I felt a hot blanket of fury closing around my head. Rage at myself for missing the story. Rage at Nick for betraying me. My finger hovered over his name in my contacts list. And then, in a flash, I remembered what had happened the last time a rage like this had consumed me: I'd erupted at a random stranger on the street, and then watched my career go up in flames.

With a shaking hand I put the phone down. I closed my eyes. I took a deep breath and let it out in a hissed *ohm*. It wouldn't fool a yoga teacher, but it would have to do.

BY THE TIME I got to the newsroom the rage had seeped from my body, leaving me as drained as a flat tire. I locked my bike outside, took a deep breath, and pushed my way through the glass door where the newspaper's name lay flaking. Apparently I worked for the *Quill & acket*. Dorothy was always promising to have it repainted.

But Dorothy was not to be trusted, as I was learning.

When I walked in, my colleagues' faces flashed up at me and just as quickly looked down. They'd all read Nick's story, clearly, and were embarrassed on my behalf. I might as well have been carrying a stool sample in a tiny plastic jar.

I slunk to my desk, my face burning. On my keyboard was a tiny Tupperware container filled with pumpkin seeds. I glanced over at Bruce, and he gave me a thumbs-up and mouthed, "It's okay." Kaydence sidled over and asked me if she could get me a muffin from Glenda's. I nodded, my lips pressed together. I was a grown-ass woman, as my son liked to say. I wasn't about to cry at work.

The door to Amir's office was open, as usual. He swung through it, one hand on the door frame and the other beckoning me. I saw Kaydence raise her eyebrows at me in a question. Maybe the question was: *What would you like for your last meal?*

I walked quickly into his office. Better to get it over with. He was standing by the window, and I marvelled again at how fresh he looked, like a bill just delivered to the bank. It occurred to me that I should not be thinking this way about my boss, especially as we were about to talk about sexual harassment allegations.

He turned to face me, and I braced myself for the shitstorm of accusations about why I'd been scooped. He sank into his own chair and pushed a printout toward me. Nick Dhalla's story, of course. "This guy's good. You've got to give that to him."

You have no idea, I thought.

"I'm sorry," he said.

The shock dropped me into a chair. "You're what?"

"I should have done more when you said you thought there was some dirty history there. I should have pitched in. Helped you find sources."

I stared at him. I'd never had a boss admit culpability. Usually they had four-year degrees in ass-covering.

We sat in silence for a moment. I closed my eyes

and allowed myself to drift off on the comforting scent of Amir's laundry detergent. I appreciated the simple cleanliness of it. He didn't rely on musky cologne, unlike some others I could—

My eyes snapped open and I shot forward in my chair.

"George Weatherbottom," I said.

"The lawyer? Is he involved?"

"I talked to him at the memorial. Just briefly, but he said, 'It's not as though they weren't paid for their trouble.'"

Amir let out a low whistle. "Anything else?"

"Weatherbottom brushed me off after that. I meant to go back and ask him." I stood up and began walking tiny circles, my mind flying ahead. "Nick heard it too. But if there were payoffs to those girls, he couldn't get it confirmed. Otherwise it would have been in his story."

"Which means it's still out there waiting for you."

"Exactly." That feeling was back, that elusive feeling: elation and excitement and fear that someone would beat me to the story. Again. But I wouldn't let it happen. I was a hawk with a doomed bunny in its sights.

Amir stood and began to pace too, the two of us spinning like gears in a machine that was finally working. "Check our archives for any stories," he said.

"Definitely. And I'll go back to Weatherbottom to see what I can get." I remembered what Natalya had said: *balance sheets don't lie*. I'd have to try to get a look at the Playhouse's books from those early years.

"Let's see if you can find anyone who was working at the Playhouse that year. Anyone who was backstage, or on the board." Suddenly his mouth clamped shut.

"What? Amir, what is it?"

He brought his hand up to his forehead, as if to ease away the wrinkles. I felt like telling him not to bother: I'd tried that and it hadn't worked. After a moment he looked up at me.

"Calvin Talbott was there."

"Dorothy's husband?"

"He was the chair of the board at the Playhouse in the first season. Dorothy told me there'd been an almighty fight in the early years. A putsch, she called it. Calvin got tossed out and Martha took his place."

In his eyes I saw the mirror of my own feelings: elation and fear. "If there were payouts, Calvin would have had to sign the cheques." The knowledge sat between us, sticky and uncomfortable. "Go and talk to her," he said. "She owes you that, at least."

As I walked past his desk, Bruce hailed me. He was hunched over his screen, the seriousness of his purpose evident in the lack of snacks nearby. Close to his shoulder sat Hannah Shim, the summer intern, who had the intensity of a ballistic missile. She was a genius with spreadsheets and spoke both French and Korean. I predicted she'd be my boss within five years.

"What's up with the Mercer story?"

Bruce and Hannah looked up at me. They were both wearing overalls, which I doubt they'd planned.

"He's out of hospital," Bruce said. "Refusing to give another interview to the police. Won't talk to us either, obviously. I got a peek at his initial statement. He claims that he dropped his phone into the fountain, and then he slipped and banged his head when he reached for it."

"And I have a bridge I'd love to sell you," I said.

"Well, exactly. It smells like my compost bin in the middle of August. And Hannah found out something very interesting."

"A couple of things, actually," Hannah said in her precise voice. I liked the fact that she was unafraid to own her accomplishments. "First, the area around the fountain was repaved at the beginning of the summer. There'd been complaints from parents that their kids were sliding around. So I called the landscaping company, and they told me they'd installed a no-slip surface around the base of the fountain. They use ground-up old tires, apparently."

Bruce sat with his fingers steepled, beaming like a papa bear whose cub had just raided her first picnic basket. "And the second thing?" I asked.

Hannah swiped at her phone, which had a picture of BTS on the homescreen. So she wasn't one hundred percent terrifying genius, at least not yet. She tapped and brought up a picture, which she turned to me. I leaned closer. The photo was dark, figures crowded together. It looked like the inside of a bar, and someone had written across the top: *Fireball Fridays, only at Shaughnessy's!*

I shook my head. "What am I looking at?"

"Shaughnessy's, out on the old Highway 2," Bruce said. "It's where the kids go. The ID policy is gentle, let's put it that way."

"Yeah, I remember," I said. "I think I upchucked some Southern Comfort in the parking lot back in the day. What's it got to do with Mercer?"

Hannah wrinkled her nose in polite disgust and spread her fingers to zoom in on the image. "That's Alec Mercer there," she said. I squinted and saw that it was indeed Alec, wearing a tight blue T-shirt, next to a table crowded with glasses. A man stood beside him, holding a shot glass.

My breath caught. "Is that—"

"Yes," said Bruce. "Declan Chen-Martin."

"But Declan's supposed to be—"

"Sober. Yes, I know." Bruce leaned back in his chair. "That's the thing about actors. They're good at acting."

My mind was spinning. The whole town was like a giant murder mystery game, except with real weapons, and real blood. Why had Alec lied about tripping? Who had pushed him? Was it the same person who'd killed Eliot? Was it the same person who'd smashed my windshield and slid a poison pen letter through the newsroom door?

Back at my own desk, I tapped out a quick email to Dorothy, asking if we could meet. I wanted to write *What the fuck?* in the subject line, but settled for *A couple of quick questions.* Then I opened Twitter and DM'd SunneeDaze29, the woman who'd said she knew something about Eliot Fraser's past. She had not yet responded to my questions.

I spun my chair to look out the window. The lake was still, with no wind on it to lure sailors; an elderly couple sat on one of the benches in Centennial Park, watching the paddlewheel make its crossing. Nick and I had sat on that very bench, talking about Fraser's death. I'd been so glad to see him. My one untainted relic of the past. And he'd been glad to see me, or so I'd thought. Now I realized he'd only been interested in the information I'd gathered—though he'd been happy to make a detour through my bed to get it.

Goddamn it. I swivelled back to my desk. I felt a rumble at the base of my sore spine, long dormant but still familiar. The combination of humiliation and professional rivalry was as potent as jet fuel. He was not going to steal my thunder.

The universe decided to pay attention for once. A notification flashed in Twitter, and I opened up the message from SunneeDaze29. She apologized for being late with her reply; her boss was an asshole and work was a zoo. But yes, she had spoken with her aunt Darlene, who had a lot of things to say about Eliot Fraser. She'd added a devil emoji.

I let out a little whoop. Finally, a crack of light. I was getting out of my chair to tell Amir what had happened when Kaydence raced into the office. She was gasping for breath, and she'd squeezed the top off the muffin she was holding.

"Whoa, wait a second," I said, and put a steadying hand on her arm. "Kaydence, are you okay?"

She shook her head frantically. A martini-shaped barrette fell out of her curls and onto my desk. On a gulping breath she said, "It's Glenda. They've taken her in for questioning again."

CHAPTER 16

"I DON'T UNDERSTAND," I said. "The police can't be *that* incompetent. Why would they suspect Glenda?"

Kaydence burst into fresh sobs, sucking in air between each strangled word. "I ... didn't ... tell ... you ... everything."

I held her by the shoulders and manoeuvred her into my desk chair. "Breathe," I instructed her. "Don't talk." I rubbed her back, murmuring "there, there, you're okay." Why did people say that? What did *there, there* even mean? And as for *okay*, I had the feeling we were a long way from it. Amir and Bruce hovered nearby, on alert.

Eventually the tempest subsided, and Kaydence emitted a small moan. "I should have told you," she said. "Glenda didn't come to her seat that night. We were supposed to be sitting together, but she never showed up."

I met Amir's eyes. He nodded. I slipped into interview mode, seamlessly. "Where was she?" I asked.

Kaydence raised her watery face from her hands. "She went to see Eliot backstage. But she didn't hurt him! She wanted him to reconsider. He'd told the theatre not to renew her contract. But it was totally unfair! She thought if she could talk to him in person and explain how important her business was to her, he would see reason."

Amir had moved closer, standing on the other side of my desk now, his expression serious. "Kaydence," he said, "I wish you'd told us this before now."

Kaydence mopped her face with a fistful of tissues. "I know," she said. "I'm sorry. It was a huge mistake. I'll understand if you have to fire me."

"Amir is not going to fire you," I said, hoping it was true.

"I am not going to fire you," he agreed. "But you need to tell us everything you know. Don't leave anything out."

Kaydence sighed. "Eliot told her he'd back down if she gave him what he wanted."

"Sick fuck," I said. I turned to Amir and then to Bruce, who had now joined the party. "Eliot propositioned Glenda on the baking show." Bruce shook his head and muttered, "What an asshole"; Amir wrinkled his nose, conveying the same sentiment.

"So someone saw her backstage and told the police," said Amir.

"They must have," said Kaydence. "She didn't think she'd been spotted. And she was the victim, not Eliot Fraser. So you can see why she thought it was better to keep quiet." I could think of several reasons, and from the arch of Amir's eyebrows, so could he. Kaydence coloured and kneaded her fingers. "But then I saw the audience footage. There are pan shots of the auditorium after Eliot collapsed. I'm in some of them. Glenda isn't. I realized it might come out if the police matched tickets to seats and she'd look guilty even though she didn't hurt a hair on his head."

"Please tell me you didn't delete the footage," said Amir.

Kaydence looked offended. "I would never. And I was going to tell Cat about it today anyway, but then Lindy phoned from the bakery and said that the police came by and took Glenda away. During the breakfast service!"

"Let's take a beat," said Bruce. "We're putting the story together. We can't be afraid of the facts."

"Well said," said Amir. "So I'm going to suggest that you, Bruce, and Cat go through all of the audience footage together and see what's there."

"I can help," said Kaydence.

Amir's voice was kind but firm. "No, you can't. I'm going to drive you home, and you're going to take the rest of the day off."

I watched him escort Kaydence out of the building while Bruce rolled a chair next to me. "Well," he said, "this is a dog's breakfast."

I nodded. "Do you believe that she didn't delete any files? Or edit them?"

"*I* do," he said.

"Hmm," I said. Kaydence wasn't a reporter, and she *was* an exceptionally loving and protective friend. If I didn't have Bruce's confidence, I wasn't going to advertise it. I opened the shared drive where Kaydence had saved all of the community videos—filed under the surnames of the people who had submitted them—along with a spreadsheet indicating which reels she had viewed and a summary of what each one contained. She hadn't got too far down the list, which was a relief. "Let's look at the ones she hasn't opened yet," I said. If we had other shots of her sitting alone, I thought, we'd sidestep the need to examine what Kaydence had or hadn't done.

We were lucky. Most of the audience footage had been shot in the auditorium after Eliot's collapse, from various angles. But some had been shot before pandemonium broke out. At least two of the reels had a clear visual of Kaydence next to an empty seat. "Glenda's not the only one missing," said Bruce. He pulled up a map of the theatre and printed it. "When we're done here, I'm going to try to locate all the empty seats and see who was supposed to be in them. In the meantime, though, let's fast-forward through the auditorium footage. Otherwise we'll be here all day and night."

"Brilliant." I meant it. Bruce didn't telegraph his skill with clever verbal shots or attention-seeking dramatics, but he was as good a journalist as Nick Dhalla in his own unassuming way. I clicked through to the next clip, expecting yet more of the same, only to find myself backstage. "Hey now," I said. "What have we here?"

Onscreen, Natalya was giving a pre-game speech in the props room about the critical importance of order and discipline. I was willing to bet that she didn't know one of her employees was engaged in unauthorized filming. Or maybe she did and was waiting for the right moment to exact vengeance. "And now," she said, "the chair of the board has a very few words for you."

Martha Mercer stepped into the frame. "I have promised Natalya that I will be brief. I only wanted to thank you for all that you do behind the scenes to make our productions among the best in the country. The board is grateful for your skill and professionalism."

So Martha Mercer had been backstage. I wondered if the police knew.

We skipped forward to the next clip, which opened with a selfie video of Madison, the actress playing Rachel in *Inherit the Wind*. "Opening night!" she said, flashing a peace sign and then flipping the view to capture the corridors backstage.

"Oh, you little beauty," said Bruce. "God bless the millennials, not a moment unrecorded."

"I think she's Gen Z," I said.

"Same difference," said Bruce.

Madison was no cinematographer, and I had already started to feel seasick when Bruce said, "Stop. Rewind to where she sweeps the corridor. Go frame by frame."

"Do you want to drive?"

"I thought you'd never ask," he said, and I surrendered the mouse. He clicked furiously, stopping with a sigh of satisfaction. "There. Look."

"Is that Alec?" As Madison passed by a door that was halfway open, the camera captured a fleeting glimpse of a male figure, facing into the room, his shaggy blond hair cascading down to his collar.

"Patience," said Bruce. "Watch." He advanced the video, and I saw Alec twist toward the camera with a look of alarm on his face. As the angle of his body shifted, another figure came into view: Declan Chen-Martin, who pulled his hand from Alec's waist as if burned and stepped out of camera range. The final frame showed Alec slamming the door shut.

"Alec and Declan?" I said. "I'm going to need some time to process that one. It's kind of weird, isn't it? Considering Alec is his boss?"

"Theatre people," said Bruce, returning the video to regular speed. "They're different from you and me."

Madison/Rachel continued down the corridor, and another door opened. Hadiya rushed out, almost colliding with the camera. Hadiya swore, and Madison seemed to stumble. When the camera righted itself, Hadiya was framed against the dressing room door. And above her shoulder, the name *Eliot Fraser* was crisp and clear.

"Well, well," said Bruce. "Good news for Glenda. She certainly wasn't the only one backstage where she wasn't supposed to be."

"I'll text Kaydence and let her know that we can put Hadiya and Martha at the scene," I said, and tapped out a brief message. "That's something, at least. Are we nearly done with the videos?"

"Unless you include going back over them to find empty seats," said Bruce. He saw my expression and grinned. "It's okay. You should go write an article or something. I'll do it." He rolled away from my desk, taking his theatre map with him.

I'd started composing a note to SunneeDaze29, suggesting a time to chat, when my phone rang. It was Kaydence. "You're on speaker phone," she said. "I'm here with Glenda, and with Glenda's lawyer, Lori."

"It's Lori Draper here," said the lawyer George Weatherbottom had described as "that girl who does divorces." Clearly her mandate was broader than advertised. "To be clear, they haven't charged Glenda with anything. And I think they're unlikely to, since it's an absurd theory of the case. But it can't hurt to demonstrate in advance that we can show reasonable doubt. With any luck, we can prevent the police from getting tunnel vision."

"Any idea why they're so interested in Glenda in the first place? She's hardly the only person in town who had a history with Eliot."

"Well, the Swine Survey certainly didn't help," said Lori.

"I told you that I wasn't involved in creating it, only circulating it," said Glenda.

"It's a bad fact," said Lori, "but we'll deal with it."

"Swine Survey?" I asked.

"A group of women were meeting at the theatre to discuss gender-based discrimination," said Lori. "Unfortunately, some unidentified members of the group decided to circulate a list of alleged perpetrators. Eliot Fraser was one of the names on it."

"I'd love to see that list," I said.

"I'm afraid I can't share it," said Lori. "There's a good argument to be made that it's defamatory."

"Sent," said Kaydence. Lori sighed, audibly.

We wrapped up the call, and I summoned Bruce to share in the latest Port Ellis scandal. The Swine Survey wasn't a long list—maybe twenty names in total—and most of them were unknown to me. Bruce, of course, knew everyone. "No surprises there," he said. "Eliot, Calvin Talbott, your new friend George, the ex-mayor, the guy who owns the Swiss Motel, the bouncer from Shaughnessy's. The usual creeps. Your bartender's there too."

"Bradley?" I said. I hadn't paid much attention to Adeline's part-time barkeep, since we worked opposite shifts. He'd seemed harmless enough to me, aside from his propensity for dropping glassware.

"He invites high-school girls to his house parties," said Bruce.

"That's … eww," I said. "Where do you hear this stuff?"

Bruce shrugged. "Most folks like to talk. I listen."

I guess I'd been so focused on establishing roots in Port Ellis that I'd let some of those folks off the hook, starting with Dorothy and her alleged perv of a husband. She'd been lying low, avoiding the office and my request for a conversation. I'd tackle that problem tomorrow. Tonight, though, I had a shift at the Second Act, the one place where it didn't seem to matter that I was a newcomer. Everyone talked to you when you were serving them drinks.

I ARRIVED AT my post a few minutes before opening to find Adeline sitting at the bar with a glass of white wine. "Join me?" she asked.

"If you don't object to your bartender drinking," I said, serving myself. "Long day?"

"They're all long lately," she said. "At least that's how it feels. I'm worried about Declan."

I could understand why. I hesitated for a moment before saying, "Someone saw him at Shaughnessy's the other night."

She seemed to fold in on herself. "He's not supposed to drink. He used to have a problem with it. But I guess you know that." I nodded. "It's all the stress at the theatre, with Eliot and now Alec. He's never been resilient. I try to help him but he won't talk to me." I handed her a bar napkin and she wiped her eyes. "I feel so helpless."

I understood exactly what she meant. Motherhood was a life sentence: you were chained to your child and carried along on their journey, for good or for ill. It could be a bumpy ride for control freaks like Adeline. "You're a great mom," I said. "He adores you."

"I don't know," she said. "He says he has anxiety because I wasn't around enough when he was small. I was always working at the restaurant." She grabbed my hand. "You should be with your son, Cat. You don't get another chance to raise them. And it's dangerous, what you're doing, snooping around the theatre with a killer on the loose. Look what happened to Alec!"

"We don't really know what happened to Alec," I said. "He says he slipped." I didn't believe that for a second, but the conversation had veered into territory I wasn't comfortable exploring. I knew Jake needed more of me, but he kept throwing everything I offered right back in my face like strained peas from a highchair. And since his future therapist was occupying real estate in my nightmares, I wasn't prepared to hand over my waking life as well. "Shouldn't we unlock the door?"

She glanced at her watch. "Five minutes to go. It should be a quiet night. Monday, no theatre." She gave me a wry smile. "They thought Eliot Fraser would boost the town's economy, and he killed it instead. The man had a talent for destruction, you have to give him that."

CHAPTER 17

I NEEDED TO talk to Alec Mercer, but after leaving several messages with no response, I was trying another strategy this morning: hitting the books. The Port Ellis Central Library was a neoclassical hulk sandwiched between a yoga studio and a café specializing in pour-overs, which as far as I could tell was just a way to charge six bucks for a filter coffee.

"Hello, young Catherine!" The voice carried across the library, and I waved a hand in greeting at Pierrette, the head librarian. She had a swirl of sparse grey hair and she wore two cardigans against the air conditioner's onslaught. She'd seemed ancient when I was a child and visited the library with my grandparents, and now she was somewhere north of Gandalf's age.

But she was wisdom itself and knew where every body—and file—was buried.

I explained to her what I was looking for; what I'd been unable to find at the *Quill*'s archives. Any reference to possible payouts during that first summer of the Playhouse, or the year after. Pierrette listened and nodded, then disappeared while I took a seat at one of the tables. Twenty minutes later I saw her emerge from the stacks, staggering under the weight of two boxes. I jumped up to help her, and we set the treasure trove down.

"I've brought you some of the *Centurions* from that summer. The paper that used to be published over in Elmdale until those fools shut it down a decade ago. There used to be another paper too, a weekly run by some anarchists—"

"Do you mean *The Rambler*?" I'd have to remember to tell Bruce that he was once considered an anarchist. He'd be so proud.

"That's the one. Unfortunately we never got around to archiving it. Only lasted a few years. People around here don't take kindly to chaos." And with that, she left. I tapped out a quick message to Bruce, asking if he'd kept any of his *Ramblers* from that summer and if he could bring them to the newsroom.

I spent the next two hours scouring the pages of the *Centurion*, and while I learned more than I ever wanted to know about the invasion of borer beetles,

I learned nothing about Eliot Fraser, sex pest. The paper had dutifully covered the opening of the festival and reviewed Eliot's performance ("a lion finds his roar"), but that was it.

Pierrette had also brought me all the programs from the years the Playhouse had been in operation. I flipped through them, feeling a pang looking at the cast of *Hair*, which I'd seen with my grandparents when I was a teenager. My grandfather had jumped up from his seat "to use the facilities" when the nudity started.

But then I sat bolt upright in my chair. In the heavy silence of the library, I could hear the hum of the air conditioner—and my own suddenly quickening breath. Carefully I fanned out the programs in front of me and tapped each one with a finger.

I wasn't wrong. The program from the Playhouse's first summer—the summer Eliot was using it as his own private playhouse—was missing.

I took the stack over to Pierrette, who sat at the main desk stabbing at a keyboard with two fingers.

"Pierrette, do you know what happened to the first Playhouse program? It's missing."

She leaned over and thumbed through the stack. "So it is," she said. "Good lord. You wouldn't believe what vanishes in this place. Just grows legs and walks away. And you can't even blame the anarchists anymore."

An hour later, I was on my way to visit the one

person who might have some answers. But first I had to pull over to take a call from my son. While the sun beat in through my new windshield, I listened intently to his teenaged melodrama.

"And then Telfer got fired for vaping in the washroom at work …" I couldn't tell any of his friends apart, since they all had names like nineteenth-century presidents—Tyler, Taylor, Telfer. He could have been saying anything and I'd still have been damp-eyed with gratitude. At least he was *talking* to me.

His face filled my phone's screen, and it was all I could do not to touch his dark eyebrows, the little beauty mark on his left cheek. There was a scrape on his chin. Was he shaving now? I pictured Mark giving our son a lesson with a razor, frowning as Jake dabbed his cut on the snow-white towels that cost a hundred dollars apiece.

Jake's hazel eyes had flickered off to the side, distracted by something offscreen. It occurred to me, with a sharp sudden pain, that I occupied a lot less of his brain space than he did of mine. Every mother through history had probably felt this way. It wasn't much of a comfort.

"That's Telf now," he said. "Probably wants to brag about how much free time he has. Gotta go, Mom. Love you."

"I love you, sweetheart, and I'll see you—"

But he was gone.

I tossed the phone onto the passenger seat. A dump truck rumbled past, and I rolled up my window against the dust that billowed in its wake. I'd pulled up outside the gates of Storytime Faire to talk to Jake. By accident or design?

The gates, sagging now on their hinges as a parade of trucks rolled through, had once been painted candy cane red and white. One of the pair of grinning gnome statues that had flanked the gates and terrified me as a child now lay decapitated in the long grass, its evil eye framed between a discarded beer can and a majestic dandelion. I'd brought Jake when he was seven or eight, but the park was mostly decrepit by then, and he'd scorned the spinning teacups and creaking wooden roller coaster.

A giant billboard by the side of the road explained that "Allegra Estates by Mercer Developments" would be opening soon, and though the development was "Nearly Sold Out," there was still time to "Buy Your Dream Vacation Property." The tri-lake area was starting to look like a mini Miami, thanks in no small measure to the Mercers.

But not yet, though. When I cracked the window again, there was the smell of my childhood summers: pine and forest floor and a hint of hot road tar. The sound of construction was far away, and nearer by I could hear a woodpecker busy on a tree. Maybe he was looking for a new neighbourhood too.

Against my better judgment, I checked Nick

Dhalla's Twitter feed. He was still retweeting praise for his scoop about Eliot Fraser's history of harassment. No new story yet, though. And no message from him, either: not a text or an email or a call. Nothing since the scrawled message on my nightstand. I felt my rage rise, a red tide that no happy woodpecker could calm.

A couple of workmen ambled past, tool belts low on their hips. They passed the billboard showing a diverse group of happy homeowners enjoying a glass of wine in their new Allegra paradise. I hoped, for once, that a billboard spoke the truth: Port Ellis could use a kick in its lily-white ass.

New developments like this one, and the Mercers' retirement Xanadu, would be good for the newspaper business too. New subscribers, for one thing, but more importantly new stories: developers disregarding wetland protections, irate women in Tory Burch dresses pulling out all their euphemisms at town council meetings. Old money versus new. Conflict and drama. And that spelled news.

The sun slipped from behind a cloud and I lowered the car window all the way. If I chose to stay, there'd be so much to write about. *If* I chose to stay. The sun caught the decapitated gnome's eye and I shivered. Eliot's bulging blue eyes. The strawberry-jam ooze under Alec's head. Suddenly I was glad that Jake didn't want to visit. I imagined him riding his bike through the forest trails, a sudden hand reaching out—

My phone rang, nearly giving me a heart attack. Was Alec Mercer gracing me with a phone call? I plucked it off the seat next to me, registering the 518 area code. Where was that? Upstate New York, I thought. Not Alec. I punched the green button.

"Hello, is this Ms. Conway? It's Cal Meade returning your call."

My mind spun through all the calls I'd made in the past few days; the tiles fell into place. "Oh yes, thanks so much for calling back, Mr. Meade. How are things at Shakespeare Heals?"

Cal Meade was only too happy to talk about his theatre group for misfit teens. Not surprisingly, he wanted to squeeze me in return, searching for any juicy details about Eliot's murder. I told him what I knew, keeping to the facts that were already public.

We tsk-tsked about the state of the world for a bit, and then I asked what he could tell me about Shakespeare Heals's famous patron Jonah Tiller.

"You mean Jonah Beaumont?" he said.

"I'm sorry, what?"

He seemed to enjoy my surprise. "Well, that's who he was when he came to us. What is it, fifty years now? He was just a kid. A kid who hadn't had many chances, like all the kids we get in the program."

"Can you tell me a bit more about that?"

"Well, it was before my time, obviously. But he'd had a rough go of it. I mean, I wouldn't want to grow up in New York with no parents, would you? He did some dumb things. The law was not on his side, to put it mildly. But there was a youth court judge who saw something in him and recommended that he participate in our program as part of his sentence."

"What kind of dumb things?"

"I honestly don't remember the details," Cal said. "But it's not a secret or anything. Jonah's talked about it. When we had our fiftieth anniversary dinner a few years ago, Jonah wrote about his past in the program for the gala."

I leaned forward in my seat. There was a band of sweat around my hairline. "Would you still have that program? I'd love to include the details in my profile of Jonah. And I'd love to mention how important Shakespeare Heals was in helping him turn his life around."

I could hear Cal murmuring to someone in the background. "My assistant's going to try to find it. We can scan it and send it to you. He doesn't talk about why he changed his name, though."

"I'll have to ask him about that."

"Well, whatever he's called, he's one of the most brilliant actors of his generation. And a generous and wise friend to young people who might want to go on the stage but haven't had the right opportunities. He's a gem." Cal paused. "You can quote me on that."

TEN MINUTES LATER I was cresting the hill above the lake. Millionaires' Hill, my grandparents called it. That was decades ago, when a mere millionaire could afford a property here—anyone who bought on this shoreline now probably had an extra zero to their name.

I turned right at a simple white mailbox with a tattered *Quill & Packet* sticker affixed to the side. The winding driveway led through a copse of trees—pine and birch and cedar. The lake vanished and appeared again as I drove, winking silver between the trees.

In front of Dorothy Talbott's house—it was too majestic to be called a cottage—there was a small circular drive, and I pulled off to a needle-covered parking pad to one side. Her mud-dashed Cherokee sat in front of the house, its hood nearly touching the wheelchair ramp that ran up the side of the porch. One of her headlights was cracked and the bumper scraped, and I wondered if Dorothy's driving days were mostly in the rear-view mirror.

Like Dorothy, the house was proudly and defiantly heading toward the end. The double dormers had surrendered their paint to winter storms, and a crack ran up one of the four columns that held up the porch roof. This was the back of the house—the real action was in front, facing the lake—but it was still disconcerting to find cracks in the queen's palace.

How angry could I afford to be with Dorothy? If I wanted to keep my job, not much. But did I want to keep my job when the woman employing me had lied about a crucial element of the most important story to hit town in years? If there had been payouts back in the day, her husband would have been involved. All I needed to prove it was the smoking chequebook.

The clapper on the front door was a bronze bear's paw, and I let it fall twice. Immediately there was a chaos of barking from within, and when Dorothy appeared a moment later, she was holding back two dogs with an outstretched leg.

"Do not give them an inch," she said as I came inside and bent toward the drooling, writhing canine tangle: one ancient border collie with a film over its eyes, and a living mop with a tail. "They'll take you for everything you have."

Then they should be at home here, I thought, standing up. I'd never been invited to the Talbotts' before, and I took the opportunity to look around. The foyer opened onto a vast living room, with oak beams above and a stone fireplace big enough to burn a martyr. A wall of windows with a view of the lake at the far end. To my left was a staircase with a stairlift fitted against the wall.

When Dorothy had finally caved to my request, she'd insisted that we meet at her house. I could see why. Here we couldn't escape the evidence of her husband's infirmity. It was hardly subtle, but I had to give it to her: she had a battle commander's grasp of tactics.

"Come on through," she said. "What would you like? Tea? Or something stronger?"

"Tea would be lovely."

She disappeared down a hallway, her long grey cardigan trailing after her, and called to someone in the kitchen. When she reappeared, she swept a magisterial hand in front of me. Outside, of course, where I could be awed by the view of her realm.

And it was awe-inspiring, as we stood on the flagstone patio, down a small stone staircase, overlooking the wide expanse of the lake. I thought of what Hugh MacLennan had written, so many years ago, about this country: "My God, is all this ours?" But it wasn't all ours. It belonged to the people who could afford the land titles. It had been the home of the Anishinaabeg, the Wendat, and the Haudenosaunee, but the squatters on Millionaires' Hill did not seem in any hurry to give it back.

Dorothy dropped into a rattan chair and I sat on its partner, noting that the stuffing was coming through the seat cushion. She reached into the pocket of her cardigan and replaced her thick glasses with an equally huge pair of sunglasses. "I can't put off the surgery much longer," she said, dabbing at the corners of her eyes.

I chose to ignore this bid for sympathy, which would have shamed Dickens. "Dorothy," I said, "you've read Nick Dhalla's story."

She turned the big dark lenses toward me and said nothing.

I took a deep breath, inviting calm. "The story about the women who were abused by Eliot Fraser and others."

She snorted. "*Abuse* is rather a loaded term."

"And not just abuse," I said, emphasizing the word. "There's evidence that there were payouts to the women involved. That's the story I'm working on now."

Her eyes were hidden behind the giant sunglasses. "And do you have confirmation of these payouts?"

"Not yet. But I'm working on it. That's why I'm here." I took a deep breath. "Your husband was the chair of the Playhouse board at the time. He would have been responsible for authorizing those payments."

Dorothy's mouth had tightened to a slit you couldn't fit a credit card through, but I plowed on. "I'd like to speak to Calvin about this."

"Calvin is infirm, as you may know," Dorothy snapped. "He has been for years. His mind lives in the past."

"Could I try to speak with him at least? Sometimes people with dementia can remember the distant past."

When I said "dementia" Dorothy flinched, as if I'd sworn. "That won't be possible."

We sat staring at each other, two boxers looking for openings. It was baking hot out on the patio, but Dorothy wrapped her cardigan tightly around herself.

After a moment I said, "So you never spoke to him about what happened during that first summer at the

Playhouse? There was at least one woman who was raped, apparently. This happened under his watch."

Dorothy snorted. "The words people use these days. It's amazing how quickly the language changes. *Rape*." Her mouth curled in disgust. "Is it rape when a girl wants the attention of an enormously attractive and famous man? Perhaps even dreams of leaving town by his side?"

I stared at her. It was as if a cocoon had opened to reveal not a pretty butterfly but a poisonous spider.

"Besides, it's Martha you should be talking to. She knew Eliot was trouble, but she married him and she brought him to the Playhouse anyway. If anyone's at fault, it's her."

"So you're telling me it was the girl's fault for being raped, and Martha's fault that her husband was a rapist?" My voice might have risen just a bit.

She gave me a look that was almost pitying. "Does everything really seem so clear to you? Black on this side, white over here. Martha was no victim. She pulped poor Eliot like an orange. Made him promise to promote her grotesque new retirement village, for one thing."

Before I could answer, a young woman came out of the house carrying a tray. She didn't wear a uniform, but she was clearly in Dorothy's employ. She put a pot of tea, a cup and saucer, and a jug of milk in front of me. Dorothy got a tumbler filled with clear liquid on ice and a wedge of lime, and I remembered the first line of the cottage-country bible: it's always five o'clock somewhere.

"Thank you, Jenny," Dorothy said.

I stirred milk into my tea, thinking. "But Eliot never promoted the retirement village. I would have noticed if he had."

"Oh ding ding *ding*," Dorothy said, her voice rich with sarcasm.

"Are you actually suggesting that Martha bumped off Eliot because he refused to shill for her new development?"

"I don't suggest," Dorothy said regally. "I observe. And I've been observing the Mercers my whole life. Maybe that's why I'm going blind."

"But that doesn't explain Alec," I said. "Who pushed him into the fountain? Not his mother, surely."

"Who says he was pushed? That boy has been … well, let's just say less than steady since he was a teenager." She mimed stuffing something up her nose.

I burst out laughing; I couldn't help it. "Are you suggesting he's a drug abuser? What else? Are the Mercers running a satanic pedophile ring?"

"I'd suggest less sarcasm and more digging."

I felt that sting, as she intended. Just at that moment, the doors to the house opened and the dogs came barrelling out and down the steps, skidding to a happy halt at her feet. Dorothy felt around and retrieved a filthy tennis ball from under her seat.

She hurled it with surprising strength into a stand of maples at the edge of the lawn and the dogs ran after it, yelping.

"If you want me to dig," I said carefully, "I should start with the hush money. Who got the payments? How much? Who still held a grudge toward Eliot? The person who knows the answers is your husband."

Dorothy stood abruptly. "I've told you, Catherine, that my husband is unwell. He is in no shape for an interrogation. I should get back to him." Her tone softened. "I'm glad you've joined us. You're a credit to the newsroom. You bring new life. New eyes."

Clearly the interview was over. I rose. She put her arm through mine and began hauling me up the stairs to the house. Looking up at the wall of glass that gave the Talbotts their million-dollar view, I stopped, squinting. Clouds were reflected in the glass, making it seem alive. But I could swear I'd seen something move, a shadow behind the window.

Port Ellis was like that, I thought, rubbing my free arm against a sudden chill. Picture-postcard panoramas, Chardonnay on the dock, fresh-baked pies, and laid-back luxury. If you looked carefully, though, it was like peering into the lake: watery depths full of warped shapes and wriggling, slimy life.

CHAPTER 18

I STOPPED BY the bar to pick up my cheque the next morning. Adeline was sitting at a table with a coffee and a laptop. I didn't know how she worked sixteen-hour days—seven days a week in the summer season and six during the rest of the year—and still managed to walk upright and speak in full sentences. I told her so.

"At least I turn a profit, which is more than my dad ever did," she said. "There's some satisfaction in that. But yes. I'm starting to think that I'm getting too old for this. I was hoping to close for the month of February this year. Go to LA, stay in Declan's apartment. But revenues are lower than I projected, and Declan ..." Her voice trailed off. "Hopefully we'll catch up a little with the income from the boat cruise. Which reminds me: can you work for me that night?"

"I'm so sorry," I said. "I'm reporting for the *Quill*. Can you get some of Glenda's staff to help out? They're already going to be there for the dessert buffet."

"I need bartenders," she said. "The guy who works on the boat makes one drink every ten minutes. The theatre people will revolt. I'll have to call Bradley."

I hesitated, and then said, "Have you heard about the Swine Survey?"

She gave me a sharp look. "What's that?"

"It's a list of bad men circulating online." I thought of Lori, the long-suffering lawyer, and added, "Allegedly bad men. The kind who allegedly abuse women. Eliot Fraser's on it, along with a bunch of others. Including Bradley."

Adeline froze. "Show me. Right now."

I was already regretting having mentioned it. "Let's keep this between us, okay? I don't think I'm supposed to be sharing it. There's at least one lawyer on it." Between my termination of employment and my divorce, I'd served my time in lawyers' offices. If there was going to be a defamation suit, I wanted to be as far away from it as possible. I handed Adeline my phone.

She clutched it, scanning the screen. "Do you believe it?"

"I don't know these people," I said. "Do you?"

She stood, her face white. "Enough to know that there's something to the rumours. Bradley can go ask his friend at Shaughnessy's for a job. I'm not going to employ a creep like that." She stood up. "Excuse me, Cat. I've got a phone call to make. Can you cover Bradley's shift tomorrow?"

BACK AT MY desk, I stared morosely at the stacks of paper I'd let accumulate. Other people could find things onscreen, but I needed the high contrast of ink on paper to locate the intriguing tidbit. You stumbled across the most interesting things hidden on page 125. *They try to bury the truth in a cardboard coffin*, Nick used to say.

I would have liked to bury him in a coffin. Preferably one made of lead.

I took a sip of my coffee and pulled the preliminary coroner's report on Eliot's death off the top of the pile. I didn't know how Amir had procured it, but he'd dropped it onto my desk with a smile that was just this side of smug. He wanted me to know that he still had it.

My eyes slid down the page. Age, seventy. Eyes, blue. Liver, approximately eight hundred years old. Okay, so that wasn't actually how the coroner phrased it, but I could read between the lines. Then my eye snagged on one detail, and I heard myself gasp out loud.

A moment later, I was on the phone to Hadiya. She answered with a surliness that suggested she was not a morning person. I jumped right in. "Did you know Eliot had had a vasectomy?"

Silence. Then she said, "Have you been reading TMZ again?"

"It's in the preliminary coroner's report."

"Now that I'd like to see."

"That could possibly be arranged. If I felt that you'd earned the right to see it."

I could practically hear her tapping a mental calculator. "I didn't know for sure, but he alluded to it once. Something about how he'd saved a fortune on condoms over the years."

"Charming," I said.

"That was Eliot." She was silent for a minute, thinking. "I asked him if he'd ever wanted kids of his own, but he said something had happened a long time ago that made his mind up for him. I tried to get some deets, but he wasn't playing after that. That's all I know. So, will you flip me the report?"

I was busy writing in my notebook.

"Cat? It's your turn to play."

"I'll put it in an envelope and drop it to you at the Playhouse. But you didn't get it from me."

I packed up for the day, tucking the envelope in my purse. Bruce and I were going to see if we could squeeze any more information out of George Weatherbottom, who was holed up at his summer cottage a half-hour's drive from town. It was a mark of his stature in Port Ellis that George owned a staid Edwardian home off Main Street as well as a seasonal property down the lake from the Pinerock. Rumour had it that he'd been hunkered down out there since the Swine Survey had leaked. As I swung open the door to Bruce's Subaru, I noticed a small pile of yellowing newspapers on the passenger seat.

"A gift for you," he said. "Thank god I'm a hoarder."

"I could kiss you," I said and picked up the first copy of *The Rambler*. It was designed like a tabloid, and it looked like it had been typeset with a machete. The front page featured a photograph of the Playhouse with a big red *X* through it. The headline was giant, in a point size that newspaper people called Jesus type: "White Elephant Craps All Over Port Ellis."

As Bruce drove us out to George Weatherbottom's cottage, I read *The Rambler*, taking photographs of a few articles that caught my attention. Someone at the paper had definitely had a hate-on for the Playhouse. It too had reviewed Eliot Fraser's performance and pronounced it "ham on very white bread." The theatre was bourgeois, boring, a drain on resources.

But not a hotbed of predators. I glanced over at Bruce. "These stories are not exactly incriminating."

"Keep reading."

I picked up the next few issues, from the winter after the Playhouse's debut season. An editorial in one issue was headlined "Women Deserve Better."

The unsigned column was written by someone who claimed to have worked at the Playhouse and spent the summer "being chased by pervy old men." When she'd complained to her boss, he'd fired her. She'd planned to take her story public, but before she could, "a cheque arrived in the mail." She had to promise to say nothing about what had happened, which is why she was writing anonymously.

My scalp prickled. Here was proof, finally, that hush money had been paid. "Oh my god," I said. "It's true."

"It gets better," Bruce said. "Check out the next issue."

I flipped open the last copy, so quickly I nearly ripped the paper. The entire third page was filled with a long story, and the tag at the top said *Rambler Investigates*. The only photo showed a balding man behind a desk, his mouth open as if he were shouting.

"Is that—"

"Calvin Talbott. Yes."

Quickly I skimmed the story. The finance committee of the Port Ellis Playhouse had resigned en masse at a board meeting, citing "irregularities in the financial structures" of the first season. The Playhouse had been an immediate hit, thanks to the drawing power of star Eliot Fraser. Performances had sold out. And yet the Playhouse's books were in the red due to unexplained deficits.

There were quotes from Calvin Talbott promising an immediate audit. And at the bottom of the story was a quote from the Playhouse's lawyer: "There were unexpected operational outlays in the first season, but the Playhouse will be back next year, bigger and better than ever."

"Holy shit," I whispered. I held up the paper and pointed to the lawyer's name.

"This place," Bruce said, shaking his head. "It's like *Goodfellas* with Muskoka chairs."

ACCORDING TO BRUCE'S spy network, George's wife had gone to Palm Beach for an extended stay at their condo and left instructions with the neighbours to check in periodically to see if he was dead or alive, with a preference for the former. As of nine o'clock this morning, Bruce assured me, George was still the latter; he'd opened the door to retrieve a newspaper in apparently good health.

Bruce pulled up next to a Norway pine and cut the engine. "I feel like I should apologize," he said. "I honestly don't remember any of this stuff happening that summer. In my defence, I was smoking a lot of hash."

"You don't have to apologize." I held up the papers. "You found it. This is how we confirm the story."

He shook his head. "It's more than that. I've been thinking about it. Why didn't it make an impression on me? The fact that these girls were complaining?" When he turned to me, his face was sheepish, ashamed. "I guess I just didn't care. It was all background noise."

There wasn't much I could say to that. Bruce hadn't been a swine himself, but he'd enabled swine. Was that just as bad?

I got out of the car and checked that I had my recorder and notebook. I expected our visit to be brief, so I took a moment to appreciate George's place, reminiscent of the one my grandparents had owned. This was an old-timey lake house, designed for use from Victoria Day until Labour Day, with unfashionable mustard clapboard and faded green shingles, several patched screen doors and a huge veranda overlooking the lake. Walking around the building, I had a view across the lawn to a sandy shore. A lone figure sat facing the water. We made our way down to him.

"Hi, George," I said.

"George," said Bruce.

"Bruce," said George, with a curt nod. He turned to me. "You can leave," he said.

"Maybe you don't remember me? We chatted at the memorial," I said.

"I remember you," he said. "That was the last peaceful night I had before women started throwing dog shit at my house. I'm tempted to throw you off my property, but you're with Bruce. Also, you're the first people I've seen in four days."

Bruce cocked his head. "Have you been eating, George? I hear Sally's out of town."

George waved him off. "I can take care of myself, thank you very much. Why are you here? Is it about that goddamned list? That thing is defamatory, you know."

"We're not here to talk about the Swine Survey," I said, and George slumped with relief. Bruce wrestled two additional chairs into a semicircle and we sat down. I reached for my notebook, and George immediately grew tense again.

He turned to Bruce. "Is it me, or has the world gone crazy?" Bruce didn't reply, and George continued. "When did everyone get so goddamn delicate? I went to the grocery store two weeks ago and told the checkout girl I liked her shorts. The girl complained to her manager and they banned me for harassing the staff. When did it become a crime to compliment a woman, I ask you? And now I'm on a watchlist? Port Ellis is becoming a fascist state."

Bruce cleared his throat. "We had some questions for you about Eliot Fraser and the Playhouse," he said.

But George was on a roll. "You know what I'm talking about, Bruce," he said. "This used to be a community. People had each other's backs."

"Hardly a universal state of affairs," said Bruce. "As you'll remember."

I glanced over at Bruce and watched him lock eyes

with George. They were silent for a long moment, and then George said, defensively, "I was doing my job."

I pulled *The Rambler* out of my purse and opened it to the investigation. "We know what happened," I said. "With the payouts, all those years ago."

George's mouth fell open. Beside me, Bruce was completely still. He knew that I was bluffing; I knew now that there had been payouts, but I didn't know the details.

I pointed to George's quote in the story. "'Unexpected operational outlays,'" I said. "That was you speaking as the lawyer representing the Playhouse. Nice way to talk about paying hush money to women who'd been raped."

He slumped in his chair, and I felt a moment of pity for this melted old man in a baseball cap. But only a moment. He'd never felt pity for anyone in his life, I was sure of it. Certainly not for the girls who'd been nothing to him all those years ago. Less than human. Merely props.

"I'm not going on the record," he whispered.

"No names," I said. "I want you to confirm what we already know. That payouts were made to women and girls after they were abused by Eliot Fraser and others during the Playhouse's first season."

His head flipped one way and the other, as if he were looking for a place to run. His feet, clad in old Crocs, began to tap frantically. No way he'd get far in those.

"Or," said Bruce, "we could ask your wife for an interview to see what she remembers."

"You people," he said, in a broken voice. "You're parasites."

"Is that a yes?" I said. "You're confirming that these payments were made by the board of the Port Ellis Playhouse?"

George didn't answer, and for a long while the only sound was a distant motorboat and the splash of water against the dock. His shoulders rose on a deep inhale, and he nodded.

"Thank you, George," Bruce said. "You did the right thing."

George did not look like he agreed. George looked like he wanted to take his beer glass and smash me over the head with it. But I couldn't leave, not yet. Not until we had more details. I said, "We think that whatever happened when Eliot Fraser was here thirty-five years ago may have a connection to his death. We want to know what went down."

"There are other people you could ask," said George. "Why me?"

"Calvin Talbott has dementia, and everyone else has a motive for murder," said Bruce. "You, on the other hand, were Eliot's friend. Whatever else you've done, I don't think you killed him."

Once again, the lawyer retreated into silence. I was beginning to think we should pack up and leave, when he said, "Martha called me a few months ago and asked for the old files. I had a folder of releases—you'd call them nondisclosure agreements now. I sent them to her."

"Did you keep a copy?"

George shook his head. "The Playhouse was the original client, and Martha requested the files in her capacity as the chair of the board. Whatever you—and the Law Society—might think, I take my obligations seriously. I'm not required to keep this stuff for decades, you know. I closed the matter and returned the documents to the client. Period. End of story."

"It's not though, is it, George?" Bruce said. "You know something. You're wondering if it got Eliot killed."

George shifted in his seat. "I know nothing. I merely wondered why she wanted them. It occurred to me that they could be used to … persuade Eliot to take a particular course of action."

"Like to promote a retirement village?" I asked.

"I couldn't say," said George, primly.

"George," said Bruce. There was a warning in his voice.

George turned away from the lake and faced Bruce. He looked older, suddenly, and smaller. "That summer brought consequences that were unforeseen," he said. "And it was the most innocent who had to bear the brunt of it. We couldn't have known."

It was an odd remark for someone with George's crusty, battle-scarred shell. Suddenly he felt guilt? I could see that the words puzzled Bruce too. I said, "Do you mean the young women, George? They were the innocent ones?" He seemed startled by my question. His lips shut tightly. A snapping turtle, planning to sink below the surface again. "We've all been paying since that summer, one way or another. Mistakes were made. Very expensive mistakes."

I had to admire his ability to hide in the passive voice. "What kind of mistakes? Who made them?"

But George's expression shuttered. "It's time for you to go now," he said. "Both of you."

We walked back to the car in silence. There was an emptiness in my heart where there should have been elation. I'd gotten the confirmation I needed, the giant scoop my editor wanted.

So why did I feel like I needed to jump into the lake and scrub myself clean?

CHAPTER 19

BRUCE DROPPED ME at the Second Act so I could get my car. There was another conversation I needed to have today, but it was one I wanted to have alone.

For the second time in as many days, I found myself driving to the Talbott house.

This time a nurse answered the door wearing pink scrubs. I told her I needed to speak to Dorothy. "Mrs. Talbott is resting," she told me.

"Please tell her I only need five minutes of her time," I said. "I won't even come inside."

The nurse closed the door. I swatted at mosquitoes and waited, my mind going in circles. What had George meant when he'd talked about the innocent ones? I couldn't believe he meant the women in Eliot's web. Everything he'd said previously suggested he thought they were fame-chasing strumpets who'd gotten what they deserved.

"What do you want, Catherine?" Dorothy appeared behind a large screened window next to the front door, wrapped in a frayed terry cloth bathrobe. She held the screen open but only wide enough for her body to fill the space. There was no invitation here; clearly, she intended to hold me to my five-minute promise.

"There were payouts," I said. "That first season. To women who were abused by Eliot Fraser. Calvin signed off on the payments."

My employer said nothing.

"It wasn't illegal," I said. "Maybe back in the day it wasn't even considered immoral. Everybody got something. The women got a payday. The town got to keep its festival. Eliot got away with it."

Still Dorothy said nothing. The evening was drawing in, and I shivered in the cool air. "But I don't think Eliot did get away with it," I said. "I think the past caught up with him."

One of the dogs, the mop with a tail, popped up beside Dorothy, and she bent to scratch its head. When she straightened up, she didn't seem quite as straight as before. "I can't say I'm happy to have the story run," she said. "But I think it should run. You did the work you needed to do. I like to see hard effort rewarded."

She began to pull the screen shut. "And now it's time for my bath."

It was an answer. Shrouded in deniability as bullet-proof as Kevlar, it was still an answer.

I was so tired. I knew I should go back to the newsroom and write the story, with all its messiness, its lingering questions. What had happened to the women? Had one of them carried a grudge for decades, a grudge that ended in murder? But I decided to drive straight home instead. I was a big believer in the healing magic of a shower, a burger, and a beer.

I popped my head through the service door at the rear of the restaurant and put my order in with Adeline before running upstairs to wash my cares away. I might not want to live above a restaurant for the rest of my life, but the advantages were compelling. As I unlocked my door, I was already feeling more cheerful than I had all day. That ended the second I walked in and saw the message in red spray paint on my living room wall:. TIME'S UP. YOU WERE WARNED.

The hair stood up on my arms. My heart pounded a warning in my ears. *Getoutgetoutgetout.* But I couldn't move. Moving meant making noise. Noise would make me a target. It's true what people say: terror makes time slow down. I stood frozen and watched a cobweb lazily twist in the breeze from the window.

The window. I looked over, trying not to move

my head. Sure enough, the cream-coloured curtains were swaying gently in the breeze. I was sure I'd closed the window that morning before I'd left for work. Someone had opened it. Someone had crept through. Someone who might still be in the apartment, waiting—

I unfroze, and ran.

AMIR SEEMED SURPRISED to find me at the bar of the Second Act, staring at an untouched plate of fries. He wasn't used to seeing me off my food. Adeline assured him that the police were on their way and that they'd told me to stay in the restaurant until they arrived. "She looked like a ghost when she ran in here," Adeline told him. "What kind of person would do this to her?"

"Someone frightened," said Amir. "Someone who knows that Cat is brilliant and relentless and about to figure out who they are."

I couldn't help thinking that he had a higher opinion of my abilities than my home invader did. The edges of the puzzle were taking shape, but the central image was still a pile of random pieces that needed sorting.

The front door opened, the velvet curtain parted, and Inspector Bell walked in like a queen with courtiers trailing in her wake: Detective Hayward, Constable James, and a woman in street clothes who

I didn't recognize. "I'm flattered," I said. "You must like me more than I thought."

She favoured me with a grim smile. "Did you touch anything?"

I shook my head. "I didn't get farther than the front hallway," I said. "I could see the living room wall from there." Thinking about what else my intruder might have destroyed on their rampage through my home made my chest ache. My stuff might not rise to my mother's standard for "nice things," but I was attached to it nonetheless. Amir, standing next to my bar stool, put a hand on my shoulder.

Inspector Bell's expression seemed to soften. "We're going to go up and clear the apartment first," she said. "Then I'll come and get you and ask you to do a walkthrough with us and tell us what's out of place," she said. "I won't be long."

Amir took a seat next to me while Adeline directed the cops upstairs. "I'm glad you called," he said, the corners of his brown eyes crinkling with concern. "You must have been terrified."

"I was moving too quickly to notice," I said. I'd been halfway down the stairs before processing that my reptilian brain had selected "flight" from its limited menu of options. A good choice in the circumstances.

Adeline returned, her distress palpable. "The police said I can get a painter in tomorrow at the earliest. I'm going to make a couple of calls and book them right now. I don't want you to be out longer than necessary. Of course, I wouldn't blame you if you never wanted to set foot in there again."

I was about to respond that no one was going to drive me from my home, but Inspector Bell's appearance made me bite my lip. I had a feeling she would have some opinions about my future accommodations, likely involving my relocation to another country. She beckoned to me. "We're ready for you."

At the front door, she handed us gloves and boot covers, which fitted awkwardly over my sandals. Amir entered the apartment ahead of me. I heard him gasp. I pushed my way in—I'd never had so many people in my living room at one time—and confronted the violent message for the second time. It wasn't any less disturbing now. The large red letters seemed to vibrate with anger. I averted my gaze and began taking stock of the damage, relieved to see that my furniture had escaped unscathed. My budget, already stretched, didn't extend to a full home makeover.

"Is anything missing in here?" asked Inspector Bell.

"Not that I can see," I said, moving down the hall. The galley kitchen was likewise as I had left it. A mess, but not a sinister one.

Inspector Bell put out a warning hand. "They did some damage to the bedroom," she said.

I quickened my step and stopped short in the bedroom doorway. The woman who had arrived with

Inspector Bell was standing at the foot of my bed in coveralls, labelling an evidence bag. But why was there a white carpet on the floor? It took a beat to realize what I was seeing: feathers from four disembowelled pillows had settled on every surface.

"I hope you don't think you're staying here." Amir's voice came from the doorway.

"I ..." The genuine horror in his face prevented me from saying that I was intending to bed down in a sleeping bag on the sofa. I followed his gaze to a point above the bed where a knife had been stabbed into the headboard, a ghoulishly avant-garde artwork. I recognized it: a chef's knife from downstairs that I'd borrowed when I'd roasted a leg of lamb at Easter. I'd meant to bring it back downstairs but never remembered. Even my absent-mindedness was ganging up on me now.

I jumped as Inspector Bell came up silently behind me. She raised her eyebrows at the knife. "I hope you've got a friend with a pullout couch."

CHAPTER 20

AS IT TURNED out, Kaydence did have a pullout couch, and I lay on it all night, my eyes open, wondering if it was fear or the lumpy mattress keeping me awake. It didn't help that there was a psychedelic 3D print of cats riding skateboards hanging over the sofa. "Kiwanis Club fundraiser," Kaydence said when I asked where she'd found this horrifying item. "You should come to the next one."

I did not need more material for nightmares, though I kept that from her. Kaydence had proved to be the best possible friend. She refrained from peppering me with questions and instead poured coffee and handed me sliced avocado on toast for breakfast. "I know it's a cliché," she said. "Whatever. You need your strength."

I could have sat for the rest of the day in her apartment, avoiding the cats' crazed eyes, but that just would have frayed my nerves even further. If my mind was empty, it would drift back to the spray-painted warning, the knife stuck in my headboard. I had to fill it with other people's thoughts instead.

I got in my car and headed to the newsroom, where Amir and Bruce were waiting. Together, we wrote and edited the hush money story, surrounded by files and a Matterhorn of takeout containers. We pored over my photos of the *Rambler*'s earlier reporting, and my notes of our conversation with George Weatherbottom. By late afternoon, we'd wrestled our story into shape, and I felt some ghosts starting to rest. I left Amir and Bruce to post it. I stayed offline all evening watching movies with Kaydence. I didn't want the online noise disturbing my fragile peace.

The next morning, I headed to the Playhouse.

Doug smiled when he saw me walking toward his booth, and this time he didn't hurl the visitor's pass across the desk; he gently chucked it instead. Perhaps our early-morning adventure had secured me a spot in his good graces. Or maybe he'd read the story about the hush money payouts online and liked it. I hoped it was the latter. I was proud of the work we had done together.

Doug's opinion notwithstanding, the effort was already worth it: news outlets around the country had picked it up, and it was spreading like wildfire on social media. SunneeDaze29 had sent me a message dense with emojis: two thumbs-up, a heart, a devil, and a turd. I took this as approval and shot back a message: *Is your aunt ready to talk now?* For my follow-up story, I needed to find some of the women who'd received payouts. Amir wanted something fast.

I headed into the theatre. A man came lumbering toward me carrying a stuffed ostrich, and I had to duck into an alcove to avoid being brained by its beak. Was there an ostrich in *Much Ado About Nothing*? Maybe Alec had changed the setting. Maybe he'd made it an absurdist play, and the duel would be fought with balloons instead of swords. I wondered if the director who'd stepped in for him would realize this artistic vision.

There was a bulletin board in the alcove where I'd taken refuge, and I stopped to look at it. There were the usual offers of apartment shares and snake oil weight-loss remedies. Beside them, a news release asked for anyone with information about Eliot Fraser's murder to contact the police. A newer notice overlapped this one, asking for anyone with information about Alec Mercer's accident to contact the police.

It occurred to me that the Playhouse was producing the wrong Shakespeare play. It should have been *Hamlet*, with its stabbings and poisonings and the stage strewn with bodies at the end.

I could hear voices coming from a door marked

"Rehearsal Room B." I eased the door open and slipped inside. A stack of flats sat propped against the wall, and I sidled over next to them, sheltering in their shadow. In the middle of the room, Declan and a young woman stood, her body tense with misery, his with anger. Several other actors formed a semicircle around them. Jonah stood at Declan's side, his face aghast. He and Declan were in street clothes, although both of them had swords hanging off their belts.

Declan clutched the actress by her upper arms. "But you are more intemperate in your blood than Venus," he hissed, "or those pampered animals that rage in savage sensuality." This was the scene where Claudio confronted his beloved, Hero, with the evidence of her alleged infidelity. Declan's eyes were wild, his teeth bared, and I watched, completely rapt. He was an astonishingly charismatic actor.

If he was acting. There was something feral about him, something savage that I hadn't seen before. The woman playing Hero was either a brilliant actress or she was genuinely terrified, because she quailed away from him.

"Excellent work!" I peered around the stack of flats to see who'd spoken. There was a woman in a folding chair holding a script, and I assumed this must be the assistant director stepping in for Alec. "Let's take ten and regroup."

The actress playing Hero pulled away from Declan like her skirt was on fire. I saw Jonah put a fatherly arm around Declan's shoulders, bending his head to speak confidingly into the younger man's ear. I could see, even from this distance, that Declan's shoulders had stiffened. He shook his head forcefully and broke away from Jonah, who stood and watched him stride off.

Declan came charging toward the door, and I popped out of the shadows and into his path.

"Jesus, Cat! What are you doing skulking in the corner? You scared the shit out of me."

I very nearly said "the feeling is mutual." Up close, Declan looked even more ravaged. His eyes were red, his unshaven cheeks sunken, and the aroma that drifted off him could politely be described as "stale."

"Not skulking, just asking a few questions." I held up my notepad like a shield.

"Well, I'm off to take a leak," he said, shouldering the door open. "So if you want to join me at the urinal, be my guest."

"I've done interviews in worse places," I said, trotting after him. I flung a few softball questions at him but he ignored them all. I said to his back, "How's Alec feeling?"

At that he slowed. When he turned to me, there was a new crease between his brows. I knew worry when I saw it.

"He's not talking about it at all," Declan said. "He

257

won't say anything, even to me. That's weird, isn't it? I mean, that's not right."

"I don't know, Declan. Trauma does weird things to people. Is he still saying he doesn't remember anything?"

"When I ask him, he just changes the subject." He slumped against a wall, and the hand he brought up to his forehead vibrated with nerves. Or something else.

I turned away to give him a second to collect himself, and realized with a sudden jolt that we were standing across the hall from Eliot's dressing room. There was still police caution tape across the door.

Declan followed my gaze. "I wonder who's going to end up with all of his treasures." His voice, so forceful in the rehearsal room, now had all the vigour of a punctured balloon. "You know he travelled with his Tony? He kept it next to his expensive Scotch. A shrine to his success. None of it means anything now."

"You liked him," I said, and I couldn't keep the surprise out of my voice.

He narrowed his eyes at me. "Why is that shocking?"

"I guess I'd just heard that he was a bit harsh to you. Maybe even a bit jealous."

Declan laughed. "Of course he was jealous. I was him, minus a few decades on the clock. All actors are petty bitches. If you don't learn that early there's no point staying in this business." He turned to face Eliot's door and stared at it for a minute. "But there was also something kind of refreshing about him. No bullshit. I knew that if I deferred to him, treated him like the legend he was, he'd come around. And then I could learn from him."

"But did you know about how he treated women here at the Playhouse? Was that still going on?"

"I'd heard the rumours, but I didn't know they were true until I read your story today." He shrugged. "It was gross, what he did. But they were all pigs back in the day. And to be honest, you get used to it, being chased all the time if you're a pretty piece of ass. You have no idea how many dressing rooms I've escaped with my honour barely intact." He paused. "Not Eliot, though. He was strictly Betty, not Eddie." He caught my look. "Straight, Cat. He was straight. And not in the closet, either. Not like some of us."

"Do you have to stay in the closet? I mean, even now?"

He raised one eloquent eyebrow at me, and I felt immediately ashamed. "Okay, fine. I have an overly romanticized view of the world. Have you talked to your mom, at least?"

"She's been showing me pictures of her friends' daughters since I was fifteen. I kind of hoped she'd get the message by now. Maybe you'd like to tell her for me?"

"She loves you more than anything—"

Declan pushed himself away from the wall. "I really need to go."

I flapped my hands at him. "Of course. Go. Go go." My mouth was now flapping too, and I snapped it shut. Declan shook his head and shuffled off down the hallway. It was as if all his vitality was saved for the stage. Off it, he was turning into a broken man.

Backstage was bustling once again, and I watched people with headsets and costumes and clipboards heading importantly to their tasks. The initial aura of sadness and shock had dissipated. Eliot's ghost, unlike Banquo's, was not haunting the halls. The human instinct for resilience was amazing. Or maybe it was denial?

I lounged against the wall, wondering how long I could appear inconspicuous outside the men's washroom before someone chucked me out. My phone buzzed deep in my backpack and I pulled it out, my heart doing a little stutter-step when I saw the name. It rang and rang, and a woman carrying an armload of flouncy dresses looked at me quizzically, her eyes asking why I wasn't answering.

Because I wasn't ready to talk to Nick Dhalla. If he wanted to congratulate me on my scoop, he could leave a message on my voice mail. Where I could listen to it repeatedly in the privacy of my own home.

I shoved the phone back into my bag and headed down the corridor, the way I'd come. Time to go back to the newsroom and look for new leads to pursue. The door to the rehearsal room was still open, and through it I could see Jonah and Natalya standing over a table holding several swords.

Jonah picked up one of the weapons, hefting it. He spun around when he heard me enter, the sword lifted uncomfortably close to the area of my body where most of the vital organs lived.

"Jesus," I said, "friend, not foe."

The sword didn't seem to hear my words. "I wonder," Jonah said.

Natalya reached over and grabbed the hilt, tsk-tsk-ing as she might with a naughty ten-year-old. "Don't worry," she said to me. "They're all props."

"You can tell my bowels that."

Jonah barked out a laugh. "I'm going to start calling you Penny," he said. "You know, like the bad penny that keeps coming back."

"Yes," I said. "I get it." He could join the line of people in this town who were unhappy to see me. If he could find the end of it.

Natalya bowed in my direction, an Old World gesture. "I'll leave you both, then."

"Natalya, wait. I wanted to ask you—" But she held up her hand, keeping me at bay. Her eyes were warm, though. "It was a good story you wrote today. A true thing."

"Can I call you to follow up?"

But I was speaking to her back. She gathered up the swords and left the rehearsal room.

Jonah tugged on the elastic that bound the sleeve of his shirt. "Was Natalya your source on that story?"

I put my finger to my lips, indicating silence. He shrugged. "It was a good story. I'd known Eliot was depraved, but not quite the depths of the depravity." He groaned, and flopped into one of the folding chairs beside the table. "Do you think those payouts had something to do with his murder?"

"I have no idea," I said. "It seems like the entire population of the tri-lake area had a motive for wanting Eliot dead." *Including you*, I thought. But I kept that to myself. "And it wouldn't explain why someone attacked Alec."

He frowned. "Alec said he tripped on a bit of wet paving. Declan says so too."

"And does Declan seem like someone who's making sound decisions at the moment?"

Jonah stiffened in his seat. His brows were drawn together in a way that suggested my next question might be my last. Now was the time to test the theory I'd been putting together. "Look," I said. "I know he's fallen off the wagon. And I know that will jeopardize both productions. I don't have any interest in writing about that. That's his struggle. But I'm concerned about him. Adeline has been a good friend to me."

Jonah's eyes searched my face, and I suddenly knew

what his scripts must feel like when they were being underlined. But then, to my surprise, his whole body sagged.

"I'm doing the best I can," he said. "When you're a sponsor, you feel such responsibility. Even if it's not your fault. Even if you've done everything you can. And the worst part is"—he raised his worried gaze to me—"you know it could be you. You could be the one taking that drink. Doing that line."

So Declan's deterioration from god to mere mortal had a chemical explanation. "What do you think made him start again?"

Jonah smiled grimly. "I can see you're not blessed with an addictive personality. Who knows what did it? Someone looks at you the wrong way. Or someone looks at you the right way, and you feel invincible. I can tell you what didn't help. Eliot goddamned Fraser."

I sat very still, not wanting to jeopardize this moment. "You mean Eliot's bullying? Did that make Declan snap?"

"His bullying?" Jonah's laugh echoed around the rehearsal room. "You've got it the wrong way round. He didn't bully Declan into having a drink. He seduced him."

He saw my confusion and shook his head. "No, not that kind of seduction. Eliot was straight as the road to hell. It was much more pernicious than that. *Come, lad, let's have a drink and talk about act two. Come to my*

263

dressing room and I'll tell you about Elia Kazan. One little drink's not going to hurt you." Jonah's face was twisted in a grimace of pure hate. "That kind of seduction. The one that's meant to destroy."

Before I could frame another question, the door to the rehearsal room opened and a young woman peeked through. She waved at Jonah and held up two fingers. He stood up, throwing his shoulders back. "Break's over," he said. "See you later, Penny."

CHAPTER 21

I WALKED BACK to my car, feeling my phone buzz in my purse. I pulled it out and saw a text from Hadiya: *How's the investigation going, Jessica Fletcher? I got the report, thanks.*

I flinched at the geriatric reference while forcing myself not to look back at the building. I felt a prickle between my shoulder blades. Was Hadiya at the windows, watching for a reaction? Had she been listening in on my conversation with Jonah? I couldn't tell if the thaw in our relationship was real or a ploy to make me like her and look the other way.

As I drove back downtown, I flipped through the radio dial while my mind raced around. Maybe I was overlooking the most obvious suspect of all. Eliot had treated Hadiya like an indentured servant; I'd seen that myself. To hear Jonah tell it, he was not only sleeping with her but intended to fire her from the job into which she'd invested her very substantial ego. She'd had daily and intimate access to him. And now she was trying to insert herself into my investigation. I felt like a less elegant Miss Scarlett, hopping from the ballroom to the conservatory as suspects vanished out of sight around the corner.

But I wasn't a detective, amateur or otherwise, I reminded myself. I wasn't in the business of finding murder suspects. I was in the business of finding my next big story, and I needed to follow the facts.

"Even if he was a dog, he's a dead dog now," the radio host was saying. "We're asking you, listeners, if we should let dead dogs lie. Or should we dig up all of Eliot Fraser's sins and rake through them again? We'll take your calls after news and traffic."

I had time to listen to two callers, both of whom felt that Eliot Fraser's golden memory was being tarnished with allegations that he couldn't respond to. And if he had flirted with a few women, well—it had been a more innocent time. Before the fun police had busted the party.

I wondered what those callers would think if they knew Eliot had tried to blackmail Glenda into screwing him. George Weatherbottom's words came back to me, drowning out the radio host: *And it was the most innocent who had to bear the brunt of it.* Which innocents, though? My mind suddenly snapped into focus, and without looking down I reached over to turn off the radio. What if some of the hush money payouts were so large because they'd been intended not just for one person but for two? For the baby—or babies—that had resulted from Eliot's priapic spree through the back-stage of the Port Ellis Playhouse?

He'd had a vasectomy, though. It said so in the medical report. But what if he'd had the operation after that summer? What if he'd had it because of that summer? I was mentally rearranging all the pieces when I heard a blaring horn behind me—I'd taken my foot off the gas and was driving like it was my first day on the road. A pickup truck rage-sped around me and vanished up the hill. My damp hands clutched the wheel. At this rate I'd be dead before the killer could get me.

I parked behind the Second Act, where I found the back entrance blocked by a delivery truck. I stomped around the side of the building to the street. I hadn't moved back in yet—the painter wasn't finished her work and the police had encouraged me to stay away for a few more days for my own safety—but I was allowed to duck under the police tape if I needed a few personal items. Today I was here for my notebooks from the beginning of the investigation. I wanted to go through them again to see if there were any leads

I'd missed the first few times I'd read them. Sometimes you had to read a document four or five times before you saw what you were looking for. A wise asshole had once told me that.

I rounded the corner of the building and stopped short. I felt a little burn in my chest, like I'd just eaten something bad for me. The wise asshole was sitting on a bench outside the Second Act, reading the *Quill & Packet* on his phone.

Nick looked up. "Did you know that Braden and Keira are having a stag and doe at the Legion on Saturday night?"

My arms folded across my chest like they were protecting my abused heart. Too late, of course.

I said nothing. He sighed, and put his phone beside him on the bench. He pulled something out of his pocket, unwrapped it, and popped it in his mouth. He held the package out to me: "Nicorette?"

"Wow, you are a charmer," I said. I couldn't keep the sarcasm out of my voice. "First you buy me a coffee, and now you offer me gum. What's next? Are you going to pick some flowers out of the garbage behind Foodland?"

He sighed. "I'm chewing a pack a day. I've been told no smoking if I'm going to ... You know. Walk the plank again."

"I'm sure your new bride would be happy to hear that you think marriage is only slightly more appealing than a watery grave."

Nick chuckled and looked up at me: the practised look of a boy who knows how to get out of trouble. Suddenly I felt my anger go, and with it any stupid hopes I might have been harbouring. I didn't want to be saddled with him, or any little boy. I didn't want to drag someone behind me, not ever again. I wanted someone who'd happily walk by my side.

I sat next to him on the bench. He held up his phone. "This is good," he said. "Really good. You found the pieces and put them together. You know I don't like to be scooped. And you didn't just scoop me. I feel pulped."

The praise wrapped around me like a comforting blanket. I ordered my traitorous ego back to its cave. He still hadn't apologized for leaving my bed without a backwards glance, or running his story without the courtesy of a heads-up. "Did you drive all the way up from the city to tell me that?"

"Well, I also really want to go to Braden's stag." When I didn't laugh, he said, "Look. You know there's a good follow to be done on your story. More than one. Claire thought you might be persuaded, so she asked me to see if you wanted to get—"

"The band back together," I finished. I looked down the street to Centennial Park, where I swam some mornings. People were walking their dogs, or lying flopped in the grass reading. Peaceful life in a peaceful town. That just happened to be home to a murderer.

It was tempting to partner with Nick. To have some cover. To play it safe. But I'd done that too often. I needed to see this through on my own and not be distracted by the emotional whipsaw of flirtation. I turned to him. "You know what? Right now I'm pretty happy to be playing solo."

I CUT THE engine and sat outside the gates of the Mercer family compound. When Jake was little, he'd overheard me say that our neighbours were building a monster home, and for years after he was terrified to walk by that house, thinking that an actual monster lived inside.

Maybe an actual monster lived inside this one too.

I leaned over to speak into the intercom discreetly tucked into one of the gate's flagstone pillars. "I'm here to see Martha Mercer," I said. "She's expecting me." The intertwined wrought-iron Ms on the gate swung away from me as it opened. I rolled down the pea-gravel drive.

Dorothy's house had the aura of a once-grand property whose owners were burning the last of the good furniture for heat. Martha's looked like the kind of place where they burned peasants to keep warm. I walked past the tailored banks of rhododendron and up through a colonnaded porch. I half expected to see Scarlett O'Hara entertaining the Tarleton twins on the steps.

Instead, a middle-aged woman in a polo shirt and chinos opened the front door and ushered me in. "I'll get Mrs. Mercer," she said, and left me standing in a cavernous hall like a kid waiting outside the principal's office. There was a portrait of Martha in the foyer: just Martha. No husband, no sons. I had to admire the bald vanity of that move.

I heard the skitter of heels on the staircase and looked up to see Martha descending. She clutched the railing and nearly bobbled on the last step. Instinctively, I reached out to steady her, but she batted me away. The diamonds in her tennis bracelet glinted.

Without a word, she strode deeper into the house, beckoning me to follow. There was a lot of following to do, because the place was only slightly smaller than Versailles, and almost as blingy. The sound of male voices grew louder, laughing and talking over each other, and we passed a sunken living room where three blond men lolled on couches, looking as if they didn't have a care in the world—probably because they didn't.

"Sons," said Martha briefly, in the way a dog breeder might say "puppies." I cast a glance at the men, Alec's younger brothers. I wondered where Alec was. Despite my efforts to contact him, he'd effectively disappeared.

Martha led me to a bar area overlooking the sunken living room and gestured imperiously at a stool. She nearly knocked over a vase full of primroses on the bar, and I wondered if she'd had a sundae with Scotch sauce for dessert. She flopped onto another stool and barked at me: "So. What is it you want?"

There was a hint of pink around her eyes, as if she'd been wiping away tears. It was a little like imagining a shark crying. Maybe she was worried that the police would soon be pressing her gilded doorbell? Immediately, I felt guilty; I had absorbed Dorothy's prejudice instead of assessing the situation on its merits. Suppressed feelings of guilt wouldn't be the only reason for her stress. She'd nearly lost a son.

She made no move to offer me a coffee, so I launched right in. "I was wondering how Alec is doing. He hasn't been seen since the accident."

Martha sat bolt upright on her stool. "Is this for a newspaper story?"

"No, just neighbourly concern," I said, and I meant it.

Her posture relaxed. "Well, thank you for asking," she said grudgingly. "It's more than Dorothy Talbott could be bothered to do. He's recovering. Upstairs, as a matter of fact. The doctor thought it would be better if there were people around who could monitor him for signs of concussion."

"And so he could have his own personal slaves to wait on him," one of Alec's brothers called out from the conversation pit, and Martha frowned. She turned back to me. "Surely concern for my son is not what brought you here."

I took a deep breath. "As I mentioned on the phone, I wanted to talk to you about the"—my gaze slid over to the tangle of young men on the couches, and I lowered my voice—"the payouts that were made to Eliot Fraser's victims."

"'Victims.'" Martha snorted. "Are you a victim if you have an affair with a handsome and famous man and then get a fat cheque out of it?"

I stared at her. Obviously, they hadn't taught the history of feminism at whatever Swiss finishing school Martha had attended. It occurred to me that she'd echoed George's and Dorothy's responses. They may all have hated each other, but they were united in class solidarity.

"I would see them," she said. "Making eyes at him. And I'd be standing right next to him. His wife! Like I was invisible. Like I was nothing." She leaned over the marble countertop toward me, and I caught a whiff: definitely Scotch. "Why aren't you over at Dorothy's, anyway? That's where you'll find answers."

"Funny," I said. "That's what she said about you."

Martha let out a hiss, the sound of decades of hatred escaping. "That is rich. That is very rich. It was Calvin who was supposed to keep a tight rein on Eliot that summer, and instead they had their heads under every skirt in town."

From the corner of my eye, I saw Martha's sons slowly sit up and I felt a twinge of pain. No one wanted to see their mother melt down in front of a stranger. But I couldn't let go: she was so close to telling me what I needed to know.

"Whose skirts, Martha? Who was chasing Eliot?"

She wiped a thin hand across her mouth. Her eyes were lost in the past. "Such stupid girls. They had no sense. They didn't even know how to protect themselves."

"Protect themselves from what, Martha? From Eliot?"

Her watery eyes turned to me. "I think that girl wanted Eliot's baby. Some sick memento. A token to remember him by." She nearly spat out the next words: "A fine payday."

Now we were getting somewhere. I inched closer. "Who wanted the memento, Martha? Who wanted the payday?"

But she was on a tangent and didn't even seem to be listening. "Calvin Talbott was a terrible board chair. What do they say these days? An enabler, that's what he was. When he thought I wasn't looking. When I took over the chair, I was determined all that would stop." Her skinny hand slapped down on the counter. "No more monkey business at the Playhouse. No more hanky-panky backstage. One grope and you're out. That's in their contracts now. I was not going to let that poison spread."

Her pink-painted mouth was trembling. I wondered

if she knew that her own son was playing a hanky-panky duet with his leading man, but I decided not to pursue it. It was the hush money I needed to know about.

"Martha," I said. "About the baby, the baby that was born after that summer. Who was the mother? Who was the girl Eliot assaulted?"

Now she was crying, and I could hear the boys stirring behind me. Even oblivious idiots couldn't ignore their mother's tears. "He was irresistible," she said, in a broken voice. "Even to me. Even after he'd been so horrible. After all the things he'd done. I still wanted him. I saw him in New York, at a performance of *Burn This*. I was with Rod by then, but still, I couldn't stop myself. I wanted to have something of Eliot for my own. To prove that he'd been mine, once."

"That's enough!"

The deep voice behind me made me spin around on my stool. Alec stood, arms crossed over his chest, a dark bruise still visible above his left eyebrow. His brothers stood behind him, younger versions of his blond beauty. They looked confused about what was going on, but Alec just looked furious.

Even angry, though, his manners hadn't abandoned him. Or he had something to say he didn't want anyone else to hear. "Why don't I walk you out?" he said. I looked over at Martha, who had ducked under the bar and was rummaging among the bottles. I wasn't going to get any more information out of her. But she'd already given me something; I just didn't know what. Her words danced in my head, loose threads that still didn't form a pattern.

The younger Mercers watched me as I followed Alec out. I wondered if they'd show their mother some love, or if her tears would just make them turn away in discomfort. I felt a horrible pressure in my chest. The eternal imbalance of maternal love. We reached and reached, and they pulled away.

Outside in the setting sun, Alec's bruise stood out in contrast to his bright hair and vivid blue eyes. He looked almost as haggard as his mother. He rounded on me. "You heard that."

I wasn't sure which *that* he was referring to. Eliot and Calvin's cavalcade of assault? The mystery baby? Martha's cryptic declaration of love for her repulsive ex? I opened my mouth and closed it again.

"I need to tell you something," Alec said. "But it's off the record." Normally I wouldn't agree to the condition without some negotiation, but I sensed that Alec was not in the mood for negotiating. I nodded.

He walked in a tight circle, his eyes on the ground. Somewhere toward the lake I heard the *thwap-thwap* of a weed whacker. I waited. Finally he looked up at me. "You know about my relationship with Declan."

I nodded.

"And now you know that it was against the theatre's rules. We could both be fired."

"Is this why Declan's falling apart?" Alec scuffed his foot into the pea gravel and said nothing. "He's a mess. Adeline's beside herself with worry." Still nothing. "I know he's fallen off the wagon again."

A shadow crossed Alec's face, a flicker of guilt. Suddenly I understood. "You were going to break up with him, weren't you? Did you know something?" In my excitement, I advanced on him, and Alec backed up. "Did you suspect something? Was Declan responsible for Eliot's murder?"

It was as if an electric charge went through his body. He started toward me, his teeth bared. "For god's sake, no. Declan's loathing is turned inward, not out. There's not a violent bone in his body. There's not." But as he said it he turned his head away so that his bruise was hidden from my sight. And in that instant, I knew.

"He did it," I whispered. "It was Declan who shoved you into that fountain."

CHAPTER 22

DRIVING OFF THE Mercer property, I had the feeling of leaving a holiday meal, stuffed past the point of digestion. Martha and Alec were treasure troves of information, but what did it all mean?

The sun was dropping quickly as I made my way back to town, shading my eyes from the dazzling orange and pink light. The Mercer place was remote by tri-lake standards; among other things, money bought privacy around here. I'd chosen an after-dinner visit on purpose, guessing (correctly) that Martha would be less cautious with me after cocktails and wine. But I hated driving on the local highways at night. I didn't know the roads well enough yet to anticipate their twists and turns, and I was unnerved by the Formula 1 enthusiasts who hit the asphalt in the twilight hours.

My car groaned as the road climbed, topping out at the scenic outlook over Lake Marjorie. To one side, a sheared rock face rose, ridged with old blast shafts; to the other, a small parking area, a favourite spot for first kisses and selfies. I averted my eyes from the spectacular view, focused on hugging the curve of the road as I began the descent. There was a little bridge over the river at the bottom of the hill, flanked by low railings and barely wide enough for two cars. Partway down, I noticed a dark suv in my rear-view mirror, rapidly closing the distance between us. It was driving too fast for the narrow two-lane road, and it had its high beams on.

I slowed down as I approached the bridge, hoping the other driver would pass me before the next ascent. Instead, it zoomed up to my rear bumper, filling my mirrors with blinding light. With my window down, I could hear the river's hissing rapids and the revving engine behind. We were nearly at the bridge. My foot tapped the brakes, more instinct than anything. A shadow flew up from behind, and I felt my shoulders hunch. Bracing for something bad. The impact was immediate. I felt my car accelerate as the suv hit the gas, and suddenly I was spinning, grappling at the wheel and pumping the brakes while the world rushed by. When the car jolted to a stop, I found myself on the shoulder just before the bridge, inches away from a drop that made my hair stand on end. Hurtling up the hill in front of me, the suv was almost out of sight.

I allowed myself the luxury of a moment's closed eyes. Another warning. Or was it? People drove hammered along these roads all the time, especially at this time of the evening. Whether it was a drunk or a murderous maniac hardly mattered. I'd almost ended up face-first in the river.

I turned off the ignition and stepped out of the car. I walked to the rear to assess the damage and immediately wished I hadn't. The bumper was crushed, the driver's-side tail light smashed, and the frame around the hatch door looked bent. I decided not to try opening it in case I couldn't get it closed again. I wondered if my new mechanic had a points card.

In the fading light I could see the black ribbons of tire marks on the road. My hands shook as I dialed Kaydence's number.

"Oh my god, Cat," she said, her eyes wide, when she pulled up in her purple Kia ten minutes later. "You could have been—"

"I know, I know." I didn't want to hear her say it out loud. "I don't want to think about it."

She gazed up the hill, following the direction the suv had taken, her expression puzzled. "Why aren't the police here yet?"

"I haven't called them. I called you instead."

"What? Why? That's crazy," said Kaydence. "Someone just wrecked your apartment." Her eyes narrowed. "Why did you call me? Be honest. It's because you don't want Bruce or Amir to know, isn't it? You think I can't stand up to you?" She put her hands on her hips, ready to prove me wrong.

"It could have been an accident, totally unrelated," I said. "Bruce and Amir would jump to conclusions."

"It was not an accident and you know it. It was most likely the freak who trashed your place and murdered Eliot. Give me one good reason not to call 911 right now." She pulled her phone out of her purse and waved it at me. I took a step toward her, feeling only slightly less panicky than I had when the suv hit. "Amir will think he needs to take me off the story, and I can't let that happen." I clenched my hands into fists. Keeping control of the consequences seemed urgent, even existential. "Do you know what it's like to lose everything you thought you had, everything you thought you were? I need to break this story, Kaydence. If I do, I feel like I can get myself back."

"You could have died, Cat." She stared at me, challenging, her chin up.

"But I didn't." I walked over and gave her a hug. "I'm fine. Let me make this choice for myself, please?"

She relented and hugged me back, hard. "I'm not going to stand by and watch you get hurt," she said. "I'll help you tonight, but all bets are off tomorrow."

"I'll take it," I said. "Doesn't your cousin have a tow truck?"

AT THE OFFICE the next morning, I filled Amir in on my conversations with Martha and Alec, leaving out the details of my latest near-death experience. The story was what mattered. I'd stayed up late drawing a map that connected all the miscreants and liars in town. I'd nearly run out of ink. Alec's bruised face had haunted me long after I'd put my pen down. If Declan had attacked his boyfriend, could he have poisoned Eliot as well?

"They're different sorts of crimes," Amir pointed out when I told him what I'd learned at the Mercers'. "Loss of control versus methodical planning. I'm not convinced." I'd always loved batting a story back and forth, especially with a generous partner. I felt purposeful, and powerful. It was good to taste that heady emotional cocktail again.

"Dorothy thinks it was Martha," I said.

Amir gave me a wry smile. "And that surprises you?"

"Obviously not. But does that mean she's wrong? I saw Martha, and she's a wreck."

"Her son was attacked. You'd be upset too."

"It was more than that," I told him. "She was going on and on about how much Eliot hurt her when they were married." Still bitter, so many years after the fact: a terrifying prospect. What if Mark had ruined me in much the same way? What if coming to Port Ellis wasn't a healing change of scenery, as I liked to package it in my rare Instagram posts, but a self-imposed banishment from any life worth having? Time would tell, but once it got around to opening its wrinkled lips, I'd be well past the point of no return. "Martha had plenty of reasons to be backstage, and a tortured history with Eliot. Opportunity and motive."

"I don't buy it," said Amir. "Having him die on opening night was a disaster for her. She needs the Playhouse to survive so it can attract buyers for her properties. If she wanted to murder Eliot, she could have done it as easily at the end of a profitable season."

"Fine. Your serve, then. Who are your favourite suspects?"

"I like Jonah Tiller, or should I say Beaumont."

It pained me to admit it, but I could see his point. An email from Cal Meade had arrived that morning, and it shed a new and unflattering light on Jonah's past. Amir tapped on his keyboard, opening the scanned program I'd shared, and read from Jonah's letter to the Shakespeare Heals patrons. "'Have you ever gone days without a meal, stealing candy bars from corner stores to survive? Have you wondered where you could find a safe place to sleep, somewhere no one could hurt you or take everything you owned in the world? Have you ever lived in circumstances where crime, even violent crime, seemed as natural and inevitable as breathing?'" Amir looked at me. "That's some serious trauma there. Did Eliot antagonize him? Trigger him? Jonah had every bit as much opportunity as Declan or Martha, not to mention motive."

There was a knock at the door, and Amir waved Kaydence in. She didn't look my way or give any hint about last night's drama, and I could have kissed her pink-frosted lips. "The guest list for the Playhouse fundraiser," she said, passing Amir a printout. "I've emailed it to you and cc'd the newsroom. The schedule's on there too."

Amir nodded his thanks. "You're ready to livestream from the boat?" He'd kept her on limited duties since her slip-up over Glenda, but he'd clearly decided that a leashed Kaydence was a useless Kaydence.

She held up her rhinestone-encrusted phone. "I even took a practice trip on the *Old Maid* to make sure the Wi-Fi's decent. We're all good. Move over, Met Gala."

Amir tilted his head, and I was worried the next words out of his mouth would be "What's a Met Gala?" Fortunately, my phone rang. I waggled my fingers at them as I left, the phone to my ear.

"Hello? This is Cat Conway."

"Hi, Cat," said a voice I didn't recognize. "This is Willow. SunneeDaze29?"

"Hi, Willow," I said, sitting down at my desk and opening my notebook. "It's great to hear from you. How's your aunt Darlene doing?"

"That's why I'm calling, actually," said Willow. "I told her about you and sent her that video of you scaring the crap out of those boys. She loved it. She said she'll talk to you." My moment of notoriety: it did come in handy sometimes. I very much doubted that I'd done more than embarrass those idiots, but I wasn't going to argue.

"That's amazing," I said. "How can I reach her?"

"She told me to give you her phone number, but you have to swear not to give it to anyone else, okay? She's pretty jumpy. My mom says that she was never the same after that summer in Port Ellis. She moved to Reno and never went back." Willow recited the number and I entered it into my phone. "My advice is to call her soon. Sometimes she changes her number and goes off the grid for a few months. Also off the wagon."

I checked the batteries in my digital recorder, hooked up the cable that let me record, and called Darlene's number. It rang and rang, and I imagined a phone on a countertop in a condo in Reno. Maybe Darlene was staring at it, working up the courage to pick up. Maybe she was passed out in the bathtub. Maybe she was at the gym. I knew nothing about her life, or the pain that had driven her from Port Ellis.

I let the phone ring a dozen times, waiting for voice mail to kick in. It never did. I sighed. I'd call her again later, from on board the *Old Maid*. There was a gala to get ready for, and my hair was not going to tame itself.

CHAPTER 23

"ARE YOU ABSOLUTELY SURE?" Bruce asked.

"I'm sure," I said patiently. Bruce had been check-ing in every hour today hoping I would change my mind and steer clear of the fundraiser. "We're going to be late if you ask me again." I wasn't going to mention the last-minute crying jag in Kaydence's shower, which I was dismissing as nerves. I had cried enough tears in my forties to float the *Old Maid* herself. I needed anger instead. I couldn't lose focus now.

I had eliminated any trace of tears with a liberal application of eye makeup. A midnight blue jumpsuit with a halter neckline, some sassy platform sandals, and a cashmere wrap completed my disguise as a glamorous and carefree partygoer. Bruce shot me an admiring glance. "Playing it cool, Cat Conway, I like it. Have you figured out whodunnit yet?"

"Ransacked my apartment or murdered Eliot?" I asked.

"Either. Both. Aren't they the same person?"

I sighed. "I don't know. But my instincts tell me it's all connected."

"I'd say your instincts are spot on," he said. Bruce was wearing his version of black tie—dark flat-front khakis, a collarless black linen shirt, and leather sneakers. He checked his watch. "We'd better hit the road."

Clouds had gathered, dark and threatening, as we got into Bruce's car. His radio was tuned to an AM station that warned us about the possibility of a torrential thunderstorm, and then warned us that a feed truck had overturned on Highway 2. "Not our concern," Bruce said, when I raised an eyebrow about the feed-truck news. "We're on the party clock tonight."

A low rumble of thunder sounded as we turned into the parking lot by the water. There was something I needed to say. I cleared my throat. "You know," I said, "I'm not the best at accepting help."

"No kidding," he replied with a smile.

"What I mean is, there aren't that many people in my life that I'd ask. I just wanted to say thank you. For being my friend."

"You have more friends than you think," he said. "Speaking of which, ours are waiting. We don't want the party to start without us. Can you run in those shoes?"

We trotted up the gangplank as the *Old Maid's* horn sounded for the final time. The giant paddle-wheel groaned and churned, and with a mighty jolt the boat shifted into forward gear, a cheer went up from the assembled crowd, and we were off.

THE RAIN HAD driven everyone inside the *Old Maid's* main cabin, where they descended on the bar as if they were on board the *Titanic* and it was last call before the iceberg. Port Ellis polished up nicely: cocktail dresses in place of Lululemon, stilettos instead of flip-flops. I wobbled on top of my platform sandals, which were already killing my feet, and cursed the first person who thought it was a good idea to put a heel on a shoe.

Or maybe I was wobbly from nerves. Death threats and break-ins would do that to a girl. I took a steadying breath and let the music that the swing band was playing wash over me. To calm my nerves, I cast my eye over the crowd and began counting suspects. What would Jane Tennison do?

Alec Mercer's head was a bright beacon in one corner of the room, and he kept a tight grip on his mother, who looked thinner and more wretched than ever. Even the best-cut Ferragamo dress couldn't hide that kind of distress. A woman came over to talk to

Martha, and Martha struggled to put her game face on.

Jonah Tiller stood in another corner, glowering at autograph hunters who came his way. The Playhouse was dark for the evening, but the actors still had to sing for their supper. Hadiya Hussein, lovely in a red sheath dress, was snatching hors d'oeuvres off a tray as if she might never eat again. I remembered that feeling.

In another corner, my colleagues had gathered: Kaydence in a dress printed with parrots and monkeys, Dorothy in orthopedic sandals and a crystal-studded muumuu. Amir looked incredible in a narrow-cut dark suit, and I watched him pluck a drink off a tray and give it to Dorothy. Bruce tried to clink glasses with her and missed. A wave of warmth washed over me: My people. My lovely, awkward people.

A sudden blare of noise from above made me jump. Over a crackling PA system, I heard someone identify himself as the captain, though he might have said "kraken." My ears strained to hear his broken words above the noise of the crowd. "Wet outside—decks—careful—life jackets." I appeared to be the only one listening to the kraken's warning.

Rain spattered against the cabin's windows. I took a step into the crowd, under a banner that read "You Bring the Stage to Life." Tonight would be the main fundraiser for the Playhouse all year. The *Old Maid* had two cabins, one set up for mingling, entertainment, and a live auction; and one for a silent auction.

The floor heaved under my feet, reminding me that we were not on dry land anymore. I felt my bare shoulder bump into someone's arm, and I turned to say sorry. And then my mouth fell open.

"Declan?" I didn't mean for it to come out as a question. But for half a second I'd wondered if it was him. He was wearing sunglasses, despite the gloom. He took one look at me and stumbled away.

The crowd closed in behind him, and I fought my way through, following his dishevelled head. A hand tugged at my arm, and I turned to see Hadiya, cheeks puffed like a hamster's, holding out a slider on a napkin. A one-bite peace offering.

"Sorry," I said, squeezing past her. "I'm trying to find someone. I'll see you soon." I stood on tiptoe, and nearly fell over. Stupid sandals. Then I saw a door open at the end of the cabin and I plowed my way toward it. I yanked it open and found myself out on deck.

"Declan!" I called, startling the small group of smokers sheltering under an overhang. I was shocked at how awful he looked. Maybe there were limits to how much an actor could fake, even a good one. Though Eliot had faked being a decent human being all those years.

I strode toward him, my sandals skittering on the wet deck. I reached for his arm, but he yanked it out of my grasp, and I nearly stumbled. Declan's teeth were bared as he brought his head close to mine.

"I know you've been talking to Alec," he hissed. "Did you think he wouldn't tell me?"

Instinctively, my hands went up—whether in protection or in surrender I couldn't say. "Declan, I'm not trying to get you in trouble," I said. "I'm just trying to figure out—"

"You think I'd hurt Alec? You're an idiot. I love him. I always will."

"What about Eliot?" The words left my mouth before I had a chance to consider how rash they were. Declan's brows drew together in one terrifying, murderous line. I took a step backwards. Over my shoulder I saw the smokers heading back inside.

We were alone.

The rain whipped hair into my eyes. I took another step back and felt the railing press into my backside. *Don't look down*, I told myself. I looked down: the water churned, green and white, far below. I could hear the groan and clack of the giant paddlewheel. Suddenly I could barely breathe.

"What do you mean, 'What about Eliot?'" Declan took another step forward, and I clutched the slippery rail with both hands. "Are you actually suggesting that I killed the old bastard?"

"No," I said, "of course not. Though it may look that way to other people. I mean, he was jealous of you. So jealous that he helped you fall off the wagon. And I know he—" My voice faltered. I glanced quickly around the deck, wondering if I could shout for help, but all the sane people were inside.

"What?" Declan's voice was deadly quiet. "You know what?"

"That he was going to rat you out." My mind raced to keep up as everything began to make sense. "He was going to tell the board about you and Alec. And then they'd fire both of you. That's why Alec wanted to break up with you. Because of the no-sex policy. The policy that he was responsible for." Declan's face was wet with rain. At least I thought it was rain. He stared at me, and I pressed on. "Eliot ruined it for everyone, didn't he? He never paid. Not until the very end."

Suddenly, he laughed, a wild, frightening sound. "Eliot really did ruin everything," he said. "You have no idea. But that doesn't mean I killed him. And you're not going to tell anyone that I did." The boat swayed and Declan moved toward me. I let out a startled yelp and side-stepped. He smashed into the guardrail, the momentum nearly toppling him over the side. Instinctively, I reached out to grab him and pull him back from disaster.

"Cat? What are you doing out here?"

I spun around to see Amir holding the door to the cabin open. I'd never been so happy to see a manager in my life. Declan wrenched himself from my grasp and staggered away, toward the boat's stern. I considered following him, and then I remembered his bared teeth, his rage. Could he have been the one who broke into my apartment, slashing and spray-painting threats?

Shivering, I followed Amir back inside. He pulled a handkerchief from his pocket and handed it to me. Of course he carried a handkerchief; the best men did. I used it to mop my face and shoulders, then gave it back to him, a sodden mess.

"All good?" he said mildly. No note of admonishment or anxiety. Just a simple question that assumed I was on top of things. I felt warmth rise through me, banishing the cold. It was amazing how good it felt to be considered competent.

"I'm good," I said. He didn't need to know that I was, in fact, terrified. That the killer was likely on board with us. Knowing Amir, he'd want to do the right thing: Call the cops. Tell the captain to head back to shore. I wasn't ready for that yet. The final piece of the puzzle was here. I just needed to find it.

"I'm going to try to dry off," I said. "I'll meet you back in the main cabin."

He nodded and left. I headed off to find a bathroom. A woman carrying a tray came flying toward me, champagne flutes jiggling dangerously. Behind her I saw Adeline, her face screwed tight with anxiety. Maybe there'd been a cheese-puff cataclysm in the galley.

When she saw me, her face fell in shock. It seemed

a bit of an overreaction, even if the rain had turned my hair into Medusa's.

"Adeline? Is everything okay?" Still she stared at me, and then seemed to give herself a shake. Her normal Adeline face was back: calm, imperturbable, efficient.

"Of course," she said. "You just look a bit …"

"Like a drowned rat?" *Thanks to your crazy son,* I thought.

"You might want to dry off," she said, diplomatically. And then she was gone, chasing the endangered tray of champagne.

I watched her go. Everyone was on edge tonight. Was it the weather? The fact that we were still no closer to knowing who'd killed Eliot? But I felt like I was closing in on something. It was an itch deep under the skin.

I stood in the tiny bathroom, attempting to dry my hair with a combination of paper towels and warm air from the automatic hand dryer, which required me to bob my head at waist height. None of this improved my appearance, but a timeout and some physical exertion gave me some mental clarity: I wasn't just cold, wet, and frightened; I was also spitting mad. I was done playing nice with the people of Port Ellis, from the glitterati on down. All it had gotten me was a trashed apartment, a car crash, and a near-drowning. Screw that. Tonight, no one could escort me out or shut the door in my face. No, the playing field had been levelled: we were all trapped in the same waterlogged nightmare for three hours. Tonight I was getting some answers.

I stalked through the cocktail party—well, okay, squelched—waving off Hadiya Hussein for a second time. I marched over to Alec Mercer and planted my index finger in the middle of his chest. "We are having a conversation right now," I said. He looked surprised, but he didn't argue. I wondered if my hair was steaming.

We found a corner that was damp enough to be deserted and close enough to the paddlewheel that no one could hear what we were saying. "Your ex-boyfriend is wasted," I said. "He's having some kind of breakdown, and he nearly pushed me off the boat just now."

Alec looked ill. "I need to find him," he said, and he turned away, his mind obviously elsewhere.

I reached out and grabbed his sleeve. "Not so fast," I said. "You know a hell of a lot more than you're telling me. Someone has been threatening me—trying to drive me off the road, breaking into my apartment, smashing my windshield, sending nasty notes—and my two top suspects are Declan and your mother, because they're the two people in town who seem to have completely fallen apart since Eliot died. Despite the fact that neither of them liked him, I might add.

Can you explain that to me?" I might not have the murder entirely figured out yet, but I was sure of one thing: Alec Mercer was loyal to the people he loved. He'd kept silent after Declan attacked him at the fountain, and he'd intervened to prevent his intoxicated mother from talking to me. And he wouldn't want either of them investigated for murder. "If you have another explanation for their behaviour, now's the time to tell me."

His lovely face was creased with worry. "You will not publish this," he said.

"I will not," I told him. "Provided it has nothing to do with Eliot's death."

We stood under an overhang, our heads protected from the rain, although it bounced off the decking and splashed up, soaking my pantsuit from the knees down. My shoes had been a write-off since my encounter with Declan. I didn't care. Blurry forms of rocky islands and windblown pine trees passed by, and I kept my gaze on Alec. I could wait him out.

Finally, he spoke. "Having Eliot here brought back a lot of memories for my mother, difficult ones. He hadn't been in her life much over the past decade, and I think she'd forgotten how much he affected her. She's not a particularly introspective person." It was a remarkable understatement, but I could give him that. I might have said the same about my own mother. "Having him in town, arguing with him about the retirement village—it was triggering for her. She was drinking more than I'd ever seen her do. She seemed fragile."

It sounded remarkably like a motive to me, and I said so. "Why are you so sure that she wasn't involved in his murder?"

"Because I've been joined at the hip with her for months," he said. "And I know that she needed him alive and well, making money for the theatre and ideally for the development as well. What she wanted was for the summer to end as a financial success and for Eliot to go back to Hollywood having made headlines for his performances and absolutely nothing else. She was still hoping he'd come around on the publicity piece, and I think he might have, once he left town. He was vain, and he didn't want to see his own image attached to a retirement community. But as long as he didn't have to see it, I think he'd have taken the money we were offering. Either way, the last thing my mother wanted was to have the international press digging through Eliot's life and relationships."

I thought about my last conversation with Martha, before Alec had stepped in and escorted me from the house. *I wanted to have something of Eliot for my own. To prove that he'd been mine, once.* She'd been teetering on the edge of a disclosure that Alec hadn't wanted me to hear. And I'd checked the dates that *Burn This* ran on Broadway, along with Alec's birthdate. "I understand why. She didn't want anyone else to guess that you were Eliot's son."

His knuckles were white where they clenched the railing. "That's a shot in the dark, and you know it. If you're looking for me to confirm it, you'll be waiting a long time. I'm warning you now: bother my mother with your theory and you'll find yourself on the end of a harassment complaint. Because hypothetically, if I were Eliot's son, Eliot wouldn't have known that fact, and consequently there would have been zero risk of him telling anyone about it, and no reason for anyone in my family to silence him."

I had just about lost him, but I wasn't done yet. "And Declan?"

"I've told you. He took the breakup very hard. He was drinking, and it made him unpredictable. But he's not a murderer. And that's my final word on the subject."

He brushed past me as he walked toward the main cabin. I called after him. "Jonah told me that Eliot was the reason Declan was drinking again. That's motive, isn't it?

Alec turned back, his face flushed with anger. "Jonah's upset because he feels he failed as Declan's sponsor, and it's easier to blame Eliot than himself. But think it through, Cat. Declan was getting a huge boost from appearing onstage with Eliot. That role was going to change his career. And now? The production's in shambles and he's under way more pressure than he can handle. Not much of a benefit, is it? If I were a journalist, I might be asking why his sponsor—the person who is responsible for helping him—is so keen to throw him under the bus."

CHAPTER 24

I FOUND THE SPONSOR in question in the silent-auction room, tucked into a corner bench, reading on his phone. "Aren't you supposed to be socializing?" I asked.

"You could argue that I'm playing the important role of drawing the guests to this part of the boat," Jonah said, with a grand gesture. "It's a fundraiser, after all."

The cabin was dotted with little tables, each cluttered with items for the silent auction. The big-ticket items—a trip to a vineyard, a week's stay in a palatial cottage—would be auctioned off at the height of the evening, when drink had loosened everyone's purse strings. I noticed that one of the items on offer was a summer internship at the Playhouse. Given what I'd discovered so far, it hardly seemed the kind of thing you'd want to buy for your kid. Unless you hated them.

The room was empty except for the two of us, a few couples sifting through the Playhouse memorabilia on offer, and a trio of bored volunteers.

"Great job," I said.

His laugh was sonorous, as inviting as a warm bath. I sat down next to him, reluctant to break the moment. "Jonah Beaumont," I said. I could see his jaw set in a hard line. "I have no interest in embarrassing you. There is only one story I'm trying to tell, and it's who killed Eliot Fraser. If Jonah Beaumont has nothing to do with that story, you can keep him to yourself. Or I can help you tell the world about him on your terms."

"I told you, I didn't kill Eliot," he said. "You're so off base if you think my past contributed to his death. I had a juvenile record. I changed my name when I got out of detention. End of story. I don't often talk about it, but it's not a state secret. There are people, like Cal Meade, who know. Although I would have expected a bit more discretion from him."

"What about Declan?" I said. "Alec Mercer thinks you've abandoned him. Is it because you suspect him of murder?"

He looked at me with distaste. "Declan's demons are his own responsibility," he said. "I've done my best to support him as his sponsor, but if he's determined to hit bottom, there's not much I can do. Sometimes relapse is part of the process. Now if you'll excuse me, I should go and do my duty, as you correctly pointed out." He stood and walked to the exit, bowing gallantly to a group that entered as he left, the door swishing behind him.

Not my best work, I thought, moving over to the auction tables. I'd always loved a silent auction, though not as much as my ex-husband, who'd once nearly come to blows with another idiot over a Loire wine cruise. My fingers slid over a set of pasties from a production of *Gypsy*, a jewelled hair clip from Desdemona's wardrobe, and a plumed hat worn by a Musketeer. There were autographed photos and programs and—

I sliced my way between a couple who were idly examining a pile of programs. The man let out a yelp of protest, but I could barely hear him over the buzzing in my brain. Everything else had suddenly gone quiet.

There it was: the program from the Playhouse's first season. The one that was missing from the library.

A sudden crack of thunder startled me, and I nearly dropped the program. A woman gave a little shriek of terror, followed by an embarrassed laugh. My wet fingers stuck to the front cover, where Eliot Fraser's blue eyes stared at me from under a knight's helmet. Prince Hal, wayward and carousing, a leader gone astray.

I forced myself to go slowly through the pages.

My jaws felt as if they'd been clamped together with rubber cement. I scanned each page carefully: Calvin Talbott's pompous message of welcome and the advertisements for outboard motors. There were photos of the actors in dress rehearsals, and the crew at work backstage.

I flipped the page and my breath stopped. I felt the boat rock under me, or maybe it was my knees giving way. It couldn't be. I wanted to throw the program back on the table, pretend I'd never seen the photo. It was too late for that, though. Squinting, I pulled the program closer to my face.

My eyes hadn't lied. But someone else certainly had.

My first instincts had been correct, I was now sure. Eliot's murder was connected to events from that long-ago summer, when he'd first arrived in Port Ellis, sowing destruction along with his wild oats. I needed to talk to someone who had been there, and who had no motive to lie to me.

I practically ran back to the bathroom, sliding the bolt to lock the door. Pulling out my phone, I found the number I'd saved earlier. I hit the call button and listened to it ring in a faraway desert on the other side of the continent, reading the graffiti on the wall as I waited. *Keira loves Braden* was scrawled in black marker, which had been augmented by the observation *Braden is a dick*. I wondered if Keira knew. She probably did. Knowing and the desire to not know could co-exist in the brain, the latter overriding the former with shocking regularity.

"Hello?" The voice at the other end of the line was thin and tired. "Who is this?"

"Darlene?" I asked. "It's Cat Conway, calling from Port Ellis. Your niece Willow gave me your number. She said you were willing to talk to me."

In the silence, I heard her light a cigarette and take a long puff. "He's really dead?" she said.

"Yes," I told her. "I was there when it happened."

"Good," she said. "Did he suffer?"

There was a knock at the door. Darlene was going to be a slow burn; I hadn't thought this through. I opened my text messages and fired off a note to Bruce, Amir, and Kaydence. *URGENT. I need someone to stand outside the women's washroom behind the bar and say it's out of service.*

"Yes," I said.

"Good," she said again. Outside the door, I heard the comforting rumble of Bruce's voice. I exhaled. Team *Quill* had this. I could take my time.

And so could Darlene. She'd lost her job as a waitress in Reno recently, she told me. She'd done her best to look after herself over the years, but three decades slinging drinks in high heels was hell on the veins. She wasn't bringing in the tips she used to. Her boss, the slimy dickweasel, had suggested that she might like to offer a few premium services to him after hours to keep her job. So she'd stabbed him in the hand with a cocktail umbrella. "It went right through the meat of his thumb," she said with pride. "And he squealed like the rat he was." I heard her take another drag of her cigarette. "Willow sent me your video, the one where you strangled that boy who disrespected you. She said you got fired too."

"True," I said. "It turned out not to be such a bad thing to leave that job, for what it's worth."

"I could see that," said Darlene. "I've been thinking about making some changes in my life too. When I heard about Eliot dying, I got to thinking about what he took from me. What I let him take. I want it all back. My dreams. My self-respect. My ability to trust other people. To feel safe."

Darlene's voice cracked. I ripped off a few squares of toilet paper to dab at my own eyes and nose. "I want that for you," I told her. "How can I help?"

"Willow says I need to tell my story," said Darlene. "Do you think she's right?"

I cared about the story, desperately, but I wasn't going to be yet another person who manipulated Darlene for their own ends. "What I think," I said, "is that healing is a process and it's different for everyone. My opinion doesn't matter. Willow's opinion doesn't matter. What matters is your own sense of what will help you. You're the expert here, Darlene."

"I think it would help if I could get people to believe that Eliot Fraser was a snake."

"I can't speak for everyone," I told her. "And I can pretty much guarantee that there will be some haters out there if you decide to go public, because that's the world we live in now. But I can promise that I'll believe you. So why don't we start there?"

"Okay," said Darlene.

The bathroom smelled like urine and disinfectant, and the dirty metal walls recorded decades of aspersions along with the occasional cartoon penis. But it felt like sacred space as Darlene began to speak. "We were all so young," she said. "That's what you have to understand. It was like signing up to be a camp counsellor. The pay was barely anything, but they offered room and board and a chance to be part of a community. We felt lucky to be chosen."

She described the work and life at the theatre, and I let her talk. "Eliot was hot, what can I say? He was the only celebrity there that summer and everyone wanted to be near him. Was he a jerk? Hell yeah. But he could be a good guy too. He'd show up for drinks with the crew and buy rounds, that kind of thing. There was a party at someone's cottage one night, and he was there. We ended up hanging out together, and after that he paid attention to me. Wooed me, I guess you'd say. And I fell for it. I thought we were a couple, exclusive. I'm embarrassed about that now, but that's what I thought. I knew he was married, but he said he and his wife had an 'understanding.' And then one afternoon, I went into his dressing room and he was there with another girl."

"Did you know her?"

"A bit. I can't remember her name now. Abigail? Amelia? He had her on the camp bed he had in his dressing room. She didn't seem to be having fun. I remember her staring at me over his back with these huge eyes. Like, pleading eyes. But I was so angry, I just stomped out." A choked sob. "Maybe I should have tried to help her. But I thought she was taking my place. And I was just a kid myself."

I respected her enough not to rush in with easy platitudes. We were silent for a moment and then she resumed with a sigh. "Anyway, I went back the next day, to give him a piece of my mind. I thought he'd grovel. That's how much I didn't get it. How young I was."

"And he didn't?"

"No. He told me I was being boring. He yawned in my face, the bastard. Then, when I started to cry, he gave me a drink. I don't know why I didn't leave, but I didn't. And then he's got his arms around me, his hands down my shorts." Her voice had started to wobble, and I waited, saying nothing. I heard the scratch of a cigarette being ground out, stabbed into the tray.

Darlene took a long breath and blew it out in a

sigh. "I guess nowadays you'd say he assaulted me. But I didn't think of it like that, you know? I'd gone in there willingly, and I didn't fight him off. The police wouldn't have believed me. That's what the lawyer said when I got fired later that day. He paid me for the rest of the summer, but I had to sign a paper that said I wouldn't say anything bad about Eliot. I needed the money for school. But then, when school rolled around, I didn't have the energy for it somehow."

I closed my eyes against the tide of pain. Darlene's pain. The pain of all those young women. "I'm so sorry that happened to you," I said. "It was wrong, in every way."

"That's what Willow says," said Darlene. "Thank you." She blew her nose. "I mean, it could have been worse. The Chinese girl, Abigail? Or whatever her name was? I heard she ended up with a baby."

CHAPTER 25

COUNT TO TWENTY.

I'd counted to twenty several times already as I tried to get my breathing under control. My head between my knees, staring at my red-painted toes in my ridiculous silver sandals. Still my head swam. Nothing made sense.

The Chinese girl had had a baby. Not Abigail, though. Not Amelia.

Adeline.

Adeline and her baby. I remembered the vasectomy and what Hadiya had told me: something in his past had made him want the operation. Like fathering a child through rape, perhaps.

As I thought it through in a dank little bathroom

with a heart on the verge of exploding, it did begin to make sense. I remembered Declan introducing Eliot to his mother that night I'd interviewed him in the Second Act. Eliot had been clueless; this middle-aged woman was just another fan. But Adeline wasn't dazed because she was starstruck. She was dazed because she'd come face to face with her rapist.

The father of her child.

The program from the Playhouse's first summer suddenly made sense too. When I'd seen the picture of Adeline backstage, standing only a few feet from Eliot, I'd been stunned. She'd hidden the fact that she'd worked there from me. Now I knew why. Because that summer Eliot Fraser had raped her and left her pregnant. With a child who would one day grow up to be as talented, and messed up, as his illustrious father.

I stood up and went to the sink, where I ran cold water into the basin. I used my fingertips to press the cool water into my temples, but it didn't do anything to calm the raging fire there. The doorknob rattled, and I heard Bruce outside: "Did you fall in?"

In the mirror, my face had the glazed look of someone who'd just been slapped. I needed time to think, but there was no time. At some point in the future I would deal with my feelings of hurt and betrayal. And rage.

But first I had to hear it from her. I stormed out of the bathroom, nearly sending Bruce flying. The boat reeled under us, and I fell against him. A server carrying a tray of miniature crab cakes crouched against the wall, clutching his precious cargo to his chest.

"You look like hell," Bruce said helpfully, but I barely heard him. How many times had I eaten those at the Second Act? One of Adeline's signature dishes, and a thousand miles from the plain, tasty food her father had served at Treasure Garden. She was a genius with the menu. A wizard with cocktails, with mixes and potions.

Now that the pieces were falling into place, I felt like an idiot for not seeing the pattern before. I'd always assumed that the money to refurbish the Second Act had come from Adeline's dad's life insurance, but now I knew better: it had come from an envelope marked "hush money."

But why? Why kill Eliot? Adeline seemed incapable of violence. She was my friend. She'd given me a receptive ear, a roof over my head. Suddenly I felt pain like a punch in my gut. I saw the slashed pillows, feathers drifting like ash. The threatening note under the door. What if Adeline was never my friend at all? What if she'd just been keeping me close so I couldn't see what was under my own nose?

The boat listed, and an acid wave of nausea rose in my throat. The captain's voice crackled over the PA, sounding as if he were speaking through a bag of kitty litter. I turned to Bruce, my eyebrows raised.

"Sounds like he said it's too rough out here and we

have to head back to port," Bruce translated. "At least that's what I think he said."

Which meant I only had a few minutes left to pin this down. I grabbed the server's arm, and he squawked as the sliders slid. "Where's Adeline?" I hissed.

The poor kid pulled away from me in fear. Apparently this was my superpower: terrifying young men. He lifted one hand from his tray and pointed to the back of the boat. "I think I saw her heading toward the kitchen," he said.

"The galley," Bruce corrected, and I left them to debate the finer points of nautical nomenclature. Rage and sorrow propelled me through the silent-auction cabin, and I stopped to pluck the program off the table, ignoring the volunteer's indignant "Hey!" I tottered through the next cabin, packed with people trying to get one more drink in before we headed for shore. I saw Kaydence raise her hand to me from across the room, but I ignored it. I was driven by a hot, blind compulsion: I needed to find the end of this thing. To see Adeline's face when I confronted her with my suspicions.

I found her in a narrow hallway outside the galley, rearranging a server's tray of hors d'oeuvres. She saw me and frowned. I was already a wrench in her well-oiled plan. She'd broken into my apartment, slashed the pillows, scattered my things. She'd hoped to scare me away.

Instead, it had lit a fire inside me. Rage was a fuel. Rage at my own idiocy, and at her. My friend.

Adeline touched the server's shoulder and she obediently moved off. The two of us were alone in the dimly lit hallway. It was dark outside now, the occasional flash of lightning through the windows illuminating the space between us. Thunder rumbled above, closer now than ever.

I held up the program, open to the page that showed her backstage with Eliot. "You were there that summer."

She squinted at the page, then started as a server came hustling out of the galley's swinging doors. She stepped away from me to let him through and said, "I'm really very busy, Cat. I have a dozen staff to supervise. I'm not interested in looking at old pictures right now."

"I know Eliot raped you."

The words hung between us like a glass in mid-fall. She stared at me, frozen. For a second I felt terrible: I'd just ambushed her with the worst catastrophe in her past. But a split second later the feeling was gone. If she was a killer, she hardly deserved my sympathy.

A commotion from the end of the hall made both of us jump. A drunk couple, joined at the tongue, had bumbled into the passageway, clearly seeking privacy. Adeline's eyes darted toward them, then back at me. "Not here," she said. "Meet me at the stern in two minutes."

I looked out the windows, dark and streaming with rainwater.

"Out back," she insisted. "I'll talk to you. But just you. Alone."

I SLIPPED OUT a side door and made my way along the deck to the stern. The wind tore at my hair and dashed rain into my eyes. I didn't pass another person as I tottered along, cursing my Elton John platforms. Even the smokers had wisely taken cover.

The aft deck was barren too. I watched as the giant paddlewheel battled the storm to take us back to port. I shivered in the wind, and I realized how empty it was back here. How open to the elements, and to danger. Some backup might not be a bad idea.

I patted my pockets and groaned. I'd left my phone in my clutch purse, and my clutch purse in the possession of Bruce, who'd looked at it as if I'd just handed him a soiled baby.

Maybe Adeline wouldn't show up. But she would know that I'd take that as a sure sign of guilt. I could write a story now, just with the evidence I had. Darlene's confession about the payouts and the baby. Martha's admission about Eliot's grotesque transgressions. The program, showing Eliot and Adeline together. I could write the story, and let the cops take it from there.

I almost wished she wouldn't show up.

A tiny yellow hole opened in the darkness as the door to the cabin opened. A small figure stood silhouetted against the light. Then the dark figure moved toward me. Dark, except for a metallic flash in the gloom.

"Oh, Adeline," I whispered. I knew she couldn't hear me over the groan and clank of the paddlewheel, the roar of the wind. I took a step backwards as she advanced toward me. All I could see was the chef's knife, huge in her tiny hand.

To think I'd been afraid of her son all this time. But I should have known: there was nothing more dangerous than a mother bear when her cub was threatened. She'd do anything to save it. Even kill her friend.

"Back up," she called. So I did. For the second time that night, I felt the boat's cold railing against my backside. Except this time, the giant paddlewheel was behind me. I suddenly remembered the old washing machine my grandmother kept at her cottage, with its terrible mangle. *Watch you don't catch yourself, Cat. It'll take your arm in a second.*

There was no one to watch out for me now.

"Why?" I called to Adeline. "Just tell me why."

She halted just a few steps away. The knife was level with my belly. Her face was blank, the face of someone who had made peace with a terrible decision. "You know why. That monster ruined my life. He wasn't going to ruin my son's."

Keep her talking. If I could keep her talking someone would surely come out on the deck. "How was he ruining Declan's life?"

She sneered at my deliberate obliviousness. "Who gave Declan a drink after he'd been two years sober? Who tried to get him fired?" The knife stabbed toward me, and I sucked in my gut. "Some men just destroy everything in their path. They eat and eat and shit out what they don't want. A trail of shit and destruction behind them. And no one stops them." Her voice rose, shouting over the wind. "It was time for someone to stop him. Even just for a minute."

Through my terror, I felt something dimly register. *Even just for a minute?* "Are you saying you didn't mean to kill Eliot? Were you just trying to make him sick?"

The knife dropped a fraction of an inch. For a second, Adeline looked lost. "I thought if I could just give him a bit, maybe he'd end up in hospital. It wasn't hard to get him to drink it. A special celebratory cocktail. A toast to his new triumph." Her eyes met mine, bitter. "I didn't know about the Viagra. Though I suppose I should have guessed."

The boat swayed and Adeline lurched toward me. I let out a squeak. Frantically, my eyes swept the deck, and the one above. No one. No one was coming to my rescue. My only hope was to keep her talking.

"With Eliot out of commission, Declan would have the lead role. You were doing it for him."

Her mouth twisted, and I wondered if it was the cold or some overwhelming sorrow. They should tell us this when we become mothers: your heart is never your own again. There's always a piece of it out in the world, undefended. Against my better judgment, I felt a twinge of sympathy for Adeline. What wouldn't I do for my own son? I'd stop at murder, but I might come pretty close.

She lifted the knife. Maybe if you've killed once, the second time is easier.

"Adeline, this is ridiculous." I choked it out, and the wind stole my words. I looked behind me at the mighty paddlewheel heaving, and gulped. "You won't get away with it twice. They might be lenient with you about Eliot, if you didn't mean to kill him. But me—"

"You'll look like an accident," she said, in a terrifyingly flat tone. "A dumb outsider who doesn't know anything about water safety. Who wears ridiculous shoes in a rainstorm on a boat and then just *pffft*"—the knife's tip drew a plummeting arc in the air. "Taken by the lake."

The knife advanced on me. It was all I could see. This was going to be my last sight in this beautiful world. I gripped the wet railing and felt a scream rise in my throat. But who would hear me over the storm? A picture of Jake flashed in my head. Had I told him I loved him in the last text I sent? Had I included a heart?

I was going to leave him motherless. This bitch was going to deprive him of a mother. The thought filled me with rage, and suddenly I was unfrozen. I reached down and slid one sandal off. The shoes might be ridiculous, but they were also a weapon.

Adeline lunged at me, and I swatted at her with the sandal. The tip of the knife caught the strap and she hurled the shoe over the edge. I watched it sink into the churning black water. She came at me again, and I hopped backwards onto the railing, feeling it cold and slippery under my bottom.

"And now over," she hissed. "Unless you want me to cut you first—"

Suddenly a dark object came hurtling through the air and smacked her in the back of the head. Adeline screamed and stumbled toward me, wildly waving the knife. I scooted even farther back, clutching the railing desperately with my wet hands. I could feel the gusts of wind and spray sent up by the paddlewheel on my bare back.

Adeline was lurching to her feet again when another object hit her, this time on her shoulder. The knife clattered to the deck. I slid off the rail and kicked out, sending the knife skittering away. I might have kicked Adeline in the head while I was at it. But only with my bare foot. I wasn't a monster.

"Cat!" I heard, and I looked up to see Hadiya and Kaydence leaning over the railing on the deck above.

Kaydence had her phone out, filming, and Hadiya was holding something large and round to her chest. On the deck, Adeline lay whimpering. There were two catering trays next to her.

A sound rose in my throat, half laugh and half sob. She'd been brought down by the tools of her trade.

"Cat, are you okay? Get the knife!" Kaydence was still filming, and I gave her a thumbs-up. All my limbs felt like water, but I stumbled over to the knife, picking it up gingerly. Adeline was trying to rise to her feet, and Hadiya called down: "Don't even think about it, bitch. I've got another tray, and my aim is deadly."

I stood, swaying, in the cold and the rain, and then I did laugh, looking up at my girls. My posse. My heroes.

FIFTEEN MINUTES LATER, I was wrapped like a mummy in layers of blankets while my friends gathered around me. Bruce offered me a piece of old licorice from his pocket, which I declined, and Dorothy offered me a shot of brandy, which I accepted. Amir knelt at my feet, looking gratifyingly sick to his stomach.

All around us, people huddled in small groups, muttering. I saw Declan in the corner, being comforted by Alec. My heart stung for him. He hadn't asked for any of this.

"Where is she?" I asked Amir.

"They've got her in the galley. The crew's watching her, but she's got no fight left."

Neither had I. The boat jerked a little as it bumped the dock. The captain was in an understandable hurry to get back to port, and to hand off his deadly cargo. Through the window, cutting through the darkness, lights flashed blue and red, blue and red.

Home. I was safe, and I was home.

CHAPTER 26

FORGET ELIOT FRASER, I was the new celebrity in town. Everyone wanted to hear about the infamous marine fundraiser from someone who'd been close to the action.

It had been four days since the worst sunset cruise in history, and I was venturing out in public for the first time. I'd been holed up on Kaydence's couch, save for the occasional trip to the *Quill* office or the police station, but today I was ready to return to whatever passed for normal life after your friend, landlady, and employer caused an international incident and then tried to murder you.

I was starting with breakfast. Kaydence had commandeered a table by the window and installed Bruce and Amir as buffers against Glenda's nosy customers. Glenda herself came over to swat several well-wishers away, and then stood on a chair and clinked a water glass to get the attention of the crowd. "Cat Conway published her story in today's *Quill & Packet*," she said. "Buy a copy at the counter if you want the scoop, but otherwise, leave the poor woman alone to drink her coffee. I'm looking at you, Fergus. And don't forget— every purchase of Wrongful Confections goes toward my legal fees!"

Kaydence had come up with the idea of packaging several varieties of chocolate-covered treats, available at the Bakehouse and online, to boost revenues. Kaydence's marketing had created a small internet sensation, and Glenda was working overtime to fulfil orders. Fortunately for her, she had help from the kitchen staff of the Second Act, who were out of work for the foreseeable future.

"Any word on what's going to happen to her restaurant?" asked Kaydence. She was being careful not to say Adeline's name around me. They all were. I couldn't decide if I was touched or furious about being handled like a piece of museum-quality parchment, even though I felt old and fragile enough to be one.

"It's being sold," I said.

"Who's buying?"

"Who knows," I said. "Maybe someone in this town needs a second act of their own."

ALEC MERCER HAD shown up on Kaydence's front porch two days earlier, wanting a private meeting. I'd declined, given that my recent experience with one-on-ones had involved the pointy end of a chef's knife, and after some wrangling, he'd agreed to let Kaydence sit in. He'd come from depositing Declan at rehab.

I was fed up with Mercers and Talbotts and their endless machinations. I was tired and cranky and wanted to go and stare at the lake from my bedroom window, far, far away from the Mercers and the Talbotts. "First things first. Alec, why are you here? What do you want from me?"

If he was taken aback by my absent manners, he didn't show it. "It's about the conversation we had on the boat, before everything happened," he said.

"Before your ex-boyfriend's mother tried to kill me? Yes, I remember."

He eyed Kaydence, and said, carefully, "Would you mind stepping out?"

"Cat?" Kaydence said.

I nodded. "Are you sure?" she asked.

"We won't be long," I told her.

"All right." She stood. "I'll be in the kitchen. I can be back here in two seconds flat." She turned to Alec. "If you upset her, I'll tell everyone you get your eyelashes tinted."

I smothered a smile. "She'll do it too. Be warned."

Alec listened to her footsteps receding before saying, "You weren't wrong."

"About you being Eliot's son?"

"Yes."

"When did you find out?" I saw him hesitate, and said, "I assume you want me to keep the incest quiet." He winced, and I felt a small stab of guilt. But only a small one. The Mercers had been dicking me around throughout the investigation. I could have been spared more than a few nightmares if Martha hadn't kept the payouts to herself. The same was true of Dorothy, but I could only process one grudge at a time. "You'll tell me the truth, or you'll leave. Your choice."

"Fine," he said. "The truth: I found out on opening night. Eliot had told my mother that I was seeing Declan. He was stirring the pot, hoping to get Declan fired for dating another employee. He loved messing with people, especially my mother. She was beside herself, came to me right away, told me everything. She knew that Declan was Eliot's child; she'd been there when Adeline was paid off in the first place."

"So you had to cut it off with Declan. But you didn't tell him the whole story."

"I thought it was better for him not to know. But he was so hurt; he couldn't accept that we were over. He asked me to meet him at the fountain to talk. He promised to quit drinking if I'd reconsider. He wanted to talk to my mother about the morality clause in his contract. He thought we could negotiate an exception if we disclosed our relationship."

"Under other circumstances he'd probably have been right," I said.

Alec tilted his elegant head. He knew the rules were different for him, but he wasn't going to be so crass as to admit it. "I turned him down, and that's when the accident happened. After that, I felt I owed it to him to tell him, to explain why we couldn't be together. So now there are four people who know the truth: you, me, Declan, and my mother. As far as my family is concerned, that's too many."

I felt a chill and considered calling out to Kaydence. "Is that a threat?"

He gave me a grim smile. "It's the opposite. It's recognition of the debt that I'll owe you if you promise to keep my family's personal business secret."

"Okay," I said.

"Okay?" He looked incredulous.

"My interest was always in the story of Eliot's murder, and I can tell that story without compromising you and Declan," I said. "The *Quill & Packet* is a serious newspaper, not a tabloid, whatever your mother might think."

"Thank you," he said, turning to go. He took a few steps, hesitated, and then came back to stand in front of me. "You had a car accident recently ..."

"One of your brothers? Or half-brothers, I should

say?" I'd had some time to think, and I couldn't make sense of a scenario that had Adeline disappearing in the middle of her dinner service to run me down in an SUV that she didn't own.

He winced. "My mother was upset. There were some ... crossed wires."

I heard the screech of metal on metal, felt a rush of dizziness. "I might have another name for it."

"I'm very sorry," he said. "Your repair bill has been paid. You don't have to worry about anything like that happening again. You have my word."

"SERIOUS" MIGHT HAVE been overstating it, but the *Quill & Packet* was *my* newspaper now. Even with a story that was being picked up, well, everywhere, and generating opportunities as it spread, it seemed that Port Ellis had snuck up on me, just as Bruce had foretold.

"I might need your help looking for a new place," I said to Kaydence, and she squealed, jumping up to hug me. Glenda did the same. I could feel all the necks in the room craning in my direction: *What news?*

Amir's gaze was steady over his breakfast. "You're staying?"

"I'm staying. But not in that apartment."

"I'm glad," he said. "Really glad."

I smiled at him. I was relieved that he'd forgiven me

for keeping him in the dark about some of the threats I'd faced. I'd expected him to be angry when he heard the whole story, but he'd hugged me instead and then apologized profusely for behaving unprofessionally. "We're friends, aren't we?" I'd asked him then. "I think a hug after a murder attempt is acceptable."

"Okay," he'd said, and hugged me again.

I'd told my new real estate agent to find me a rental with two bedrooms. Jake had called me the morning after the news broke about my near-death experience. His voice was full of guilt, or at least as much guilt as a fifteen-year-old is capable of feeling. He'd told me he wanted to stay with me for the whole month of August, and even as he said it, I could feel my heart knitting back together in my chest. I'd drawn up a mental map of all the ice-cream parlours in the tri-lake area. We were going to eat disgusting double-fudge sundaes at every one of them.

My phone rang. "I'll meet you back at the office," I told the group. "I have to take this." I stepped out of the café and into the soft morning air. "Hi, Nick," I said, crossing the street to my favourite park bench. "The answer is no."

"You haven't even asked why I called," he said.

"I don't have to."

"Maybe I called to check on a friend and tell her I'm glad she's alive and well."

"Uh-huh," I said.

"And to compliment her on cracking the Eliot Fraser case."

"That would be very gentlemanly," I said. "And appreciated."

"And to invite her to come downtown for a chat with Claire Silverberg about her future."

"Ah, there's the rub," I said. "I'm otherwise committed."

"Cat, there isn't going to be another big story up there. You know that. Eliot Fraser's murder was a freak occurrence. Fate is extending you an invitation. Accept it, please. I'm telling you this because I respect you as a person and a journalist. Don't waste your chance to have the life you want."

"Don't worry about me," I told him. "I'm doing exactly what you always recommended. I'm doing what's best for me." I disconnected, smiling to myself.

From my bench, I watched my crew spill out onto the sidewalk in front of Glenda's, still chatting as they ambled west along Main toward the newsroom.

I ran across the street to join them.

WIDOWS AND ORPHANS

In Port Ellis, there's no off-season for murder.

Journalist Cat Conway is looking forward to an easy assignment for once. She's covering a major wellness and self-actualization summit at the Pinerock Resort, featuring Bliss Bondar and Bree Guthrie, creators of the Welcome Goddess empire and widows with attitude. Cat's mother, Marian Conway, bestselling author and defiantly mediocre parent, is on the agenda—and so is murder.

When one of the influencers turns up dead, suspicion falls on the high-profile guests. Could the killer be a jealous business partner? Or the Instagram-famous poet with a bee in her sonnet? The academic who takes vicious aim at the wellness movement? The empowerment guru whose wife hates him? Or Cat's mother, who has a reputation to protect and a shocking secret to hide?

Cat's pulled into investigating a celebrity death while struggling with the possible demise of her livelihood: The *Quill & Packet* is struggling financially, and may be headed toward its final edition. A convoy of protesters, angry at Cat's reporting, has besieged the *Quill*'s newsroom. Can Cat rescue her mother and her newspaper, or will the killer stalking Port Ellis beat her to the deadline?

ACKNOWLEDGEMENTS

OUR PURPOSE IN writing this book was to have some fun after two years of pandemic living had turned us into withered husks of dread. We hesitate to admit exactly how much fun we had (a lot) as we probably broke some cardinal rules about writing and suffering.

Our agent, Samantha Haywood, encouraged us to dive into crime writing together and cheered us the whole way along. We appreciate Sam's exceptional team at Transatlantic Agency, particularly Megan Philipp, who keeps us in the loop. Huge thanks also to the crew at House of Anansi: Leigh Nash, who acquired us; Shivaun Hearne, who pointed out our bad habits in the kindest possible way and saved us from our own literary impulses; and the editorial and design folks who fixed all our mistakes and made the book beautiful—Michelle MacAleese, Jenny McWha, Greg Tabor, Lucia Kim, Linda Pruessen, and Gemma Wain.

We are indebted to all the people who read and (gently) guided us. Veteran journalist Bruce Stapley offered his newsroom insights and reminded us that there's no such thing as a free lunch. Christina Donaldson, a career detective in the Toronto Police Service, made sure that we didn't push the bounds of credibility too far with our policing scenarios. Roz Nay brought her expertise as a bestselling crime novelist to her brilliant first edit of our manuscript. Doug Saunders cast a seasoned journalistic eye over the second draft. Beta readers Sasha Akhavi and Margo Hilton gave us a boost of confidence. It goes without saying that any remaining errors are entirely our own.

Bury the Lead is dedicated to journalists. We respect the hell out of you. Thanks for your efforts to save the world. Thanks also to booksellers everywhere, who provide oases of peace and sanity in our communities. Lastly, we appreciate the mighty network of fellow writers with whom we share the peaks and pits of our chosen profession.

Kate is grateful to her husband, Sasha; her kids, Jack and Charlie; her stepdaughter, Chaya; and her fur angel, Shelby, for thinking this job is cool and worth doing. You are all good eggs, even if you don't clean the countertops. She also appreciates her extended family of parents, sisters, brothers-in-law, and nephews, with a shout-out to Sam Macintosh, who invited her to his grade-two class to teach writing. She learned a lot. Most of all, she can't believe her luck at being able to write with Elizabeth Renzetti, who in addition to being an absolute icon is a darling, generous, wise, hilarious friend.

Elizabeth wants to thank her late parents, who adored mysteries. Beginning with their subscription to *Ellery Queen's Mystery Magazine* and continuing right up to their purchase of the latest Donna Leon novel, they taught her to love a red herring and a dark alley. Elizabeth is also grateful to her husband, Doug, and her children, Maud and Griff, for not being too irritated when she's got her nose buried in a book. She considers herself blessed to have found the perfect partner in writing, empathy, laughter, and fun in the brilliant Kate Hilton. Finally, she is awed by her former colleagues at the *Globe and Mail* for their continued dedication to truth-telling in a confounding world.

© Betsy Hilton

KATE HILTON is the bestselling author of three novels: *The Hole in the Middle*, *Just Like Family*, and *Better Luck Next Time*. When not writing, Kate works with psychotherapy and life-coaching clients in the area of transformational change. No stranger to reinvention herself, Kate has had prior careers in law, university administration, publishing, and major-gift fund-raising. She lives in Toronto in a blended family—including a husband, two sons, a stepdaughter, and a rescue dog.

© Jessica Blaine Smith

ELIZABETH RENZETTI is a bestselling Canadian author and journalist. She has worked for the *Globe and Mail* as a reporter, editor, and columnist. In 2020 she won the Landsberg Award for her reporting on gender equality. She is the author of the essay collection *Shrewed: A Wry and Closely Observed Look at the Lives of Women and Girls* and the novel *Based on a True Story*. Her book *What She Said: Conversations about Equality* will be published in 2024. She lives in Toronto with her family.